W9-BDJ-710

Beyond the Wind

Acclaim for
Beyond the Wind

"Rob Hood spins a good yarn with lots of action that brings readers face to face with the problems of gay, lesbian, bisexual, transgender (GLBT) children who, in addition to the problems all children have while growing up, must also deal with the fact that they are different and subject to emotional and physical hostility from a homophobic society. Hood goes beyond stereotypes and creates real people whose thoughts and actions are believable. Readers will learn a great deal, yet still feel that they have read a good story, not had a sermon preached to them."

—Bill Fuller
President, PFLAG
Lincoln, Nebraska

"Beyond the Wind is a psychosocial and emotional look at HIV/AIDS, gay and lesbian youth living in the heartland, teenagers, friendship, and families. Although written as fiction, it contains insight and truth about issues many of us have dealt with in regards to growing up, sexuality, religion, love, and relationships between friends, family members, schools, politics, and society. It is engaging, entertaining, emotional, and educational."

—Pat Tetreault, PhD
Sexuality Education Coordinator–University Health Center
Community Health Education Department,
University of Nebraska–Lincoln

NOTES FOR PROFESSIONAL LIBRARIANS
AND LIBRARY USERS

This is an original book title published by The Harrington Park Press®, an imprint of The Haworth Press, Inc. Unless otherwise noted in specific chapters with attribution, materials in this book have not been previously published elsewhere in any format or language.

Beyond the Wind

HARRINGTON PARK PRESS
Southern Tier Editions
Gay Men's Fiction
Jay Quinn, Executive Editor

Beyond the Wind

Rob N. Hood

Southern Tier Editions
Harrington Park Press®
An Imprint of The Haworth Press, Inc.
New York • London • Oxford

Published by

Southern Tier Editions, Harrington Park Press®, an imprint of The Haworth Press, Inc., 10 Alice Street, Binghamton, NY 13904-1580.

© 2004 by The Haworth Press, Inc. All rights reserved. No part of this work may be reproduced or utilized in any form or by any means, electronic or mechanical, including photocopying, microfilm, and recording, or by any information storage and retrieval system, without permission in writing from the publisher. Printed in the United States of America.

PUBLISHER'S NOTE
This is a work of fiction. Names, characters, places, and incidents either are the products of the author's imagination or are used fictitiously, and any resemblance to actual persons, living or dead, business establishments, events, or locales is entirely coincidental.

Cover design by Lora Wiggins.
Cover Model: Ryan Harmon (at left)
Photographer: Mark Lynch

ISBN 0-7394-5238-X

To those who are in
the deepest pit
of the
Valley of Shadows

And to Drew, who went home
way too early

From the Journal of Christopher Talbot

Tuesday, September 4th

There's an old railroad bridge on the outskirts of town. It spans the dark waters of Stephen's Creek in a wooded section of the countryside. Years ago, someone painted a message on one of the cement walls beneath the bridge. Most kids who read the faded words don't grasp their meaning. To them, the writings are just senseless babble, totally insignificant compared to more colorful works of graffiti on the concrete canvas. But when I first read them, they struck a chord in me. It was like someone had passed this way and left behind a message I was destined to find. I copied them down in case some moron eventually sprayed over them. The words of the unknown author read like this:

> Life is a war. We all get knocked down once in awhile. Some get back up, determined to win. Some fold, surrender, and quit. The difference between the two is those who get back up are too damned stubborn to stay down.

I tried to pass those words on to Kyle tonight, because the latest battle in his life had nearly wiped him out . . .

Chapter One

It was midnight in the quiet countryside. September breezes mingled with the mist rising from Dog Lake, and massive banks of fog drifted between the hills of the abandoned missile silos. Above the ghostly mounds, a solitary owl banked in midflight, his golden eyes fixed on Kyle and me. As we burst through the mist beneath him, the startled owl glided away, then vanished like a silent, winged wraith.

Alone out there, far from the city, we probably looked like two kids involved in some bizarre role-playing scenario. The silo grounds on the outskirts of Lincoln, capital of Nebraska, were said to be cursed, a dark and evil place for late-night quests. But this was no game. This was serious. Life-and-death serious.

Kyle had a gun. He wanted to use it. I wanted to stop him.

He laughed wildly, drifted to the right, glided to the left, and slipped into the fog like a magical creature quickly fading.

Watching him vanish, I shouted, "Kyle, stop! Listen to me!"

He didn't respond, but I heard his rapid footsteps not more than ten yards ahead of me. Sucking in a ragged gasp, I honed in on the steady pounding and thrashed my way blindly through the swirling whiteness.

Suddenly, Kyle cursed in pain. I heard the weird screech of rusted metal, like a banshee crying out in the night.

I knew at once what Kyle had discovered.

I shivered, knowing also that the missiles had been removed long ago, that most of the silos were 300 feet deep and flooded with murky water. I cried out, "Don't go in there! Most don't have floors! Nothing but air beneath your feet!"

A spark of light appeared thirty feet ahead of me. Wielding his flashlight like a lightsaber, Kyle sent golden shafts slicing through the swirling vapors. For a moment, I was mesmerized by dust motes dancing crazily in the lemony haze, then realized Kyle had discovered a doorway in front of him. As I sprang forward, he offered me an imp-ish grin, and flicked off his light.

Plunging ahead, I ran blindly for a moment until the dark shape of a grassy mound suddenly appeared before me. I spotted the yawning mouth of its open door.

I had barely cleared the passageway when Kyle's light beam stabbed me in the eyes. I froze, blinded.

Kyle warned, "Don't move, Chris! You were right. No floor! Just a straight drop to the bottom of the shaft!"

Kyle lowered his light. I looked down. Inches beyond the tips of my tennis shoes, a large hole sent chilly air up into my face. I spotted Kyle ten feet in front of me, sweaty strands of white-blond hair plastered to the sides of his pale face. Surrounded by the yellow glow of his flash-light, he seemed to be floating like a ghost above the deep pit.

"Should I jump?" he asked, balancing precariously on an iron beam running from the open doorway to the far wall, twenty feet away.

I asked firmly, "Where's the gun, Kyle?"

Hoping that maybe he'd dropped it behind him in the fog, I groaned in disappointment when he lifted the tail of his flannel shirt, revealing the .22 revolver tucked into the waistband of his jeans.

"I wouldn't need it, though," Kyle softly said, "if I stepped to either side of this beam."

I carefully shuffled my feet out onto the narrow beam, scared to death of falling but committed to saving Kyle.

"Keep away, Chris. No sense in both of us falling into those black waters down there!"

"Knock it off, Kyle!"

Raising his light to illuminate the beam, he showed me what awaited us if we moved an inch in the wrong direction. We peered down to the moss-covered walls which had once encased a long mis-sile. At the center of the shaft, blackness defied Kyle's meager light, and both of us knew that whatever lay beyond that mass of darkness promised pain, suffering, and death.

"They say," whispered Kyle in cryptic tones, "that these silos are buried in unholy ground. Some local scuba club used to dive out here. Ever heard the story of the diver who died when his air tank screwed up? Supposedly, he was down at least ninety feet! Or did you hear about the kid who slipped off a beam? He fell two hundred feet into water so black they never did find him!"

I quietly responded, "Yeah, Kyle. Heard those stories."

Kyle grinned sadly. "Lots of kids trespassed here, exploring the underground passages, until that kid fell. He didn't make a sound, didn't even call out for help. One of his friends said one moment he was balancing in the center of an iron beam—the next, he was gone. No noise. No words. No nothing. Slipped off and silently plunged to his death."

Kyle peered down into the shadows. I inched my way toward him. Hearing my shoes slide across the rusty metal, he looked up. I froze, only a foot away. Our eyes met briefly. Aiming his flashlight to create a pool of yellow at my feet, Kyle snapped, "Come no closer, Chris! I mean it! Stay back!"

But I had come too far to turn back. Saving Kyle had become my mission, and I wasn't going to fail him. I raised my hand and Kyle swung his flashlight. Our wrists connected with a hollow *smack.*

"Damn!" cursed Kyle as the flashlight flew from his grasp and I latched onto his wrist.

Struggling to maintain our balance, we watched as the circle of light drifted down through the blackness, its golden sphere swiftly becoming a spark the size of a firefly.

A splash echoed faintly in the black depths, and Kyle and I peered down to the yellow speck swirling round in a whirlpool like a tiny fairy creature madly fighting the suck and pull of the undercurrents below. The spark spiraled one last time, gave up the fight, and vanished.

"Let's get out of here," I whispered.

Surprisingly, Kyle allowed me to lead him back across the beam and out through the silo's doorway.

The moment we stepped back into the world of mist and gentle breezes, I spun Kyle around and snatched the pistol out of the band of his jeans. He didn't resist. He simply stood there, his shoulders sagging, a sheepish frown on his face.

"Just what are you trying to prove?" I asked, holding his dad's revolver up between us, the muzzle pointed to the ground.

Kyle shoved his hands in his pockets and muttered, "What am I supposed to do, Chris? How am I supposed to cope with . . . with everything that happened?"

I saw his eyes stray to the pistol in my grasp. Thinking he might do something rash, I flipped open the cartridge guard on the .22 Ruger and spun the six-shot cylinder, finding only one bullet. I thumbed it out, flicking it into the mist, and gave Kyle a puzzled frown.

"Thought I'd let God decide, like in Russian roulette," Kyle said, his eyes fixed on the shifting mist into which the bullet had vanished.

I shook my head and was just preparing to tell him about the message beneath the bridge when Kyle began to cry, muttering about the string of events that had spiraled madly out of control earlier that day.

I placed my arm around his shoulders, and we stood there in the moonlight, remembering them together.

Tuesday, September 4th
(Earlier That Day)

Kyle froze as the words echoed across the gym: "Damn! He's got a boner!"

It was Kyle Taylor's most embarrassing moment. He had been on the mats wrestling with Bobby Miller, and as he spun around and rose to his feet, other wrestlers in the gym spotted Kyle's erection. At first, a few kids began to snicker.

Of course, Bobby Miller and his big mouth didn't help matters. Backing away from Kyle in disgust, he latched onto my arm and shouted, "Hey, Chris, did you know your friend was a faggot?"

Freeing myself from Bobby's grasp, I stared down at the floor. Pointing out Kyle's misfortune, Bobby began working the crowd. Obnoxious heckling erupted. Then several others began hollering, "Fag!" and "Look at the homo!" The explosion of foul names and crude words ripped through me, especially since Kyle and I shared the same secret, one that those in the gym would never understand.

Kyle hung his head and slowly began the long walk out of there. As he strode through the roaring masses, his tear-filled blue eyes fixed on the locker-room door, a few of the kids began focusing on me. I did my best to ignore their cold, hard stares.

Most kids at school knew that Kyle and I hung out together, but we never gave them reason to suspect that we were anything more than best friends. Kyle claimed we had nothing to be ashamed of, constantly reminding me of David and Jonathan in the Bible. *Special friends,* he called them. I, though, was always nagging him about being discreet, painfully aware that we were unlike most fourteen-year-old boys living in the middle of the heartland.

Kyle was halfway across the gym when old fat Mr. Phillips burst out laughing. Everyone stared at him in curious silence as he crudely snorted, "Little playing with the boys got you excited, huh?"

Laughter once again broke out among my fellow students.

I thought, *Go! Go, Kyle! Just get out of here! Ignore them. Keep going. Get yourself dressed and get out of the locker room. Before . . . it's too late!*

Kyle trudged into the locker room, and a few minutes later when old man Phillips shouted, "Showers!" the whole mob went howling in there after him.

As I started across the gym, Mr. Phillips looked at me with his brown, lifeless eyes and growled, "Hey, Talbot! Better tell your friend to get his turn-ons somewhere else. I'll be damned if I let him get a rise in my class!"

"You'll be damned, for sure," I quietly whispered.

"What's that?" Phillips barked, his barrellike chest all puffed up like a fighting rooster. "You say something worth repeating, Talbot?"

I flicked my long, dark bangs out of my eyes, trying hard not to glare as I glanced back. "No. Not worth repeating, Mr. Phillips."

He angrily muttered as he scooped up his clipboard and waddled to his office. Under my breath, I growled, "Dumb ass!" but then realized if Phillips was perceptive enough to recall that Kyle and I were friends, the wild mob in the locker room would soon be in my face about that fact, as well.

Special friends, I thought as I walked. *David and Jonathan.*

Kyle really believed that stuff, too, and had found a site on the Internet that backed up his theory with scripture. Inside my head, I could hear those words as I approached the locker room: *"Jonathan's soul was knit with the soul of David, and he loved him with his own soul."*

Placing my hand on the door before me, steeling myself for the confrontation ahead of me, I recalled the tragic deaths of Matthew Shepard and Teena Brandon, and thought, *Words, Kyle. Words. And because of the way some people interpret words from that same book, two scrawny, gay kids like us from Nebraska could easily become the victims of a royal ass kicking!*

I pushed the door open before me and started down the hallway leading to the locker room, thinking about one of the main reasons I don't like violence. When I was younger, trying hard to please my dad, I was forced to take karate lessons at a local dojo. Then one day, Dad decided it was time to put my four long years of training to the test. Signing me in at the state tournament, he said, "Be your father's son! Go out and kick some butt!"

I could have refused that tournament, but I would have let my dad down, so I competed. My opponent was a gangly kid with messy blond hair. After several rounds of sparring, I took him down with a perfect leg sweep, following through with a heel to his chest. The ref should have called it. The kid was thrashing about on the mat, gasping for air. Then two dads began calling to their sons: "Get back in there and finish him, now!"

I gave my own dad a puzzled look. I thought I *had* finished him. In pain and crying, the skinny kid looked over at his dad as well. He clawed his way to his feet. As he staggered back toward me, I imagined that kid riding home after the tournament, hunched down in his seat, dealing poorly with his father's wrath. And with that image in my head, I let him beat me.

My dad and I haven't gotten along very well since then. All because I felt pity for that kid who needed to win more than I did. My dad would have never understood that. Hell, on the ride home he said, "You should have beat that damned fairy!" It made me totally paranoid. I wondered if my dad suspected I might be gay since I didn't seem capable of pulverizing that kid. I knew then, if my dad even *thought* I was gay, he would disown me in a heartbeat.

Chapter Two

As I entered the locker room, I heard the loud pops and cracks of wet towels being snapped. I heard pain-filled curses, followed by wild howls of laughter.

Naked in the shower area, Kyle was in serious trouble. More than a dozen lunatics snapped at him with wet towels. Red welts rose on his back, his shoulders, and his bare butt.

I quickly moved in between him and his attackers, shouting, "Get behind me!"

Snap! Pop! Two more kids lashed out with towels, and Kyle slid down the wet wall, cradling his head in his arms.

"Leave him be!" I hollered, taking up a stance in front of him.

Jeff Sandler, a husky, acne-faced kid, lunged at me, his fist passing dangerously close to my nose. I simply moved away with catlike grace, stepping to one side of his direct attack, and drove the extended knuckles of my right hand into Jeff's solar plexus. Jeff went down, clutching his chest, his eyes bulging.

It became quite obvious that anyone who wanted a piece of Kyle had to go through me. Five kids came at me in a mad rush. Karate or not, there was no way to defend against their barrage of fists and feet. On the screen, Jackie Chan might brutally demolish greater odds, but I couldn't avoid all that firepower. My vision was blurred by a fist in my right eye. A forearm smashed into the side of my head. Someone's foot connected with the shin of my left leg. I finally managed to raise my hands and, with a series of quick snapping motions, deflect several more punches that would have knocked me senseless. Slowly, my attackers backed off.

My face hurt. My ears were humming. I could barely breathe. Another thunderous volley of punishing fists and I would have been out of the fight. Then Tim Elliker spotted Kyle crouching behind me. He savagely kicked at him. I simply reacted.

7

Lunging forward, I swept Tim's fists to either side, then threw a rapid punch directly at his face. Tim's eyes widened as my knuckles connected with his nose. He groaned, closed his eyes, and fell backward next to Jeff. A stillness descended on the locker room as the mob looked down at Tim holding his bleeding nose and Jeff gasping for air.

I really felt bad. I didn't want to hurt Elliker like that. He and I used to tell each other jokes in math class. I liked Tim. He was a decent kid. He was just following the pack.

"What the hell's going on?" came the thunderous voice of old man Phillips. "What in the name of Judas happened in here?"

He shoved half-naked boys aside, looking down at the stars of his wrestling team sprawled on the floor before him. It was quite a blow to the cantankerous old fart. I almost felt sorry for the man as he kneeled on the wet floor, not knowing whom to help first.

Certain that his state of confusion wouldn't last long, I helped Kyle to his feet. "Get your clothes from your locker and head for the nurse's office," I whispered urgently.

"What about you?" he asked in concern.

"I'll be fine. I'll come get you later."

Kyle forced a smile then slipped out of the shower room and ran to his locker, where he quickly began to dress.

Old man Phillips shot up off the floor, jabbing a finger at me as he shouted, "You are in deep shit!"

"That's fairly obvious," I quietly muttered.

Phillips then jumped in my face, his bad breath invading my nostrils, his saliva spattering on my chin. He made it crystal clear that I was to go straight to the principal's office. When he finished ranting and walked away, I gathered my clothes from my locker and hastily dressed. Kids around me harshly whispered. Some flipped me off, while others made threats. With *after school* echoing in my ears, I hastily left the locker room.

A few moments later, on my way to the main office, I sighed in relief as I saw Kyle slip safely into the nurse's station. I began wondering how Principal Durban was going to react when I explained why I punched out Tim and Jeff. I had never been in this kind of trouble before, but Durban would probably suspend me. Though Kyle had been bashed, I knew our school was in the dark ages regarding intolerance. But I sure as hell wasn't going to get suspended without pointing out to Durban that if Phillips had reacted differently, I wouldn't have had to defend my friend.

As I sat in the office, waiting to be dealt with, I reflected on our friendship. Kyle and I had been best friends since kindergarten. Growing up together, we lived in the same neighborhood, played on the same Little League team, joined the same Scout troop, and attended the same Sunday school. Ours was a special bond formed by years of childhood memories. We'd built tree forts, played pirates, rode bikes, launched skateboards, skinny-dipped in Stephen's Creek, fished at Dog Lake, and camped out in each other's backyards.

During one of these camp outs, we shared the same sleeping bag, knowing if we got caught, death wouldn't be punishment enough. We were just two young kids experimenting. In the darkness of a pup tent, we never even thought about words like *homosexuality, oral sex, anal sex,* or *mutual masturbation.* Hell, neither of us knew what the word *gay* really meant until we turned twelve, which is when we began to wonder about our many secret encounters, scared to death that someone in our town might suspect that we weren't just two average kids.

I mean, one could never look at us in a crowd and figure out our sexual orientation. *Ordinary kids,* most folks would conclude. We're both fairly average in looks and size, slender and not very tall. My hair is dark and Kyle's is white-blond. We both wear it a little long with feathered bangs and wisps that flip up above our collars. But for the most part, we appear as fairly typical kids.

Growing up, until this point in our lives, hadn't been all that difficult either, but after Kyle's unfortunate situation that day, little did I know life was going to change for both of us.

Durban sent me to the media center until he could decide what my final fate would be for assaulting Tim and Jeff. So I was already stressed out when Bryce Carlile startled the hell out of me as he growled, "Talbot! You're a dead man!"

I was greatly relieved, however, to find Bryce standing before me, a smirk on his face. Bryce was not your typical student at Danbury High School. If he had been a year older and had a license, Bryce would have been a biker, as his father had been until he crashed his Harley one night in a fatal accident. Bryce's family came from a different culture than the majority.

Tall, lean, and broad shouldered with raven-black hair, Bryce was one of the toughest kids at school. Even the aggressive jocks and ill-mannered skinheads respected him. Bryce could handle himself, but it was also known that his older brothers ran with a local bike gang. If anyone messed with Bryce, they would have sixty bikers looking for them.

"I heard an ugly rumor in the hall just now," said Bryce, spinning a chair around backward. Plopping himself down, his legs spread wide on either side of the chair, he looked directly into my eyes.

Feeling somewhat safer now that he was there, I quietly asked, "What did you hear?"

Bryce answered, "That Kyle rubbed Bobby Miller while they were wrestling and that he was running naked around the locker room with a hard-on."

I groaned, then softly said, "Not true. I just went through a grueling interrogation in Durban's office. Durban wouldn't listen to me! He's convinced that Tim Elliker and Jeff Sandler were telling the truth. Both claimed that Kyle did a reach-around on Bobby Miller! Durban's talking about Kyle being charged with sexual assault!"

I explained to Bryce what had happened in the gym. Though Bryce was straight, he knew Kyle and I were gay. I often wondered why he hung out with us. He had been our friend since fourth grade. I think it stemmed from our relationship with his little brother. Only a year younger than the two of us, Johnny had been our shadow. We'd treated the younger kid like the brother we never had. After Johnny died in a tragic car accident, I often suspected Bryce put up with us because we'd been cool to his little brother.

Bryce actually confided in me once, telling me that he'd caught Johnny and another kid playing around in a tent in their backyard one summer evening. Johnny tearfully begged Bryce to pummel him senseless rather than tell their parents. Bryce did neither. I'm still not sure if Bryce was simply being tolerant of his brother's behavior or if he was just too shocked to act.

Bryce looked at the two kids who appeared behind us in the media center. Knowing about the rumors spreading through the halls, one of them pointed at me and whispered something, then burst out laughing.

Bryce shot to his feet, glaring at them. Both boys froze. "Hey, man. Peace!" muttered one kid as they beat a hasty retreat out of there.

"Bastards!" snarled Bryce. "Gonna be a lot of them flipping Kyle crap on the way home. You two better wait for me at the middle doors before leaving school. Okay?"

"I was hoping you'd say something like that. Thanks."

"You can thank me if we get Kyle home in one piece."

I asked, "Couldn't you phone your brothers? I think this is that serious. If the mob after school is anything like the pack in the locker room, Kyle's gonna get hurt."

Bryce considered my request for a moment. "I don't think my brothers would support such a cause. They're not quite into 'Support your Local Homo.'"

He grinned sheepishly. "No offense."

"None taken," I said.

Bryce exited the media room, leaving me alone with my troubled thoughts.

After school, we were swarmed by an angry horde in the center of the track field. Despite the fact that Bryce warned them to back off, the mob steadily tightened the ring they formed.

"Grab my crotch, faggot, and see how long you live!" a burly kid shouted as he stepped in close and slapped Kyle's shoulder.

The sudden blow caused Kyle to stagger forward. Another kid spit a glob of mucus in the center of Kyle's back.

"Knock it off!" snapped Bryce, moving between Kyle and the two pimple-faced bullies.

Bryce struggled to keep his anger in check, knowing that any sudden show of violence on our part would ignite a spark and further enrage the entire mob. So far, he'd managed not to use his tightly clenched fists on any of the kids who were circling around us like sharks waiting for blood.

A group of kids scattered behind us as a tall, redheaded boy barreled up on his bike. *Whap!*

We all heard the noise as the kid slapped Kyle's back with a leather belt. Kyle cried out and sank to his knees.

Bryce reacted instinctively. He latched onto the belt, gave an angry yank, and jerked the kid back and off his seat. The boy landed on his tailbone, yelping in pain. His bike rolled down the hillside and crashed into five boys who didn't scatter in time. A lot of cursing followed, and three of the older boys focused on Bryce as they moved toward us.

"Gonna get ugly," whispered Bryce, his expression scaring me more than the idiots swarming dangerously around us.

I scooted close to Kyle and took a fist directly in my chest. Bryce put one kid down with a swift punch, and then the mob attacked from all sides.

Suddenly, there came a loud honk. Everyone froze, gaping at the Mustang barreling out of the distant parking lot. As the blue Ford shot onto the field, kids scattered in all directions. Wide-eyed with fear, they forgot about us as the maniac in the car became their immediate concern. Fortunately, no one was run over as the driver of the Mustang cranked a hard right, spun the car sideways, and skidded to a grass-ripping halt ten feet in front of us.

"Just like the cavalry!" shouted the girl behind the wheel. She ordered, "Get in here! Or stay and get thrashed by these assholes!"

Feisty, dark-haired Jen Lawford glared at the kids scattered about the field and snapped, "Does my brother need to come visit any of you?"

No one answered. It was their turn to feel humiliated. Jen's brother was a badass from the lower east side of town. On weekends, he served as a bouncer for local parties and had a reputation for being downright lethal. Skinheads, bikers, jocks, and even gang bangers knew better than to crash parties protected by Johnny Lawford. The crowd on the field knew they'd been pressing their luck by attacking Bryce, that he might send his brothers after one or two of them. But Jen's threat carried more weight. If she insisted that Johnny hunt them down, he would. Every last one of them.

Under her breath Jen asked, "You three just going to stand there gape-mouthed and bug-eyed? Get in!"

The three of us moved quickly. As we scrambled into Jen's Mustang, Bryce made sure Kyle climbed in first, then offered me the front seat. I declined, slipping in the back next to Kyle.

As Jen gunned the car and shot away from the seething crowd, I said, "Thanks, Jen. Good timing."

Too busy swerving in and out of scattering kids to glance in her rearview mirror, Jen responded, "I'd just made a U-turn in the east parking lot when I spotted that angry mob. What the hell was that about? Why are they so pissed off?"

"They were born angry," muttered Kyle under his breath.

"What?" came from Jen as she braked to leave the field and enter the parking lot near the school.

"Nothing," murmured Kyle, wiping tears from his cheeks.

Bryce told Jen what had taken place earlier in gym class and filled her in on the ugly rumors kids were spreading.

Two years older than me, Jen Lawford had been a good friend since third grade. Then, she had long, silky hair, usually braided or worn in pigtails. Now, her dark hair was cropped short around her pixielike features, and though she wasn't what some might call beautiful, Jen was attractive in her own way. She had smooth, dusky skin and very green, catlike eyes that bored into your soul when she fixed you with her steely gaze. Her eyes softened, however, as she glanced in her mirror at Kyle and asked, "Are you okay?"

Seeing that Kyle was about to break down and cry, I changed the subject. "Were you looking for Cindy? I saw her earlier. She was heading toward Quik Mart with—"

And then I stopped myself as I saw the creases appear around Jen's eyes in my view of her from the mirror.

"With Brenda Gage," she flatly stated.

I could see Jen was hurt. Cindy Halsey had not been kind to her lately. Jen had told me days ago that Cindy had doubts about their relationship, that Cindy was no longer certain she was a lesbian. Jen had been hurt then. She was even more hurt now. Cindy had probably ditched her on purpose.

"Sorry, Jen," I softly said. "Some people are just heartless."

Jen sighed, forced a smile as our eyes met in the reflection of the mirror, and replied, "Heartless and cruel. That's for damned sure!"

Chapter Three

Kyle didn't return to school after the assault on the track field. During the weeks that followed, Principal Durban demanded an investigation into the incident in the gym, and everyone, including Kyle's parents, believed he had actually fondled Bobby Miller. Sexual assault charges were hanging over Kyle's head, and he was just too depressed to go to school.

School officials requested that Kyle's parents take him to a counselor. They didn't want him back if he posed a risk to other kids. Kyle's dad hadn't spoken to him since the call from Mr. Durban. He simply ignored Kyle, acting as if he didn't exist. Kyle's mom did just the opposite. She constantly nagged at him, demanding, threatening to take him to a counselor or a therapist.

Kyle was in no state of mind to comply, though. He just put up with her nagging and began living a miserable existence, except when I came to visit him after school each day. I had been keeping a close eye on him since the night I took his dad's gun away from him at the missile silos. That had been a close call, and I didn't want Kyle to try any other desperate stunts.

Jen was the only one I told about Kyle's suicide threat, and she encouraged me to keep checking in on him. Since she'd rescued us on the track field, Jen had been providing Bryce and me with a safe escort to and from school. Things had not cooled down yet, and there was talk about me finally getting the beating I'd managed to escape from due to Jen's intervention. Frankly, I wasn't sure what would prove to be more dangerous—facing my vengeful enemies or flying down the streets in Jen's Mustang, for she was notorious for her wild and crazy driving.

On the way over to Kyle's one afternoon, I thought of the discussion I'd heard in health class, and shared it with Jen and Bryce.

"Mr. Hefner spoke about AIDS in health today. But he kept associating it with sexual activities among promiscuous gay men. After the lecture, John Beams claimed that AIDS was God's way of sorting out the good from the bad. But Martha Grimes started a debate when she claimed the real sorting out would take place one day in heaven."

Seated in the front next to Jen, Bryce said, "Heaven? You guys actually believe that gay men go to heaven when they die?"

I shook my head because his question caused Jen to stomp angrily on the gas as she firmly asked, "Would you be surprised, disappointed, or angry if you discovered God allowed a gay man in *ahead* of *you?*"

Bryce didn't quite understand Jen's question, so Jen tromped on the gas again and asked, "Surprised? Disappointed? Or angry?"

Bryce shrugged and said, "I guess, angry."

"At God?" questioned Jen. "As if it would even be your business! You think being straight gives you the right to judge and condemn?"

"Well," argued Bryce, "at least I don't do things with other guys!"

Jen responded, "There's much more to being gay than having sex!"

To that, Bryce said, "Sex between a man and woman is the only right way. Between two guys? Hell, AIDS is spread that way! That's how it got started!"

"AIDS," snapped Jen, "is also spread through heterosexuals! And no one really knows for certain how it first got started. It's wiped out more heterosexuals in Africa than homosexuals! Besides, unlike some *people* I know, it doesn't *discriminate!*"

Bryce looked over the seat at me. "So, how do you think God feels about you being gay, Chris?"

I answered, "I don't know."

But I did clearly remember the first time the word *gay* came up between Kyle and me, and my mixed emotions at Kyle's suggestion that we were in fact gay.

When we were nine, we'd watched a movie with sex scenes flashing across the screen. Afterward, in a tent in my backyard, we talked about screwing girls. "Do you get horny when you look at a *Playboy?*" Kyle had asked me.

"Sure," I answered, but I was ashamed to tell him that I never had pictures of naked women flashing through my head.

But that night, on that campout with Kyle, I had my first experience with sex. Kyle had simply reached down into my sleeping bag and . . . we ended up naked together inside a single sleeping bag.

Something changed, though, after I turned twelve. One night, visions started rolling through my head of Kyle and me beneath those summer night stars. I tried imagining several girls from school performing the same acts, but there was just no spark; nothing even clicked. I just couldn't find pleasure in thinking those same thoughts about girls. I found myself attracted to boys.

After a few more experiences with Kyle, he finally posed the question, "So, we are gay, right?"

At that point, I wasn't ready to accept it. Kyle assured me, "Chris, it's all right to admit—between us—that we're gay. I'd never tell another soul. Swear to God."

I shook my head, saying, "Now that you brought up God, what about the stuff they say at church? Sodomy means butt screwing, right? God destroyed Sodom. God sends homos to hell. You still want to claim we're gay?"

Kyle had leaned over and squeezed my shoulder. "Chris? Do you really believe that God would condemn us for how we feel about each other? I mean, set sex aside and think about it. Isn't God love? Do you really think he'd turn against us because we loved each other? Sounds like a big contradiction to me."

My thoughts of those earlier days faded quite suddenly, as Jen and Bryce began arguing in the front seat of her Mustang.

Jen snapped, "Get past the part that HIV passes through bodily fluids and what do you have? A virus! A mean and nasty virus. A virus like Ebola. The two originated in the same place, anyway. And Ebola is a deadly virus, too. One takes you out slowly and the other takes you out savagely. But both are killers. Yet no one looks at Ebola and names it a gay virus or a homosexual plague. It's simply a murderous disease!"

We waited for Bryce's witty comment, but he looked rather pale. "Yeah. I saw a film on Ebola in health. That's some sick stuff! But that doesn't spread through sex, does it?"

"What difference does that make?" responded Jen. "Don't you see what I'm saying? It's not how either virus is spread. It's the fact that they both kill people. Besides, HIV isn't spread only through sex. The virus can be passed through needles and also blood transfusions. HIV is an opportunist. It will travel from person to person through blood and bodily fluids, but travel it will, infecting millions!"

Bryce shrugged. "You make it sound like it's waging war on us."

"It is!" replied Jen, looking over at him like he just didn't get it. "And if you look at HIV that way, as a ruthless enemy out to destroy the human race, then maybe you can get a sense of what it will take to combat and conquer it."

A few moments later, when Jen dropped me off at Kyle's house, neither Bryce nor Jen heard me say good-bye, for they had launched into another heated debate. When Kyle met me at the door, I could no longer think about AIDS, God, or sex. Kyle was so depressed he gave me a hug and began to cry.

Wednesday, October 3rd

Until the fateful day of that wrestling match in the gym, Kyle didn't have much of a reputation. He certainly didn't have one that needed repairing. Kyle was just one kid among hundreds who passed quietly down the halls until fellow students suspected he was gay. And rather than endure the cruel remarks or the threats of physical harm, Kyle simply faded out.

I visited him every day after school, and for those first weeks, Kyle desperately needed assurance that I still supported him. He was like a lost puppy, lonely and needy.

School officials finally informed Kyle's parents that the police would not be filing sexual assault charges in regard to the incident in the gym, but all the truancies eventually caught up with Kyle. His parents were required to attend a meeting at the school administration building, and officials there recommended a therapist who could help Kyle deal with his feelings. Kyle's dad forced him to see the therapist, angrily proclaiming, "It just might get this fag thing straightened out!"

Though Kyle unwillingly attended two sessions a week during that first month, he still skipped school. Two days after the social worker visited with Kyle and his parents, telling them the many truancies had been turned over to juvenile court, Kyle let me know I was going to lose him.

"I'm running away, Chris," Kyle said.

We were in his room, playing Nintendo. I put down my controller and joined him on his side of the bed. "Kyle." I spoke his name calmly, placing one hand on his shoulder. "What are you saying? Where would you run to?"

Brushing my hand off, Kyle leaned back and propped pillows beneath his head. "To the Big O," he declared, tears glistening in his eyes.

I was shocked. "Omaha? What? And become a street hustler like Ronnie Hatchett?"

Kyle sniffled, fighting back tears. Then he answered, "Yeah, something like that. I talked with Hatch the other day. He says he makes good money doing the streets." Slowly, he added, "He's going back to Omaha on Friday."

"And you're going with him? Kyle, you can't be serious. Come on, there are other choices to be made."

Kyle sat straight up. "Are there, Chris? What choices? You tell me! According to my therapist, being gay is a matter of choice! She claims I *choose* to be gay! She claims I can just turn my gay feelings on or off, sort of like messing with a light switch! God, does she actually think I wanted to shame myself that day in the gym? Does she think I'd purposely want to disappoint my parents and be called a 'queer boy' and 'light in the loafers' by my own dad? Is that my choice? She believes that one day I just woke up and said, 'Oh my, I think I'll be gay! I think I'll become attracted to boys!' Like I had a choice in the matter!"

I sat there, totally stunned by his hostility.

"She doesn't believe that gays and lesbians are *born* with such a sexual orientation," he said. "She thinks they *choose* their lifestyle in hopes of finding love that they failed to find in a *normal* relationship."

Shaking his head and blowing upward, which parted his bangs, Kyle added, "She asked, 'Have you ever thought a girl looked pretty? Did you ever feel attracted to a girl?' And then she tells me I ought to try having a *normal* relationship with a girl!"

Kyle sadly whispered, "But I just can't. I don't feel anything for girls. Not like I feel for you, Chris."

I forced myself to smile. I scooted closer, opening my arms to offer Kyle a hug. It hurt when Kyle pushed me away and slid off the other side of the bed.

"*Who* did decide?" snapped Kyle, spinning around to face me. "Who decided that I would be gay? Is this God's joke? Does he sit up there each time a baby's born, scratching his bearded chin and deciding which one's going to be straight, gay, or lesbian? I can imagine him saying, 'Let's see, I think I'll give this one a challenge and allow him to be gay.'

"Is that how this works, Chris? Is there a grand decision? Who makes up the rules? Who decided to make me gay? Because I can tell you now, it wasn't *my choice!*"

"Nor was it mine," I responded, glancing up toward the ceiling, imagining God was actually listening to our conversation. "I have to live with it, though. I have to accept that I am, Kyle. And I pray to God that I don't go to hell because of it."

"Hell!" snarled Kyle as he pointed to the crucifix hanging on his bedroom wall. "How could God be so cruel as to let us suffer a living hell on earth and then send us to hell when we didn't have a choice in the matter? Where's the love of God in that?"

Snatching the crucifix off the wall, Kyle heatedly said, "Or is this gay thing one of the sins Jesus died for? Is it true what my mom says? That all we have to do is confess our sin of being gay to Jesus, and we'll be cured, healed, and made straight?"

I hung my head, feeling a tear sliding down my left cheek. "I tried that, Kyle. I actually kneeled down one night in my backyard and told God I was sorry for my gay acts and that if he would help me, I would change and not be gay."

Kyle tossed the crucifix on the bed. Jesus lay there, looking up at both of us. "God didn't change you, though, did he?"

"No," I whispered, my eyes filling with so many tears I could no longer see Jesus lying there on the cross. Everything in the room—in my life at that moment—became one big blur.

I added softly, "God might have made us this way for a reason, Kyle. Maybe we were destined to love each other even though the world and the church claim differently. Maybe against all odds, God that's beyond the wind, the sun, the moon, and past the stars, has a different plan for us."

"Beyond the wind and past the stars, who's watching us?" asked Kyle. "Is he angry with us? Does he still care about us? Just how does he look at us?"

I remained silent.

Kyle declared, "Choices have little to do with it. I wish my therapist could talk to God about these choices. He'd straighten her out."

"But not us," I added, trying to apply humor to the tragically sad exchange we were having. "No *straightening* being done to us. We are who we are."

I blamed myself long after that day. If only I had tried to reach out once more to embrace Kyle. If only . . . but I didn't. I was too emotionally drained to attempt one more hug. I do remember kissing him lightly on the forehead, and little did I know what that good-bye would mean for both of us.

Chapter Four

Monday, October 22nd

I looked up over the monitor to see Jen standing there in the media center. Peering at me with her dazzling green eyes, she reminded me of a very intelligent cat. "What's up, Christopher Robin? You look like you lost Pooh back in the woods somewhere."

Kyle had been gone for nearly three weeks now, and both she and I knew he'd gone on run with Hatch. Kyle was somewhere up in Omaha, and I was crushed.

Jen said, "Come on, Chris. You can't up and die on me. He'll come back, begging you to forgive him, and you guys will go on as if he never left."

I gritted my teeth, wanting to say, *Oh yeah? He'll come back to me just like Cindy came back to you, right?* But I didn't. I couldn't hurt Jen that way. It had been four weeks since Cindy left her to discover what boys were all about. Jen had been brutally crushed, but somehow she managed to cope. She'd loved Cindy for nine months. The two were never without each other. Then Cindy met Matt Lane and Jen got dumped.

"He's been gone three whole weeks, Jen!" I reminded her.

"His loss, not yours! Don't let him pierce your heart that way. Kyle will start missin' you, sooner or later."

"It's the *later* that worries me," I told her, noticing the small purple mark on Jen's neck.

Jen saw me look away a little too quickly. She grinned and deep dimples appeared on her cheeks. "Yes, Chris, I'm seeing someone new. She's a cutie, too. So right now I'm emotionally stable enough to tell you, 'Everything will be okay.' Crock of shit, right?"

I shook my head and ran my hand through my hair. "I just want him back, Jen. I miss him. Sometimes I wake up and—"

"Shh!" she urged, reaching out to place two fingers on my quivering bottom lip. She knew how badly I was hurting.

"So," Jen said, "why don't we just go find him?"

Fighting back tears, I looked at her. "Drive up to Omaha and search for him?"

"Yeah. Go to the Big O and go questing for Kyle. I'm free Saturday. How about you?"

"Are you serious? How would we go about finding him?"

Jen straddled a chair and eased herself down, her chin resting on her folded arms. "Kyle took off with Hatch, correct? Well, Ronnie Hatchett is rumored to be the most expensive street whore in the Old Market stretch. We find Hatch and you can bet we'll find your Kyle."

Only he's not truly my Kyle anymore, I nearly said. *Not if he's selling his body to other men or boys.*

"You don't know what Kyle's been doing these past three weeks," I said, more heatedly than I meant to. "But what do you suggest? Travel to Omaha and start asking for a whore named Hatch?"

Jen shook her head. "Might be more simple than that. I know Ronnie's sister. She probably knows where he sleeps. He's got to crash somewhere."

Jen noted the worry in my eyes. She reached out and ran a comforting hand down the length of my forearm. "It'll be okay, Christopher. You'll see. It'll be okay."

I hoped so and silently prayed. But I was wondering if God ever really listened to me anymore.

Bryce met me at Smoker's Corner after school that day. In fact, Bryce had become quite serious about being my protector ever since Kyle's fateful incident in the gym. Bryce was more than just a good friend. He was a real knight in shining armor. He might have had biker brothers as role models, but Bryce had heart. He was rough on the outside—with his shaggy raven hair and his faded jeans, skin-tight pocket T-shirts, and scuffed-up boots—but inside, Bryce had a soul of gold.

Bryce was sure of himself, too. It was as if Bryce knew exactly who he was in the world. I wished to God I could be just like him. I was a long way from being sure about myself. Hell, one has to at least like oneself to have self-assurance. I was a long, long way from even doing that.

"Hey, bud," Bryce greeted me. "Jen talked to me about your quest. Let's go see what we can come up with, okay?"

He pointed a finger directly at Toby Greenfield, a tall, lanky boy near the front of the crowd of freaks and grunges smoking on the curb. "Give me a smoke, Tobias."

Toby rolled his eyes yet complied at once. He handed a cigarette to Bryce, his eyes straying to the Marlboro box clearly visible in Bryce's T-shirt pocket.

Bryce lowered his voice so that the rest of the crowd on the corner couldn't hear. "What I really want from you is a favor." Placing the cigarette between his teeth, Bryce continued, "You and Hatch were friends at one time, right?"

Toby blurted, "That queer? Ronnie Hatchett's a damned—"

"Shh!" Bryce glanced at the crowd on the corner.

Toby looked directly at me. "Sorry about the comment. It's just that Ronnie tried to—"

Bryce cut him off, asking, "Got a light?"

Toby fished a lighter out of his jeans and proceeded to light Bryce's smoke. I stood there, not knowing if I should have been offended. Kids at school labeled Kyle as gay, not me. I was just known as the "homo's friend." No one as yet had placed the tag on me.

One of the grunges on the corner eyed me and whispered to her three friends. They looked at me and began laughing.

Oh yeah! I thought, my face turning beet red. *They think I'm gay too. I couldn't have hung out with Kyle all of these years and not have known about him being gay!*

Bryce blew three perfect smoke rings. "Tobias, at one time you were going with Hatch's sister. True?"

Toby nodded. "Yeah. Becky. She's been hacked at me since I punched her brother out. Thinks I'm an insensitive bastard just because her queer brother tried to—"

"She got the bastard part right," said Bryce, smirking.

"Hey," said Toby, "what would you have done if the brother of the girl you were dating tried putting the moves on you?"

"Probably punched him out like you did," replied Bryce.

"Hell, yes!" snapped Toby. "Damned faggot!"

Toby noted Bryce's stern gaze. Looking at me, he said, "Sorry about that. About the fag thing. Sorry."

I stared at him, speechless. What was I to say? *Don't worry about it? I've put up with homo jokes all of my life? I'm not offended because I'm not a street whore like Hatch?*

I became angry, thinking, *Does this ass think that all gay boys flaunt themselves like Hatch? Does he believe that I would be so desperate as to throw myself at him? I'm not a slut like Hatch! I would never give up my body for someone else's gratification like Hatch does!*

Bryce noticed my rigid stance. "Okay, Tobe. Enough about Hatch. Could you talk to Becky, find out where her brother is?"

Toby asked, "What you want with him? Last I heard he was up in Omaha, selling himself on the streets—"

Bryce placed a finger on Toby's chest. "Talk to Becky. Tell her Jen wants to speak with her about Ronnie. They were friends. She knows she can trust Jen."

"A lesbo and a gay-wad!" chuckled Toby. Looking at me, he grinned impishly. "Oops! Sorry!"

"Here," said Bryce, taking a slip of paper from his pocket and handing it to Toby. "Ask Becky to call Jen at this number. It's important, so get it done for me, okay?"

Slipping the paper into his pocket, Toby answered, "Sure. I'll call her when I get home. But she might still be torqued at me."

Bryce tapped him in the center of the chest, looking intently at him. "Get it done, Tobe. I'm counting on you. Sooner is better than later."

Bryce removed his Marlboro box from his T-shirt pocket. Slowly he took out a cigarette. He smiled as he handed it to Toby. "Thanks for the smoke."

Toby grinned, put the cigarette in his mouth, and walked back to the crowd. Every freak and grunge on the corner watched as Bryce and I walked away.

"Thanks," I offered Bryce, hoping he knew how much I really appreciated his loyalty and that he would even be seen with me. I thought, *What are his friends back there thinking? Do they think maybe Bryce is gay too? Isn't he the least worried about his own reputation?*

"We'll find our little bro, dude," Bryce said, tossing his cigarette butt over one shoulder. "Find him and bring him home."

He caught me glancing back at the crowd on Smoker's Corner as I asked, "What do you think they're saying about us right now, Bryce? I mean, you looking for Hatch? And you, me, and Kyle always hanging together? What do you think they're saying about us?"

Bryce caused me to admire him more than I already did as he gruffly said, "Them? Hey, my heart is bulletproof to their snide remarks and ignorant accusations! They can only hurt me if I let them. So, really, Chris, they can just piss off!"

I came through the back door so quietly that the folks in the living room didn't hear me. I'd spotted Kyle's mom's car in our driveway the moment I reached Carson Street. I almost turned and walked the other way. Instead, I decided to see what was up.

Easing the door closed, I stood near the kitchen counter and listened to my mom trying to comfort Katie Taylor. "It must be terrible. You hear about kids running away, but it never occurs to you that your own child might leave without a word of warning or even a note—"

"Kyle did leave a note," Katie interjected. "He apologized for embarrassing us. He was thinking of *us* and what *our* friends thought after that horrible incident at the school, worried about *our* feelings. He must have heard us talking about this homosexual thing. And do you know what he apologized for in his note, Lori? Kyle was sorry that Jack and I would never be grandparents! Kyle actually overheard my comment about grandchildren! Jack, you see, isn't taking any of this too well. His only son, a homosexual? What father would be pleased with that kind of announcement?"

My mom said, "I'm sure it must be difficult."

Katie Taylor continued, "And Kyle told us he's felt this way ever since he was a little boy! So Jack and I talked about the fact that maybe—and, God, we prayed—that Kyle might be going through a phase, that he might find the right girl eventually, marry, and have children."

"Kyle heard this conversation?" asked my mom.

"Yes. Now that he's gone, do you think I should have been worried about grandchildren? That seems so ridiculous now."

My mom tried to comfort her. "He must be so confused. Maybe a good therapist might help him."

Katie laughed with no humor. "The therapist only made Kyle angrier. Kyle told us she didn't understand him and didn't have a clue about why he was gay."

Mom asked, "Have the police been helpful? Lincoln's not all that big. Would his friends hide him?"

"His friends?" said Katie with a little snort. "He didn't have many. His constant companion was your son, Lori."

It became quiet in the living room. In fact, it became quiet throughout the entire house. I held my breath, counting seconds until I heard my mom ask, "What are you saying, Katie? Are you thinking Chris might be—"

"No! No, Lori, I didn't mean that. I was just saying if Chris doesn't know where Kyle is, then who does? Have you talked to him about it lately?"

"Some. Chris is really quiet lately. I'm sure he'd talk Kyle into returning home if he knew where he was."

"Yes," responded Katie, "the two boys were fairly close. They've practically grown up together."

I knew where this was going even if Mom didn't as she replied, "Yes, from kindergarten up to now, ninth grade. I used to call them Butch Cassidy and the Sundance Kid."

Oh, Mom, I thought, *say no more! Steer her away from talk about Kyle and me. Don't you see where she's going with this? And Sundance Kid? Come on, Mom! Don't put "kid" and "dance" in the same sentence when you're talking about her gay son, for the love of Jesus!*

"Do you ever suspect your Chris?" asked Katie, very quietly.

Mom gave a nervous chuckle. "Of being homosexual? Christopher being gay?"

Come on! I wanted to shout. *Defend me! Say no! No, Mom! You and Dad haven't actually suspected all along, have you? Haven't I kept this part of me hidden well enough? Didn't I kick butt for Dad in karate tournaments? Don't I laugh loudly when Dad and Uncle Mike tell gay and lesbian jokes at family reunions?*

Katie cleared her throat and said, "Kyle's only had two girls call him these past three years. Two! How many girls has Chris dated? How many girls phone your house, asking for your son?"

Busted! I thought. *It's going to become so clear to Mom, and later to Dad. This is bad and going to get worse. Hell, I might have to run away myself! No wonder Kyle didn't get any support from them! Katie Taylor is a digger and an analyzer!*

"Well," I heard Mom say, "Chris is fairly shy when it comes to girls. He's also very private. John and I don't pry, nor do we keep track of his friends calling. Chris is just an average, normal kid."

Katie didn't like what she'd just heard. Her voice was crisp as she snapped, "What do you mean by that, Lori? How would you define normal? I admit Kyle has a problem and needs psychological help, that this homosexual thing is very wrong. But are you saying your son is normal, that mine is not?"

Mom let out a little sigh before saying, "Oh, Katie, no. I'm so sorry. I didn't mean it that way. It's just that—"

Sounding more and more like the Wicked Witch of the West, Katie blurted, "Face it, honey! Our boys spent way too much time together! They were hardly ever separated! And remember all those sleepovers during the summer?"

Oh, my God! I thought. *How can you let her say this, Mom? Shut the damned hag up! Tell her to go straight to hell! Don't let her convince you that Kyle and I were doing things with each other. Please don't let her convince you that I'm gay.*

And that's the way the heated conversation ended. Two seconds later my dad came in the front door, oblivious to the exchange taking place in our living room. He greeted both ladies cordially. Katie and my mom returned his greeting, Mom downplaying how she obviously felt and Katie excusing herself, claiming she hadn't realized the time and that she needed to be getting home to her own husband.

Chapter Five

Dinner that night was sort of a blur to me. I knew what my mom was mulling over in her head, and I purposely kept my eyes fixed on my plate as I felt her glancing in my direction. I kept wondering if Mom had talked to Dad about Katie's unpleasant visit. I had the sneaking suspicion that she had, and that I was now under close scrutiny. To describe my mom and dad, I would have to say Mom looks like a younger version of Sally Field and Dad reminds me of Mel Gibson with a thick mustache. Neither one could "act" like those two movie stars, though, and I could tell something was up between them. I figured Katie had definitely done her damage.

After I ate, I went for a walk down to the park three blocks from home to clear my head.

Stars were brilliant in the October night sky. The moon was a golden globe slowly rising among the specks of silver. I imagined it was an elfin vessel made of phosphorous light, sailing along a river of stars. The night definitely had a Tolkienish quality to it—an early autumn evening when hobbits might pass unseen through moonlit meadows. These thoughts gave me peace.

Ever since reading *The Lord of the Rings* back in fifth grade, I've never gazed at stars or the moon again without feeling some magical presence in the air around me. Anyone who has ever read the fantasy trilogy penned by J. R. R. Tolkien can probably relate to what I feel. For some reason, that series of books touched me in a profound way. Sometimes, I lose myself in daydreams where I slip away to Middle Earth and become a grand hero on a bold quest. It's certainly more fun than the life I really live.

"Hey!" a loud voice startled me, shattering my thoughts. My stargazing had kept me from remaining alert, and I suddenly found myself surrounded by three kids as they slid like wraiths from among the pine trees in the park.

Moving directly in front of me, the largest boy snarled, "What do we have here? If it ain't the Karate Queer!"

Two of the kids, Tim Elliker and Jeff Sandler, had been there that day in the shower room at school. I had hurt them as they had tried to assault Kyle. Both more than likely sought vengeance for me putting them in their place.

"Fag?" questioned the kid in the center as he glared down at me. I had to look up at him because he was just that tall. He was broad also, like a heavyset linebacker. I couldn't see his face too clearly, but I could tell that he had a buzz cut that had a marinelike quality about it.

Marine Boy thrust his bulky chest forward, daring me to so much as touch him. "You a packer like your friend? You a little pole smoker?"

Tim and Jeff snorted with snide laughter as they hedged me in on either side. I could feel one breathing hot air on my neck. The other one had breath that smelled like sour onions.

I stood perfectly still. It was definite. I was going to get hurt. The three were positioned too well to allow me any slippage.

"Grab his arms, guys!" thundered Marine Boy. And as Jeff and Tim latched onto my arms, the brawnier kid grabbed ample folds of my flannel shirt with his massive hands.

"My boys here tell me that you stuck up for your homo friend! So I wanna know, why? You partial to packers or are you just one yourself?"

He laughed as he pushed his face an inch away from my own. "I'm doing a report in my health class, and I want firsthand information on *homosexuality!* Can you handle that?"

"Can you handle this?" came a voice from the shadows among the nearby trees. I saw a dark form glide up beside a very startled Marine Boy. One second later and a fist plowed into the side of the big kid's head.

"Damn!" cursed Jeff in disbelief, his hold on me loosening.

"Oh, hell!" gasped Tim as Bryce moved into the silver moonlight and planted another fist on the side of Marine Boy's head.

The big jock fell like a dropped ox. One second, he was standing there grasping handfuls of my shirt; the next, he was simply crashing to the ground. Bryce's second punch had hit him that hard.

"Damn, man!" cried Jeff, his eyes shifting quickly from the bigger kid's inert form to Bryce coming directly at him.

Before Bryce launched a punch at Jeff's blocky head, I performed both twisting and snapping motions with my wrists and freed myself from the clutches of my stunned captors.

Smack! rang loudly through the evening air as Bryce's fist cracked into Jeff's left cheek. Jeff immediately reached up toward the source of his pain. I gave him something else to feel as I performed a spin kick, catching him in his lower right calf. Jeff collapsed, grasping painfully at his leg.

"Bryce!" exclaimed Tim. "I'm not messing with you!"

"No, you're not," declared Bryce in even tones.

Three quick, successive jabs from Bryce, and Tim dizzily wheeled away and took off stumbling across the park.

Bryce and I both turned as one when we heard gravel crunching noisily beneath Jeff as he struggled to get to his feet. Still worked up by their assault on me, Bryce started forward, his right arm shifting back to jack Jeff up again.

I caught Bryce by the sleeve of his jean jacket. "Let him be, Bryce."

Pulling free of my hand, Bryce took two steps forward anyway. He raised his fist, and Jeff dropped all the way to the ground. Bryce snorted in contempt as Jeff threw his hands in the air to signal his surrender.

"Come on, Chris," grunted Bryce, turning to check on the still unconscious Marine Boy. Satisfied that two of my attackers were down and the third was already halfway across the park, Bryce walked away, his fists still clenched tightly at his sides.

Bryce asked, "That had to do with Kyle, didn't it?"

I answered, "Yeah. And I want to know something, Bryce."

"What's that, kid?"

I hated it when he called me that. Bryce was barely a year older than I, and yet when he used that kid stuff on me, I felt like I was about five years old again. I know he used the term in a friendly manner, so I didn't say anything. Besides, it wouldn't have mattered. If Bryce knew it annoyed me, he'd probably use it more often.

"Well," I said, "how come you don't just space us off? I mean, why bother to defend Kyle or me?"

Bryce fell silent as we made our way out of the park. I thought maybe I'd offended him. I was almost afraid to say anything more. I didn't ever want to lose the protection Bryce offered. People at school left me alone because of him. If Bryce one day decided not to watch my back, I'd definitely take a lot more crap.

"Look," Bryce finally said, "Jen spoke with Becky Hatchett earlier tonight. She got an address for us to check on Saturday. So hopefully we'll find Kyle and bring him home."

I saw Kyle's face in my mind for a moment. I sighed, "If he'll come back with us."

"Oh," stated Bryce, popping his knuckles as we walked toward my house, "the boy will come along or he'll be sorry he didn't!"

"What then?" I asked. "Superglue the kid to his bed? Lock him up in his room? I mean, he won't stay put if he doesn't want to come home."

"That's when you'll be there for him," declared Bryce.

Bryce then answered my previous question. "Do you know how I felt about my little brother when I caught him messing around with Billy Jackson in that pup tent?"

"Shocked?"

"Yeah. I really wanted to beat him. There he was, buck naked! I hated him for it because I was the one who caught him."

Bryce paused. He shook back shaggy strands of his dark hair. "If it had been Chad or Jason who discovered their baby brother with another boy in our backyard? Hell! Johnny and his playmate would have been marched out into the street, paraded around in front of all our neighbors, and had their bare butts beaten!"

I asked, "So you were mad because you found him? Why, because you weren't hard core like your older brothers? Or because you had to keep Johnny's secret?"

Bryce's dark eyes darted to the ground. He winced, having a hard time harnessing his emotions.

"My own little brother a homo, though, Chris," he whispered.

I wanted to say, *Sorry you had to find Johnny doing it. Sorry if Johnny was gay. Sorry he got hit by that car. Sorry you have to stick up for me and Kyle. I'm so damned sorry!*

But suddenly Bryce said something that made me not want to be sorry anymore. "The reason I watch your back is that I was able to accept my little brother because of you. I mean, because I knew you, Chris, and how cool you are, even though you're gay. That's how I coped with Johnny doing it with another boy in that tent in our backyard."

Bryce's words made me stop and think and for long moments afterward, I felt okay with myself. Not *good,* but *okay.*

I thought, *Cool even though I was gay? Bryce isn't even aware he's saying, "Even though you're queer, you're still cool; despite the fact that you're a homosexual, you're still okay."*

I could accept that. Coming from Bryce it was a compliment.

He added, "If I hadn't known you, Chris, and known that you're just an ordinary kid, I wouldn't have been able to quit hating my little brother. How do other people do it, anyway? When they discover their brother or sister is gay, how do they deal with it?"

I didn't have an answer. So I said, "Johnny was lucky you were so tolerant that night you found him. Johnny was lucky to have had a brother like you."

And I'm lucky to have you for a friend, I nearly said, yet I didn't. I could never be so forward with Bryce.

"Look," I said, gazing up at the stars, trying not to make eye contact with him, "my life sort of sucks. You might think I'm proud to be gay. The whole damned thing is so ironic, Bryce. Take the word for instance: *Gay,* it's supposed to describe happy and lighthearted feelings. Who picked that word, anyway? I am gay, but I'm so sad and mixed up inside that I'm far from being lighthearted and happy! I don't even like myself."

Bryce waited for me to continue. I forced myself to tear my gaze from the stars and look directly at him.

"The thing that's so cool about you, Bryce, is how you treated your little brother. You didn't harass him or beat him up when you caught him. Think how you'd feel, if you had made the last years of his life miserable. I'm glad you're who you are, Bryce. So was Johnny, I bet."

Bryce lowered his gaze, then grinned and said, "Well, I like you, too, Chris."

Then he punched me none too gently on the arm. "Just don't get no ideas."

I smiled and gingerly rubbed my arm. "You're safe with me, Bryce. You're not my type. You're way too macho!"

Bryce flexed his muscles, striking a bodybuilder's pose. He then turned to leave. "Got to go, man. You sure you're okay?"

"What? After my encounter with those three back at the park? I'm in a lot better shape than they are, thanks to you."

I leaned against my garage and silently watched Bryce move down the shadowy sidewalk beneath the trees lining the street.

When he was about twenty feet away, he glanced back over one shoulder. "I'm not talking about the squabble at the park. I'm sorry for the way you feel about yourself, man. Really, Chris, I am."

He turned to face me as he said, "Look at me. I'm considered cool by almost everyone, but even I don't always like myself. I can't imagine what it's like for you. You got to live with yourself, so I hope for your sake you eventually come to accept yourself. Sure would make your life easier, Chris."

With that said, Bryce moved off into the night.

I gazed at the stars long after he was gone, trying hard to find something to like about myself. Believe me, knowing myself as well as I did, it was not an easy thing to do. I could have been there until the sun came up because I'm always too honest with myself, and truth cuts sharper than a razor blade.

I wanted to pray for some reason, but instead I simply asked a question, thinking, *Why me, God? Out of all the millions of souls, why did I have to be born gay? Can you hear me, God? Or because of who—and what— I am, are you ignoring me?*

Afterward, I started for the back door, and as I did I saw a falling star whizzing its way across the night sky.

I heard words drift my way like mist in the night winds:

How do you think God feels about you being gay, Chris?

Isn't God love? Isn't his greatest commandment to love him and love one another?

You really think he'd turn against us because we loved each other? Sounds like a big contradiction to me.

Could God be so cruel as to let us suffer a living hell on earth, and then send us to hell when we didn't have a choice in the matter? Where's the love of God in that?

Maybe against all odds, God that's beyond the wind, the sun, the moon, and past the stars, has a different plan for us.

One more shooting star passed through the night sky, and just before stepping into the house, I waved good night to God.

Chapter Six

Jen spun the steering wheel of her Mustang, forcing her car into a sharp turn. In the backseat, I slid sideways, nearly knocking heads with Bryce, who was smart enough to reach up on his side of the car and latch onto the leather strap attached to the Mustang's roof.

Straightening out the Mustang as we shot out onto Interstate 80, Jen glanced at Bryce and me in her rearview mirror. "Sorry, dudes. Just trying to kick this night into gear! After all, Bryce, you did say you wanted a little excitement!"

"Excitement," said Bryce, "not a trip into the nearest ditch."

Jen grinned at Molly next to her in the passenger seat, then at Bryce in her mirror. "Think you can do better?"

Bryce looked hopeful. "Sure. Are you serious, Jenny?"

Jen dramatically placed her right hand over her heart. "Hear that, Molly? He called me *Jenny*. He's sweet talking me, thinking there's a chance I'd let him drive this machine."

Only I saw the frown on Bryce's face as he said, "Real funny, Jen. I thought you were serious. Don't screw with me that way."

Jen and Molly laughed, and after offering Bryce a wink over her shoulder, Jen leaned toward Molly and gave her a quick peck on the cheek.

Seated there on the start of our journey to find Kyle, I felt a little torn. There was Jen, finally happy again because she'd found a new girlfriend. I was pleased for her because Molly, with her long, silky blonde hair and her delicate features, appeared content to be with Jen. I hoped, for Jen's sake, their relationship lasted.

Bryce, however, was not a happy camper. He'd committed himself to our cause of driving up to Omaha, sixty miles from Lincoln, to find

Kyle. I felt sorry for him. Rachel Collister had called Bryce earlier, inviting him to a movie. Bryce turned down the long-anticipated date, telling Rachel he was grounded, rather than the truth, that he'd promised to help his gay friends. I admired Bryce for not ditching us. The least Jen could do to make up for Bryce's sacrifice was to let him drive her Mustang.

Jen whipped her car into the passing lane, soaring past two slower vehicles as she said, "Once Kyle's safe in that backseat, reunited with Christopher, I'll let you drive us home, Bryce."

Bryce seemed content with that, and he grinned at me. We rode for a while simply staring out at fields on either side of I-80. Jen turned the radio up when Melissa Etheridge came on. As she and Molly listened to Melissa belting out her tune, Bryce and I peered out opposite windows.

I searched the sky on either side of the road for red-tailed hawks that winged their way along the interstate. Usually, when you spotted one hawk hovering above an open field you'd spot its mate close by. I'd read somewhere that hawks mate for life, and though I couldn't be sure, I figured the pair I spotted were mates hunting for their meal. Watching them spiral, bank, and soar through the blue skies, I felt comforted. I envied them. Mates for life. I could only wonder what that must be like.

Yet it also made me aware of how alone I was in the world. I had bonded with Kyle, and if it was up to me I'd stay connected to him until the day I died. But in my heart, I doubted Kyle would remain faithful to me throughout the coming years. I knew I'd be setting myself up for great disappointment because he was so unpredictable. I wouldn't hurt Kyle by leaving him for anyone. I guess, in regard to a relationship, I had the heart of a hawk, one mate for life.

"Cool!" I heard Jen say as she and Molly spotted a single hawk gliding over the interstate directly in front of the Mustang.

The four of us watched the raptor drop to the grassy bank to our right and pounce on an unfortunate mouse.

"Gross!" grunted Molly in disgust.

"Sick!" agreed Jen, turning her face, refusing to watch the rodent squirming within its talons as the hawk beat a hasty path toward the cornfield beyond.

"Too cool!" stated Bryce, fascinated by the mouse dangling from hawk talons.

Awesome! I thought as I saw the second hawk rising from the branch of an old oak at the edge of the field. Gracefully, it fanned its wings as it rose to meet its mate. The hawks met in midair, the two of them circling within the same current.

God, I thought, *it must be great to have that special bond, to become so closely attached, for life.*

When Melissa's song ended, Jen said, "She's so cool! Got a great career and knows who she is!"

Bryce said, "A lesbian, right? Wasn't she involved in some same-sex union where one of them had a kid? What'd they do, adopt? Lesbians adopting and raising kids? I don't know about that."

Pierced by Jen's intense stare, Bryce said, "What?"

Jen responded, "Be enlightened. Lesbian couples can make very good parents, Bryce. Artificial insemination is usually how one partner becomes impregnated by a sperm donor. Most same-sex couples who have a kid raise the child in a loving environment, unlike homes where parents bitterly fight or beat their kids and turn out alienated, hostile youth!"

Jen thanked Molly for reaching over to adjust the steering wheel while she'd given her commentary. Satisfied that she'd made her point, Jen looked back to the road and took over.

Then everyone looked at me as I spoke my thoughts: "Same-sex couples would have hell to pay if they wanted to marry in the state of Nebraska."

Bryce snapped his fingers, directing Jen's attention back to her driving. "Eyes on the road, girl! Don't look pissy at me. Wasn't me who said it. Shoot your pissy looks at Chris!"

"I'm not angry," stated Jen. "Just bummed, because Chris is right. Four-one-six, which was passed in the year 2000, prohibits the state of Nebraska from recognizing any same-sex union or domestic partnership. It's in the Nebraska constitution."

Molly nodded in agreement. "Yeah, and several groups are so opposed to same-sex unions that they're determined to see that any minister who performs a same-sex marriage is defrocked."

Bryce made a sour face. "Defrocked? That sounds painful. Which body part do you have to cut off to consider yourself . . . defrocked?"

Jen took her eyes off the road again. Molly reached over to steer for her as Jen glared at Bryce. "This is serious! What man has the right to break apart what God has joined together? People are destined, after all, to find each other and commit themselves to each other. So if God places someone in my path one day that I want to spend the rest of my life with, how can anyone pass a law that hinders me from doing so?"

Bryce stared straight back at her. "Why not just say vows in secret, like William Wallace did in *Braveheart*? Because how many churches allow gay marriages in their buildings?"

Jen took over the wheel again. "Not many. But the Methodists are fairly outspoken, saying that the church should reevaluate its stance on same-sex unions. And there are many more Christian folk wondering what's so wrong with marrying people if they truly love each other."

Molly looked over at Jen. "Yes, but look at all the trouble that Methodist minister, Jimmy Creech, got into for performing a marriage between two men."

"What?" said Bryce. "The pope fired him?"

Jen and Molly laughed. Bryce looked puzzled.

I grinned at Bryce. "The pope is the head of the Catholic Church, not the Methodist. Hell, most Catholics believe homosexuality is morally wrong and expressly forbidden."

Jen agreed. "Right now in Nebraska it's only open-minded Methodists and the Unitarians who are taking any sort of stand at all, though in other states I heard there are Jews, Lutherans, and even Greek Orthodox folks who are boldly going where no man—or woman—has gone before."

Bryce asked, "What's the big deal about being married? Can't you just *believe* you're married to your partner? What difference does a piece of paper make? A secret ceremony—"

"Secret ceremonies are fine!" blurted Jen. "But in a same-sex union, partners are not able to share the same rights as other married couples—health care benefits, financial security, and so forth. We want that to change!"

Bryce smirked. "We? You sound like a lesbian activist."

Jen nodded. "It's something I have to care about. I'm sixteen now, but what happens when I find the love of my life? Do I want the right to be united with her? Damned right I do!"

Hawks don't need anyone but God to allow them to be mates for life, I thought as Jen continued voicing her thoughts. I was feeling a little depressed. Kyle and I being together forever didn't seem likely. I then wondered how hawks found each other in the country skies, if it was easier for them to find a mate than it was for us humans. I wished, for long moments after that, that I was a hawk. Maybe I'd have a better chance of finding a mate for life. Hawks were lucky that way.

Hatch was not easy to find. Omaha was much larger than Lincoln, and it took nearly an hour to locate the place he was supposedly staying at. We figured Hatch would be living in a roach-infested apartment in a run-down neighborhood. So, we sat staring in disbelief at the neatly trimmed hedges and the field-sized lawn of the mansion before us.

The Tudor-style, two-story house looked like it belonged in the English countryside. In fact, surveying the lush green grass, neat rows of shrubs, and the many arbors dotted with thousands of red and pink roses, I thought, *J. R. R. Tolkien's manor house!*

Bryce whistled loudly. "Becky must have given you the wrong address. What in hell is Ronnie doing living in a castle like this?"

Jen eased up on the brakes, allowing the car to roll slowly up the driveway between giant pines. "This place is cool! Maybe Hatch is the butler or something!"

Bryce said, "Or the bed boy for a rich businessman."

I cringed when I heard this, hoping Kyle wasn't living under this same roof under that type of arrangement.

"Hey, look!" said Bryce, pointing at the four-stall garage at the end of the drive twenty yards away. "That guy's waving at us! Looks like a chauffeur in that blue blazer he's wearing."

Jen disagreed with Bryce. "Not a chauffeur. Looks more like an FBI agent. I bet he's a security guard."

I was about to say he looked more like a real estate agent, when suddenly the guy in the driveway drew a pistol from a holster beneath his suit jacket.

Jen stomped on the brakes and the Mustang screeched to a halt. Bryce and I bumped our chins on the seats in front of us. Molly hit her knees on the dash and cursed under her breath. "Sweet Jesus!" gasped Jen. "He's coming toward us!"

Before Jen could shift into reverse, stomp on the accelerator, and send us tearing back out of the driveway, I hollered, "Wait! He's not aiming the gun at us. He wants us to drive up there."

The man in the suit, his pistol pointed at the ground, stood there glaring but also motioning for us to advance up the drive.

We then heard a loud clang. The four of us nearly threw our necks out of joint as we swiveled around in our seats to peer at the massive iron gate now blocking the entrance to the driveway some distance behind us.

"We're captured!" stated Bryce, forcing a smile, though I saw him quickly examine the high stone wall encircling the property.

Jen let on up the brakes and the Mustang slowly rolled forward.

"Now there's three of them!" groaned Molly, directing our attention to the two new arrivals moving down the sidewalk from the house. Jen braked and we came to a stop.

Bryce whispered, "Diamond Dallas Page!"

And, indeed, one of the men was a huge dude who looked like the wrestling star from TV. Only this guy was dressed in a three-piece suit, not Page's typical faded, ratty jeans. He was big and blond and sported a reddish-gold beard. A small gold hoop hung from the lobe of his left ear.

He squatted down beside the passenger's window, flashing Jen a wolfish grin as he casually said, "Nice wheels! A sixty-eight Mustang! You inherit this classic?"

Jen managed to stare back at the big guy. "My grandfather gave it to me. It was a birthday present."

"Nice," said the guy, admiring the car for long moments. He then studied each one of us with sea-green eyes that brooked no nonsense. "Sorry, kids, but the senator accepts guests by invitation only."

Jen hesitantly responded, "The senator?"

The big man nodded as he stood up, removing a small control box clipped at his belt. He pointed the box at the gates. Slowly, they began to slide open, and the big blond guard said, "You *know* whose place this is. With the Forum in town, every nosy kid in Omaha wants to get a peek at the house inside these walls! You want to speak with Senator Ash, you need to set up a meeting with his secretary."

Jen offered the man a puzzled frown. "Martin Ash lives here? *The* Martin Ash?"

Before the big guy could respond, Bryce leaned forward, saying, "We're not from here. We drove up from Lincoln looking for a friend of ours. We had no idea whose place this was."

The man studied Bryce for a moment. He then stepped around to the front of the Mustang to check the plates. Grinning once more like a wolf, he moved back to the passenger side of the car. "Lincoln it is, then. Thought you were some pesky kids inquiring about the Forum. Don't mean to be rude, but the gates are now open and you can be on your way."

But Bryce peered up at the big guy and boldly asked, "Why the hell did that dude over there pull out a gun?"

Molly glanced back at Bryce. "This is Senator Martin Ash's house, stupid! We're trespassing!"

"Senator Ash?" questioned Bryce. "He so important, he's gotta have wanna-be cops waving guns around and scaring the crap out of us?"

With a humorless chuckle, the big blond turned to look up the driveway to the guard with the gun. "Harris? Put that damned thing away! They're just a bunch of kids, not assassins!"

He fixed Bryce with a steady gaze. "There. That satisfy you?"

Jen, sensing that Bryce was now in one of his moods, decided to intervene. "Sir, we don't mean to be a pain, but we're looking for a kid named Ron Hatchett. We were given this address. Is it possible he's staying here?"

We all noted the way in which the guy suddenly went very still. He stared steadily at Jen for a moment. Before he could answer, though, one of the other guards called to him from the front walk. The big man held up a finger indicating we were to wait there, then turned to speak to the other two guards. One of them removed a walkie-talkie from his belt, handing it to the big guy. Slowly, he turned to face the front window of the house nearly thirty feet away as he spoke into the mouthpiece.

"Whoa!" whispered Bryce. "You'd think we'd stumbled onto the White House lawn! This is bizarre!"

"Shh!" warned Molly. "Don't you ever listen to the news? We happen to be at Senator Ash's residence. He's a major activist in the AIDS crisis and the most outspoken Nebraska senator when it comes to health care for victims of the disease. Because of his stance, there have been several threats on his life. No wonder the guard drew his gun!"

Warily watching the three security guards as they continued to talk among themselves, Jen whispered, "Why would a senator even associate with a street punk like Hatch?"

Bryce snorted, "Go figure! If this dude is so into gay rights, doesn't it make sense?"

Jen turned to face Bryce. "Don't even go there if you're insinuating that all gay men prey on young boys! It's just not true! Martin Ash deserves better than that!"

Before Bryce and Jen could start an argument, the Diamond Dallas-looking guy returned to the car. He squatted down again and said, "Senator Ash wishes to apologize for the covert manner in which we conduct business. We take our senator's security seriously. But as to this Ron Hatchett you were searching for, sorry, never heard of him."

Jen must have seen the sorrow in my eyes in her rearview mirror. "Sorry, Chris. We just have to look elsewhere for the boy."

She then apologized to the man for our intrusion and started to back up. Bryce whispered, "He's lying! He does know Hatch! I can see it in his eyes!"

"Shush!" urged Jen, turning around in her seat so that she could steer us back down the driveway, past the gates, and out into the street. She gunned the Mustang and took us out of there.

And then we spotted Hatch walking down the sidewalk on our side of the street. Or so we thought. The blond-haired kid could have been Hatch's twin. As we pulled up beside him, he looked at us in confusion.

"Sorry," Jen said to the rather startled kid. "We thought you were someone else."

Then he surprised us. Looking at the driveway we had just come out of, he grinned and leaned in Molly's window. "And just who did you think I was?"

Jen explained our purpose for being in Omaha. The kid denied knowing Kyle. But when Jen mentioned Hatch, he got this strange look on his face. He studied all of us a moment as Jen became a little more brutally honest about who Hatch was and the kind of things he did to make money. "A street whore?" he said with a rather wicked grin. "How disgusting!"

He stepped away from the car, saying, "A good place to find this Hatch fellow is probably somewhere in the Old Market area, more than likely, hanging out at Thirteenth and Howard Street. That is, if there is such a kid by that name. Might also find your friend there."

Jen thanked him and we drove away.

Chapter Seven

As we slowly cruised Howard Street in the Old Market area of Omaha, we gawked at the rustic storefronts. The place had that Old Chicago kind of feel to it—streets paved with bricks, buildings badly in need of fresh paint—like a place frozen in another time. At the end of one block was a pub with an open-air dining area. People sat there eating and drinking beneath huge umbrellas, candle pots illuminating their features. They appeared oblivious to us as we cruised past them in Jen's Mustang.

Venturing deeper into the market, we passed a record shop, a bookstore, an antique mall, an exotic clothing outlet, and three ancient train cars turned into a restaurant. As we approached 13th and Howard, Bryce spotted three boys standing in the shadows of an awning in front of one of the buildings.

"Is that how it's done?" asked Bryce.

"How *what's* done?" I responded as I peered closely at the kids, trying to see if one of them might be Kyle or Hatch.

"How they sell themselves," replied Bryce, pointing at the boys. "Ain't that what they're doing?"

Jen and Molly studied the young kids as well. "Looks like they're just hanging out," remarked Jen, yet just as she said this a tall man approached the boys and began talking to them. As Jen pulled slowly into a parking stall and turned the car off, one of the boys joined the man and the two walked off down the alley together.

"See," said Bryce, rather smugly. "I knew that's what they were doing. Don't they call it cruisin' or something like that?"

Jen shook her head, staring rather sadly at the man and boy as they moved off into the shadows. "I call it *pitiful*. Anyone see Hatch or Kyle? This is where that kid said we might find them."

We looked to both sides of the street, peering into shadowy doorways and dimly lit alleys.

Suddenly a voice came from just outside Molly's window. "What's up?"

Molly gasped in surprise. The rest of us turned quickly in our seats. One of the kids who had been standing beneath the awning had silently strolled up to the car. Grinning like the Cheshire Cat, he seemed amused at the alarmed looks on our faces.

Glaring up at the slender, sandy-haired boy, Bryce snapped, "You got a problem?"

The boy gave a slight chuckle. "Good question. Business is slow tonight. You looking for some action?"

At this, Bryce angrily snarled, "Look, you stupid son of a—"

Jen turned around and shoved Bryce back into his seat. "Cool your jets!" she warned, snapping her fingers beneath his nose.

The kid outside the car looked warily at Bryce. "Sorry, dude. I was just trying to be friendly. Thought maybe you were looking for a job or something. I was just inquiring. That's all."

"He means a blow job!" growled Bryce.

"I know," I said. "Don't take it so personally."

Jen climbed out of the car and approached the boy. He looked as if he might run if she so much as sneezed. "Sorry about that," she offered, gesturing toward Bryce who sat fuming in the backseat. "Our friend's not interested. However, we might donate ten bucks to your . . . cause, if you can help us find a kid we're looking for."

The boy hesitantly shook hands with Jen as she introduced herself, telling him that we were from Lincoln and searching for Hatch. The moment she said the name, the kid became friendly and gestured to the other boy still standing in the shadows near the mouth of the nearby alley.

This kid was even younger, looking to be around twelve or thirteen. In fact, he was so skinny and had such ratty dark hair, I thought at first he was a girl. As he joined the other kid, he shot nervous glances at us.

"Hey, Bobby," said the older boy, "these guys are looking for Hatch. They're friends of his up from Lincoln. They'll pay us ten bucks if we tell them where he is. What do you think?"

The smaller, scrawnier kid hunched down so that he could get a better look at the three of us in the car. "Don't know if we should do that, Ben. Hatch is doing that thing tonight. If we mess that up, he'll be mad as hell."

What thing? I wanted to ask.

My heart sank as I heard the younger kid say, "He's been up there working as a bellboy for two weeks, him and that girlie-boy who's always hanging around with him. If we send these guys up there, they just might screw things up. If Hatch found out we told where he was, he'd hunt us down, Ben."

Girlie-boy? I thought. *Does he mean Kyle?*

Jen looked down at the younger kid, but handed the older one ten dollars as she said, "We won't involve you guys. We just want to find our friend. We don't want to cause any trouble."

The ten spot vanished the moment she handed it over. The taller kid smiled. "Thanks. Ten more would help Bobby to overcome his fear, though. You see, Hatch is doing this special service tonight, and he'd be hacked at us if we blew things for him. Understand?"

I climbed out of the Mustang and joined Jen on the sidewalk. Hastily, I reached into my pocket and pulled out two five-dollar bills. "You'll walk away with ten apiece if you tell us where to find Hatch. And could I ask you a question?"

The two kids eyed my money greedily. "Ask away," said Ben.

"Who is this other kid you're talking about? Do you know his name?"

Bobby smirked. "He's Hatch's new girlfriend. Name is Kyle. He's from Lincoln, too. He's cute, but he's such a pussy."

"And what would you call yourself?" asked Bryce from his place in the backseat.

Bobby looked uncertainly at Bryce. Jen snapped, "Knock it off, Bryce!"

"Here," I barely managed to whisper as I handed my money over to the bigger kid. I was really feeling bad about what I'd just heard. I thought, *Kyle has become Hatch's lover? How could that have happened in these few short weeks? How could Kyle betray me like that? Maybe this kid's got it all wrong. God, how could this have happened?*

Bobby didn't look back as he sauntered over to the shadows beneath the awning. But Ben pocketed my cash and told us, "Hatch is doing a job up at the Black Lion Inn. Lots of things happening in that place tonight. Good luck. Remember, though, you didn't hear a thing from us. The Lion is up three blocks from here on Thirteenth and Farnum."

As we pulled away down the street, Bryce looked back at the two kids in disgust. "That's probably the easiest money they've ever earned. Pair of punks like that, selling their scrawny butts! They ought to be ashamed."

Jen glanced back sadly in their direction and said, "I'm sure they are."

As hotels go, the Black Lion Inn was classy. The building took up two entire blocks and stood at least thirty stories tall. It had an awesome glassed-in elevator and, after sneaking past security guards, the four of us rode up and down all thirty stories half a dozen times. Peering out through the thick panes of glass, we could see all of downtown Omaha. On the downward trip, the elevator dropped so suddenly that my stomach did flip-flops all the way to street level. On each trip, though, the four of us stood with our noses pressed to the panes, looking down at people and cars that appeared the size of ants and Matchbox toys far below.

Finally, on our seventh trip down, the elevator stopped on the third floor and several people entered as the door swished open. They were all yakking away, involved in friendly bantering. We tried to blend in, acting as if we had as much business being there as they did. However, in a matter of moments, the three ladies and two men fell silent as they noted our rigid stances.

"Hey, kids," one of the middle-aged women said as she gave us a smile, "you here for the Forum? You from one of the support groups of a local school? We're heading there now. If you've become separated from your group, you're welcome to join us."

Ever since the big security dude at Senator Ash's place mentioned this Forum, we'd been curious. On our drive to the Old Market district we speculated that it was probably some meeting involving politics.

Bryce blurted out, "Just what is this Forum, anyhow?"

The men and the women peered suspiciously at Bryce and then back at Jen.

"You kids aren't here to cause trouble, are you?" asked one of the men, a short guy with a receding hairline.

An older lady with swirls of gray in her long dark hair studied us before saying, "You're not students here to represent your school, are you?"

"Lady," Jen began, "we're just—"

"I'll tell you now," warned the short guy, "security escorted a group of obnoxious activists out of the meeting earlier tonight! Though they were from the Christian League of Human Dignity, all twelve of them received citations for trespassing!"

The elevator stopped on ground level and the door opened. Two of the women and one of the men exited without so much as a backward glance, but the older lady and the short and balding guy stood there before us, literally blocking our way.

Jen offered a disarming smile as she told the lady, "Honestly, we're not here to cause trouble. We're searching for a friend we were told works here. We did, however, hear about this Forum earlier tonight, something to do with Senator Martin Ash."

The elevator door started to whoosh closed. The short, stocky guy hit the button on the panel so that it swished back open. Keeping his hand on the button, he stepped through the open door to exit the elevator. "Debate starts in five minutes, Cora. If you don't want to miss Landan's opening statements, you'd better get moving. I'll escort these kids to the security desk."

Jen looked curiously at Cora. "Senator Landan is here, tonight? And he's holding a debate with whom? Senator Ash?"

Cora offered Jen a slight smile. "Yes. I'm surprised you're not up to date on current events. Haven't your teachers discussed the Forum with you at your school? It's been in the papers for the past two weeks."

"We're not from Omaha," Jen told her. "We're visiting from Lincoln. Is this Forum that big a deal?"

"Some folks think so," answered Cora. "It has a lot to do with educating kids about the AIDS epidemic. Ash and Landan are two Nebraska senators who have caused enough controversy this past year about Proposal Two Twenty-One. Surely you've heard of Two Twenty-One!"

Jen nodded slowly. "Proposal Two Twenty-One?"

Cora responded, "It has to do with an educational prevention plan that's not been accepted by the public schools. Ash is for it. Landan is against. It should prove to be an interesting debate."

Cora stepped off the elevator, moving past the balding man. "Have a nice evening, children. Come along, Douglas."

Douglas gave us a shrewd look as we stepped off the elevator. The four of us stood there looking stupid as he followed Cora down the hallway. I was about to suggest that we move off in the opposite direction when a beefy security guard appeared at the other end of the hallway. He approached us, scowling like he was constipated.

Sternly, he growled, "Okay, boys and girls, the amusement ride on our elevator is over! I've been watching you on the monitors for the past five minutes. I should issue you tickets for trespassing, but if you leave through the front doors now—"

"Ma'am?" Jen called out to Cora, who was watching us from down the hall. "How do you go about getting an official invite to this Forum?"

"Jen!" protested Molly. "We can't go to this meeting!"

Bryce whispered, "I'm here to find Kyle, not hear politicians blather about a bunch of crap!"

Cora and the scowling security guard now studied us with a mixture of curiosity and bewilderment on their faces.

Bryce lowered his voice. "Jen, are you nuts? I'm not about to go to some boring meeting! Let's just go search for Kyle and get out of here!"

Jen turned to face the three of us, defiantly placing her hands on her hips. "Jen, this is not for us," I told her, noticing that Cora was now coming back in our direction.

The woman folded her arms as she stopped about three feet away. With her green dress and her long, gray-black hair, she looked like some regal queen appraising our worth as she asked, "Are you seriously interested in the issues? Would you like to listen to the debate?"

"Yes," answered Jen.

I was about to tell Jen she could go by herself if she thought we were going to abandon our quest to find Kyle, but I shut my mouth as the hefty security guard cleared his throat. "Uh, ma'am? I think I'd best escort these kids—"

"Sir?" said Cora. "These *students* are with us. They'll attend the meeting and then . . . I'll be responsible for quietly escorting them to the front entrance."

The four of us were relieved, but I wondered where Jen's crazy scheme was going to lead. Moments later, we followed Cora and her friends into the crowded Captain's Hall of the Black Lion Inn.

Chapter Eight

Bryce leaned over and whispered in my ear, "This guy is an anal-retentive moron!"

We'd sat for the past thirty minutes in the back row listening to Landan and Ash debate, and it was far from boring.

Senator Landan reminded me of one of those late-night TV evangelists, his blond hair slicked down with 10W30 motor oil and shining so brightly in the media lights that I imagined I could see my own reflection in its glare.

"It's a major sin you're asking us to condone," Senator Landan spouted. "As a Christian—one who takes the Word of God quite literally—I cannot accept these teachings you're attempting to convince us are based on love. God did not send his Son to die on the cross so that those who lust after each other's bodies can continue to sin and then excuse it by calling it . . . an act of love!"

To argue against Proposal 221 and stop a particular AIDS prevention program from being incorporated into the Omaha public schools, Senator Steve Landan had first blasted his opponent with talk about the destruction of Sodom and Gomorrah and the evils of pornography. It was a lame approach, but he tried to associate the porn industry with the homosexual lifestyle, claiming it was society's acceptance of gays and lesbians that caused the pornographic industry to literally flood the Internet.

"If we begin to close our eyes to homosexuals and their continued sin," declared Landan, "then we open the floodgates when it comes to accepting the pornography that is displayed on our own home computers! Tens of thousands of smutty pictures flood the Internet because we've become tolerant of these gay activists who constantly whine about their rights and prey upon our sympathies, asking us to accept them!"

I couldn't believe it when I heard Landan say, "Most gay men have over a dozen sexual partners in their lifetime! What does that tell you about the lusts of these depraved men? No wonder the AIDS epidemic has spread so rapidly! The carriers of this disease couple with one another with a burning desire to continue such behavior. And with promiscuous sex running rampant in homosexual communities, AIDS is God's way of punishing these unrepentant homosexuals—"

"Don't even go there, Steve Landan," said Senator Martin Ash, "if you're trying to say AIDS is God's plague on homosexuality! What went wrong with his plan when it spread to heterosexuals? Consider the millions of heterosexuals who have died of AIDS. What is their sin that they deserve this punishment?"

Applause erupted from folks near the front of the hall.

As I focused on Ash, seated so casually before us on the stage, Bryce leaned over and whispered, "Steven Seagal!"

The dude did look like the actor, with his long, black hair in a ponytail and his Italian looks. If he'd been dressed in a black suit, he would have looked like one of those Mafia guys out of a *Godfather* movie. But he was dressed in jeans, a long-sleeved white shirt, and a black leather vest. He looked like he'd be more at home on the range than debating in front of all these stiff necks in a posh hotel in the center of Omaha.

Martin Ash swung around in his chair and looked evenly at his opponent. "I don't want to take our focus off of the proposal, but it seems I must. My opponent has focused on abstinence—no sex at all—which I consider unrealistic in teaching students about the dangers of this crisis.

"Proposal Two Twenty-One supports safer-sex practices—including the use of condoms—and so Senator Landan attacks this AIDS prevention program, pointing an accusatory finger at one component of its teachings. He calls this the *gay agenda,* loudly declaring that producers of this program accept the gay and lesbian lifestyle, hoping to rally all who strongly oppose same-sex relationships.

"I beg to differ. Students need this program—gay and straight alike—and there is much more to be gained by accepting it, for the sake of our youth, than ignorantly rejecting it."

Senator Ash turned to look directly at Landan seated behind him on the stage. "Do you believe in magic, Senator Landan?"

Landan made a sour face. "Magic? What are you talking about, Ash? The Bible says—"

"I know what the Word says," declared Ash. "If your investigative sources were any good, they would have informed you I was a Catholic monk for thirteen years. Besides, I'm not referring to sorcery. I'm simply asking you a question. Do you believe there is magic—mysterious and wondrous forces—in the world? *Miracles,* if you need to keep this in a scriptural context. Senator, do you believe in miracles?"

"Why, of course!" replied Landan.

Ash spoke then in a clear and steady voice. As he did, he slowly rose from his seat and spread his arms in a gesture that reminded me of Saint Patrick about to cast the snakes out of the misty woodlands of Ireland.

Martin Ash said, "There was a care home for the elderly in Tennessee. The director and his staff often struggled with the fact that despite their efforts, many of their elderly residents battled against overwhelming depression. The director wondered how to prevent such depression from sapping the residents of their will to live. He implemented a strategy to combat what he deemed a severe mental health issue.

"He visited a local humane society and adopted several dogs. He then had the care home residents select which dogs would share their rooms. Bonds were formed between elderly folk and animals, and moods and attitudes improved dramatically.

"God did a wonderful thing when he created a dog. Such creatures are capable of giving and receiving love. Once a bond is established, a dog can actually empathize with the person it loves, sensing sadness, anxiety, contentment, and even anger. There's true magic in that."

Ash paused, then said, "And such magic spread like wildfire through that particular care home. You see, love was allowed to nurture, to empower, to heal, and to touch the lives of those who desperately needed it. No boundaries were set on the forces of . . . love."

His long ponytail whipping over his broad shoulders, Ash swung around to face his opponent as Landan snorted.

"Bear with me a moment longer," whispered Ash. He then swiftly launched into another tale.

"In western Montana, there was a rancher who adopted a herd of wild horses rescued by a preservation team. The rancher hoped to tame these horses and sell them to possible buyers. But breaking such free-spirited animals was not an easy task. Having had no contact with humans, these horses were feral beasts.

"Months after undertaking this endeavor, the rancher had not come any closer to reaching his goal. The expense of keeping such a herd was becoming an increasing burden. The rancher began to consider alternatives, yet his options were fairly limited."

It became extremely quiet in the room. The crowd waited expectantly for Ash to continue his story.

"The alternative plan that the rancher came up with," he explained, "was to bring in a group of delinquents from a local detention facility. The rancher assigned each wild and troubled kid to an equally wild and troubled horse. The kids fed, watered, and curried the horses. It took many long hours, many long days. But finally, after several weeks of constantly touching these wild beasts, these determined kids connected with them. And with the bond they formed, the wild horses were tamed and eventually saddled and ridden."

Ash turned and faced Senator Landan, saying, "Once again, magic happened, where love was not restricted, where no boundaries were set for that force which flows through all of us—straight or gay.

"So, I ask you to consider these two parallels. When you say that this power known as love should be limited and shared only between a man and a woman, what gives you the right? Love should be allowed to nurture, to empower, to heal, and to touch the lives of those who desperately need it. Yet you judge, condemn, criticize, and take on a godlike role when you attempt to demoralize those who only want to share their lives together! What if God actually *preordained* these unions that you, as a man, try to persuade us to believe are evil? What if God decreed that love—the power that is the source of all relationships—wasn't to be restricted?"

Ash smiled. "Have you ever sat in a circle and played Telephone? It begins with one person whispering a certain message into another's ear. By the time that message is passed around a circle of twenty people, it's changed from its original version. People will edit it, paraphrase it, put it in their own words, reinterpret it, misinterpret it, and fail to repeat it word for word.

"Did you know that the Bible was first written in Hebrew, then translated to Greek, then to Latin, and then to English? Which Bible do you base your beliefs on? King James? Revised Standard? New English? Jerusalem Bible? Living Bible? They all contain different translations."

He smiled again. "In Second Peter, Chapter Three, verses sixteen and seventeen, Peter warns, 'There are some things hard to understand, which the ignorant and the unstable twist to their own destruction, as they do other scriptures. You therefore, beloved, knowing this beforehand, beware lest you be carried away with the error of lawless men and lose your stability.'

"If you're basing your condemnation of same-sex unions on scripture, be careful that you don't twist those scriptures out of context. Don't deceive yourself into thinking you have godly authority to win your case based on translations that might not mean what *you* think they do!"

Senator Landan angrily snapped, "But it's a sickness!"

To which Ash responded, "According to whom?"

The tall, dark-haired senator spun away from the podium to switch on an overhead projector. Pointing to a screen behind the stage, he said, "The concept that homosexuality is a mental illness has been repudiated by . . ."

And on the screen, we all read:

The American Medical Association
The American Academy of Pediatrics
The American Counseling Association
The American Psychiatric Association
The American Psychological Association
The American School Health Association
The National Association of Social Workers

Landan peered up at the screen. "And so, you want to promote among our youth that homosexuality is acceptable?"

"I want," declared Ash, "to educate youth—gay and straight—about the AIDS crisis without coming up against such resistance and intolerance from people with views like yours!"

Ash slipped a second transparency onto the glass screen of the projector. He said, "From the National Statistics on Teens, among gay and lesbian youth, we have . . ."

And once more, we all looked to the screen to see:

30 percent of teen suicides
40 percent of throwaways and runaways
28 percent are high school dropouts
50 percent rejected by families
80 percent report severe isolation problems
97 percent hear antigay comments in school
50 percent claim they are assaulted in schools

Ash glanced back at Landan. "In Matthew, Chapter Eighteen, verse six, Jesus says, 'But whosoever shall offend one of these little ones which believe in me, it were better for him that a millstone be hanged about his neck, and that he were drowned in the sea.'

"I say, be careful with your intolerance, your condemnation, your misunderstanding, and your rigid stance on this matter, that you don't further complicate the life of a youth who is already confused or distressed about his or her sexual orientation."

Senator Ash then said, "In considering your vote on Two Twenty-One, remember these words, 'They condemn what they do not understand.'"

Landan came out of his seat at this statement. He looked as if he was going to charge across the stage and tear into Ash. I hoped he would. Senator Ash looked capable of pounding Landan into the ground. And as I thought of Bryce's comment earlier, about Ash resembling Steven Seagal, I had to grin. It would've been cool to watch Martin Ash perform a spin kick and send Landan crashing to the stage on his pompous ass.

But to my disappointment, there was no physical contact between the two men. The confrontation that erupted remained verbal as the senators launched into a heated debate.

I shook my head and decided I needed to get out of that meeting hall. I liked Ash's tales about magic and I could relate to how he talked about the power of love in any kind of relationship. But I really had to take a leak.

I leaned over and whispered to Bryce, "I'm going to the can. Be back shortly."

Hatch ran directly into me as I exited the hotel bathroom. "Hey!" he shouted. "Watch where you're going!" I snapped back.

We took a step backward and looked at each other. Ronnie wore a red suit jacket, black dress pants, and a pair of leather shoes. Tossing his head back, he flipped long, blond bangs out of his dark eyes. "Chris? What're you doing here?"

"Looking for Kyle. Do you know where he is, Hatch?"

Hatch cocked his head and smirked. I noticed he had changed in the past three months. The bellhop suit nearly swallowed his skinny frame, blotches of zits covered his cheeks, and wiry hair protruded from his chin. If rumors were true that Hatch was a well-paid street whore, I wondered what men saw in him.

"Kyle is busy," Hatch told me. "He's about to go to work. But if you're good and can keep quiet, I might let you come along."

He's about to go to work? I thought, those words cutting me deeply. *What sort of work? Hatch has him selling himself?*

"What do you mean, Hatch? What is Kyle going to do?"

Hatch gave me a wicked grin. "Come along, if you dare," he said, entering the bathroom.

I followed him. After using a urinal, Hatch zipped up and strolled over to the sinks, where he began combing his hair. "You by yourself?"

"No. Bryce and Jen are with me. They're inside a meeting hall listening to something known as the Forum. Where's Kyle?"

Hatch wiggled his fingers at me as he started for the door.

"The Forum." He laughed as if he knew some personal joke. "Exactly why we're here tonight. Come along, Chris. But if you interfere in our work, I'll put a hurt on you."

I wanted to drop Hatch right where he stood, but I knew it would ruin my chances of finding Kyle. Reluctantly, I followed him out of the bathroom and over to the hotel elevators.

Chapter Nine

I asked, "Who is he waiting for?"

Hatch sat in a chair before a two-way mirror, adjusting buttons on a camcorder attached to a tripod. He looked up to peer at Kyle sitting on the edge of a bed in the opposite room. "You'll see," he smirked.

Tapping a button on the video camera, Hatch glared at me. "You can leave anytime. But don't even think about screwing this up, Talbot! This is something that's been planned for a long time. Kyle and I are making a lot of cash off of this deal!"

I peered through the mirror and studied Kyle's features. Tears came to my eyes as I realized how much I had missed him. Seated there in the opposite room, dressed in the same type of bellboy uniform that Hatch wore, he looked so lost. Whatever scheme Hatch had gotten him mixed up in could not be good. The two-way mirror creeped me out, and I wondered who had gone through so much trouble to install such a contraption.

"Have you guys done this sort of thing before?" I asked.

Hatch peeked through the eyepiece of the camcorder. "No. Nothing like this, anyway. We've worked this place before. Lots of money with clients to be made. But this?"

He pointed at the camera and the two-way mirror. "Hell, this is high tech! Our employer wants film on the man to convince him he needs to change his view. I'd like to be there later when he sees this flick!"

I asked, "The man? What man are you talking about, Hatch? And is Kyle actually gonna—"

Suddenly a loud knock came from the door in the opposite room. I watched as Kyle nearly leaped off the bed, fidgety as a startled cat. Kyle opened the door and stood back, allowing a stocky dude dressed in a dark suit to enter the room. The short man had long, greasy hair and carried a briefcase. He muttered a greeting to Kyle and then walked over and placed the leather case on the bed.

"Close the door, kid," ordered the beefy guy as he opened the case, revealing neatly ordered stacks of money.

Peering through the camera, Hatch whispered, "Sweet Jesus! That's a lot of green!"

We watched in total silence as the stocky guy slipped a fifty-dollar bill from one of the money stacks. "Here," he said, turning to face Kyle. "Your payment, kid."

As Kyle stashed the fifty in his jacket pocket, the man poked him in the center of the chest with a stubby finger. "Don't go messin' up any part of this because I won't tolerate screwups!"

Kyle nodded and watched as the man removed two letter-sized envelopes from the briefcase. One was blue, the other bright red. He handed both to Kyle. "Don't get these mixed up. The blue one goes to Landan. The red you give to Senator Ash. Got it?"

Kyle placed both envelopes in an inner pocket of his red suit jacket. "Blue to Landan. Red to Ash. I got it."

"Good," said the man, peering down at his wristwatch. "The Forum will be ending shortly. Get down there, and do this right! Know what to do? Or do I need to rehearse it wit' you?"

Kyle started for the door. "Hand the first envelope to Landan. Then wait for five minutes and hand the other one to Martin Ash. Okay?"

The greasy-haired man looked to Kyle standing there about to open the door. "Right. Only thing is, when that meeting breaks up, gonna be a chaotic crowd in that room. Before you get close to either senator, you'll get intercepted by one of their security specialists. So play your part as the stupid bellboy and say the envelopes contain an urgent message from a mutual associate. Got it?"

Kyle opened the door, then paused as the guy sternly said, "Once you leave this room, don't come back! Got it?"

Kyle muttered something neither Hatch nor I could hear as he went off down the hotel hallway and the door closed behind him.

We watched as the man in the opposite room quickly returned to the bed, where he closed the briefcase. Leaving it there on the bed, the short guy then hurriedly left the hotel room.

For the next ten minutes, I demanded to know what kind of scheme Hatch had involved Kyle in, but Hatch refused to tell me. Five minutes more, and Kyle reentered the room beyond the two-way mirror. I stared in puzzlement as he tossed the red envelope in a trash can beside the bed and made a thumbs-up sign at the two-way mirror.

Still peering through the camera's viewer, Hatch grinned and whispered, "Yeah! So far, so good! But hurry and get things set up, Kyle! You've got less than five minutes!"

Though Kyle couldn't have possibly heard Ronnie, he hastily crossed to the desk in one corner of the room and removed a notebook computer and a long length of phone line from its top drawer. Carrying them over to the bed, Kyle placed the computer next to the briefcase, then plucked the existing jack from the nearby wall, and inserted the jack of the independent line he held. Rushing back to the bed, he strung the line out behind him.

As Kyle flipped open the notebook computer and inserted the other jack into the back of it, I asked, "Why did he come back? You guys stealing that money? What in hell is going on?"

Ignoring me, Hatch peered through the camcorder, and quietly spoke as if he were talking Kyle through his next actions. "Hit Enter on the notebook. Then the cuffs. Lock down the treasure. Hurry! Dump the key, put the note on the briefcase. Then get out of there! Go, Kyle! Go! Go! Go!"

I peered through the two-way mirror. Kyle tapped a key on the computer and the screen lit up. He then removed a pair of handcuffs from a pocket of his red jacket. Quickly, he secured the briefcase to one of the bedposts with the cuffs.

Hatch quietly commanded, "Now the key, Kyle. Don't forget the key! Then the note! Then get out of there!"

I watched, still totally confused, as Kyle dropped the tiny silver key to the handcuffs into a flower vase on a cabinet next to the bed. Digging into his jacket pocket, he removed a neatly folded slip of paper and placed it on top of the briefcase.

"Good boy, Kyle!" sighed Hatch in relief. "Now, get your butt out of that room!"

Kyle was nearly to the door when suddenly, it swung open.

"Oh, Jesus H!" whispered Hatch.

I stood there, staring in stunned disbelief as Senator Steve Landan stepped into the room, closing the door behind him.

Shaking my head, I quietly asked, "This wasn't part of your plan? Can we get him out of there?"

Swearing under his breath, Hatch made certain the camcorder was still trained on the hotel room. "Too late! Gonna have to play itself out now!"

"What's this all about?" Landan demanded.

Hatch and I watched as Kyle stepped away from the bed while Landan angrily examined the briefcase, the computer, and finally the note he had snatched up.

After reading it, Landan looked at Kyle with fire in his eyes. "'Enter the code, then you'll receive the key.' Just what the hell does that mean?"

Wheeling away from Kyle, Landan popped the latches on the briefcase and flipped it open, revealing the neatly stacked bills. "It better all be there!" snapped Landan.

Fingering the chain linking the wrist bands of the handcuffs, Landan then looked down at the crumpled note he still held. Kyle pointed at the notebook computer next to the briefcase. "You're supposed to . . . "

Landan glared at Kyle. "Supposed to what? Whoever hired you, son, put you in a dangerous position! You wearing a wire?"

Kyle answered, "No, sir. I was just supposed to leave you with this computer so you could type in some sort of confirmation—a guarantee—that you would stick to the plan."

"Confirmation?" hissed Senator Landan. "What am I expected to do, type them an e-mail and promise—"

"The code," Kyle firmly stated. "You're supposed to type it in on the notebook. Before they tell you where the key to those cuffs are, you're supposed to make a trade."

Senator Landan studied the paper he still held. "Trade? What sort of trade? I'm not playing any games here!"

Crumpling up the paper and tossing it to the floor, Landan moved to the head of the bed. The irate senator snatched up a pillow and peeled it out of its case. "I'll just create my own carrying bag!" he growled as he eyed the money in the briefcase.

He snatched up his first handful of the cash when Kyle bluntly said, "It's not all there."

Senator Landan froze. Slowly, he turned to face Kyle, a dangerous gleam in his eyes. "How much is *not all?*"

"Only half," responded Kyle. "The rest is in some account. That's why they want you to make an online confirmation before you walk with that, and before they deposit the other half."

Muttering furiously, Landan snatched up the crumpled paper from the floor. He scowled at Kyle and then focused his attention on the notebook computer on the bed. Suddenly, the door to the room swung open, and a dark-clad man barged into the room, aiming a Glock pistol directly at Landan.

Hatch and I watched the scene unfold in stunned amazement. Landan wheeled away from Kyle to face the bearded man with the gun. The burly gunman roughly shoved Senator Landan aside. He lashed out and slapped Kyle, sending him spinning and sprawling face first onto the bed.

"You want to live, kid," the gunman hissed at Kyle, "keep your face buried in that pillow! I've nothing against you, just this self-righteous, hypocritical bastard!"

Fortunately for Kyle, he did as the man ordered. His blond hair splayed in every direction, Kyle burrowed his face deeper into the pillow.

Senator Landan faced the man, his hands raised. "What—what do—what do you want?"

The gunman raised his pistol so the tip of the silencer was only a foot away from the senator's terror-filled features. He said, "I want you dead."

With that, he aimed the Glock and pulled the trigger three times in rapid succession. *Pft! Pft! Pft!* Hot lead spiraled down the barrel of the pistol and the gunman got his wish.

Senator Landan was dead before he hit the floor.

"Should have changed your policy," spat the dark-clad man as he glared down at the prone body of Steve Landan. "Should have taken a different stance on the issues!"

Out of the corner of my eye, I saw movement. Kyle's blond-haired head lifted slightly from the pillow on the bed.

"Face down, kid!" growled the tall, dark-haired man.

Kyle froze. He mumbled, "I can't breathe."

"Suck it in and keep your head down!" snapped the gunman. "Do as I say and you'll live. Move your head again and die."

I watched from the next room, slowly letting out my breath as the man slipped his Glock into a shoulder holster beneath his black leather jacket. A butterfly knife then mysteriously appeared in his hand, and I thought the man meant to stab Kyle. He worked the knife back and forth in his grasp.

Click! Snick! Click! The sounds of the blade whipping about echoed throughout the room. Kyle flinched as the man slid his knife along the pillow and directly up against his face. "Where's the key to these cuffs?"

Kyle told him at once, and the man smashed the vase on the bed stand to get at the tiny key. He freed the briefcase from the bedpost, closed its lid, tucked it beneath one arm, and started for the door.

"Count to ten, kid," said the man, putting his knife away and slowly backing toward the door. "To ten and then you can look up and breathe! Then get yourself out of here, understand?"

Kyle's face remained buried in the pillow. I prayed he would stay that way as I watched the man leave the room, a wicked grin etched upon his bearded features.

"I can't believe this!" came a voice from the shadows beside me. "I got that on tape! I got this on film! He actually killed him!"

I looked away from Kyle in the other room, his face still buried in the pillow, to peer down at Hatch seated behind the video camera beside me.

"I can't believe this!" Hatch repeated, more excited than appalled at the sights we'd just shared.

"Go!" Hatch said as he fumbled with the camera, removing the tape. "Go in that room and get Kyle out of there! We've got to get this tape to Riley, man! We're gonna be rich! Blown away just like that! I still can't believe this!"

I didn't hesitate. I left the darkened room at a run. My legs felt like rubber and my hands were shaking uncontrollably. I'd just witnessed the killing of another human being. It was just way too much for me to handle, yet I knew I had to get Kyle out of there. We all had to get out of the hotel before someone discovered the dead senator or . . . worse. We had to get out of there before we became implicated in the man's murder.

Chapter Ten

I entered the room and discovered Kyle frozen in shock. Seated there on the edge of the bed, he offered me a dazed look. "Chris? What are you doing here?"

I held my breath as I stepped over Senator Landan's body. "I'll explain later, Kyle. Let's just get out of here!"

Kyle lowered his gaze. Tears began to form in his blue eyes. "Did you see that? Were you with Hatch? Did he get this on tape?"

Gently, I placed a hand beneath his quivering chin. Glistening tears slid down his cheeks as I said, "Not now, Kyle. Hold yourself together. We've got to get away from here."

I pointed over my shoulder at the corpse behind us on the floor. "We got to get away from him before someone spots us!"

Kyle asked, "How did you find me, Chris? You came all the way up to the Big O to find me? You amaze me."

Kyle looked slowly to the mirror on the wall beside the bed and sadly muttered, "You saw what I was doing, didn't you? I suppose Hatch told you everything."

Staring down at the dead senator, Kyle said, "I didn't know this was going to happen, though. Really, Chris, I didn't!"

He broke down then. Tears spilled down his face and sobs racked his body. I reached out and fiercely embraced him. *It's okay,* I wanted so badly to assure him. But it was far from okay. We were in serious trouble and had to get out of there.

CRACK! suddenly echoed through the room as the mirror behind us shattered. Glass exploded as Ronnie Hatch's lean form came hurtling through the two-way mirror. He landed with a loud thud on the floor at our feet.

Standing in the shadowy room beyond was the gunman who had just shot and killed Senator Landan. Sneering at us like a demon, he began to climb through the frame that had housed the mirror. "Give me that damned tape!" he snarled.

Hatch sprang to his feet, the tape in hand. "Let's get the hell out of here, boys!"

Kyle gaped in fear as Hatch dragged him toward the door. I started to follow them when suddenly the gunman fell into the room, dropping rather clumsily to the glass-covered floor before me. As he started to rise, fumbling beneath his jacket for his holstered pistol, I snatched up a lamp from the bed stand and promptly slammed it down on the guy's head. The glass base of the lamp broke upon impact, and with a loud groan the man went down.

Hardly believing what I had done, I spun around and took off running out of the room. By the time I reached the end of the hallway, Hatch and Kyle had the elevator door open and both were loudly urging me to run faster. Feeling the floor beneath me shudder, I glanced back and caught a glimpse of the dark form behind me. Blood streaming down his forehead, the gunman was nearly on top of me.

I dove for the open elevator door and Kyle and Hatch stopped me from crashing into the rear wall. As the three of us collapsed in a pile on the floor, our legs and arms tangled, the door started to close behind us.

Whump! We looked up to see the man clawing at the closing elevator door. "You're dead! Do you hear me, you little pukes! Give me that tape or you're dead!"

The man forced the door open, and with one final grunt, he caused it to recede back into place with a loud click.

Kyle and I scrambled toward the back of the elevator. Hatch rolled over on his back, peering up at the gunman blocking our escape route. The man pointed his Glock at us and held out a massive hand. Reluctantly, Hatch held the tape up and the man snatched it out of his grasp.

Grinning sadistically, the bearded guy laughed, and said, "Say good-bye to this world, boys."

But as the man raised his gun and pointed it directly at Hatch, the elevator door moved out of the recesses of the doorway, distracting the leering gunman. As he used one shoulder to force the door back into place, Hatch made a desperate lunge, attempting to dive out through the open doorway. The man body-blocked him, but as they collided the tape went spinning out of the man's grasp. Taking advantage of the distraction, I sent my fist crashing into the plate of glass on the case beneath the control panel and latched onto the fire extinguisher inside. Taking it in both hands, I swung it at the gunman and *bonk* echoed loudly as I slammed the extinguisher against the side of his head. The man's eyes crossed and his knees buckled, yet as he fell, his trigger finger jerked and the gun went off. *Pft!*

Hatch dove sideways only a second before hot lead sent splinters flying from the wall behind him. "Holy hell!" he cried as he snatched up the videotape and cradled it against his chest. He rolled back toward Kyle, eyes fixed on the gunman as he toppled over backward directly in the center of the open doorway.

Hatch scrambled to his feet. I helped Kyle to stand. Dropping the metal container on the floor beside the still and silent gunman, I said, "Come on! Unless one of you wants to touch this bleeding creature and pull him out of the doorway, let's use the stairwell at the end of the hall!"

All three of us jumped in alarm when the prone gunman let out a loud groan. Thinking he might suddenly surge to his feet like one of those unkillable psychos in a horror flick, we leaped over him and raced off down the hall toward the stairs.

We leaped three and four steps at a time to hastily descend the stairway to the lobby below, and dashed through the lobby and past the security guard stationed near the hotel's front door. Outside the front entrance, we spotted Bryce, Jen, and Molly standing on the sidewalk. All three looked relieved to see me, and Jen was about to greet Kyle with a hug until she saw the terror in our eyes. Latching onto Jen and Bryce, I gasped, "We've gotta get outta here! Let's go! Now! Head for your car, Jen, now!"

The six of us took off running, though Bryce and Jen did so only because I fiercely pulled them along with me.

"Would you guys tell me what the hurry is?" demanded Jen, as we came tearing out of a darkened alley and ran toward her car parked in the middle of the block.

Hatch, still cradling the videotape like a priceless treasure, held it up and whispered, "We're running for our lives! Believe me, Jennifer! We just witnessed a murder!"

"What?" cried Molly as she slid into the side of the Mustang.

"Get off it, Ronnie!" snapped Jen as she, too, slammed into the side of her car to keep from skidding on loose gravel and falling to the street. "What are you talking about?"

Bryce and Kyle both grabbed onto my arms as I slipped and went down on one knee. As they skidded to a halt and kept me from taking a dive to the pavement, I gasped, "It's true! We just saw that Landan guy get blown away! I swear, I'm not lying!"

Jen turned around to face us. "Senator Landan? Landan, the man from the Forum? You saw him get shot?"

While Jen fumbled with her keys and Molly ran around to the other side of the Mustang, Hatch peered down at the tape he held. "This thing here is going to be worth lots of money, you guys! I mean, lots of money!"

Bryce gave him a puzzled frown. "You got this shooting on tape?"

I answered, "Yeah, Bryce! He filmed the entire thing!"

Hatch began acting really strange then. "Oh-ho! I'm gonna make a mint off of this! I'll make way more now that the shooting went down! Man, I can't believe this! This is great!"

I looked at Hatch in total disgust. "A man just got killed and you think it's great? What's your problem, Ronnie?"

I watched Hatch's eyes. They darted from my face to Kyle's as Hatch warned, "Not a word out of you! I'll cut you in on the deal, but keep quiet!"

Kyle didn't back down from Hatch, though, as he snapped, "Did you know someone was coming to shoot Landan? Did you put me in that room, knowing someone was coming to kill him?"

Hatch shook his head. "No way! I had no idea! We were there just to get Landan taking the money, that's all! I swear!"

Bryce guided me to Jen's open car door. "Let's just get out of here and talk about this somewhere else!"

I moved toward the car with Bryce towing me but then looked directly at Kyle. "Coming with us?"

"Yes!" snapped Bryce as he released me and took three quick steps to grab onto Kyle's arm. "With us! And as for you, Hatch, you can come or stay. It makes no difference to me!"

I was relieved to see that Kyle wasn't resisting as Bryce gave him a slight shove to get him into the backseat of the Mustang. I climbed in behind Kyle, meeting his uncertain look with a forced smile. Bryce was just about to follow us when we all heard a loud voice: "Hatch!"

Standing there in the street, Hatch groaned, "Oh, hell! Oh, damn it all to hell!"

Watching from the backseat, I saw two figures materializing out of the shadows of an alley across the street. The man in front was the security guard from Martin Ash's place, the big blond guy that reminded me of Diamond Dallas Page. Behind him was the other security guard who had pulled his gun out as we drove up Ash's driveway. Both men were dressed in finely tailored suits and looked out of place there on the darkened streets.

The big dude nailed Hatch with a steely-eyed glare. "You have something that belongs to us, Ron Hatchett."

Hatch turned slightly and whispered to Bryce, "Get in the car!"

As Bryce climbed in beside Kyle and me, Hatch leaned casually against Jen's open door, closing it as he used the side of the car to support his slight frame. "Nick, my man, I've got a proposition for you. Want to hear it?"

There were at least thirty feet between the two men and Hatch, but I thought it was too close for Hatch to be acting so flippant. Nick, if that indeed was the security guard's name, looked quite capable of swiftly closing the distance to place his massive hands around Hatch's scrawny neck. And I could tell by the hostile look in the man's eyes that he wasn't pleased with Hatch's attitude.

Nick snapped, "I don't want to hear any propositions from you, Ron. Did you accomplish your task? If so, hand me the tape!"

Hatch slid his hands behind his back. As he continued to lean against the car, he dropped the tape into the backseat. It struck Bryce on the knee as it fell to the floor.

"What's this all about, anyway?" asked Bryce as he looked past me to Kyle. Kyle merely shrugged and remained silent.

"Hatch!" came a shout from the opposite end of the street.

We all looked in that direction. Two more men stepped from the shadows between two buildings. One of these guys was built like a bear. He had huge shoulders and an enormous beer belly. A headband held his long dark hair in place and his beard hung to the middle of his broad chest. Dressed in jeans, a cutoff jean jacket, and a ratty T-shirt, he looked like a biker. The other guy was shorter and stockier, and dressed in a black suit. It was his greasy hair, though, that caught my eye. It was the same man who had brought the briefcase of money to the hotel room.

In the alley across from us, Nick said, "You playing two sides, Hatch? Trying to pull one of those highest bidder moves? You don't want to play that way with me!"

Twenty feet away from the car, the other two dudes came to a stop. The smaller guy snarled, "Stay out of this, Nicholas! The kid's got more there than you hired him for! More went down than you know about, Riley!"

Nick took two steps forward, moving out of the mouth of the alley and into the street. He sized up the other two men, placing his hands on his hips. I saw him glance at his partner as he whispered, "Harris. This might turn lethal."

Harris nodded and placed a hand beneath his jacket. He didn't draw his gun, but I could see he was just itching to play cowboy.

Nick glared at the small, greasy-haired man across the street from him. "What are you rambling about, Giles?"

The larger, bearlike man mumbled something we couldn't hear and took a deliberate step forward. The smaller guy stopped him, though. "Hold on, Deek. Let's not spook anybody. Let's just play it cool, okay?"

There we sat, not sure what to do. On our right, at the mouth of the adjacent alley, stood Nick and Harris, less than ten feet from the Mustang. And on the sidewalk to our left, twenty feet away, were the two motley-looking guys. I wanted to urge Jen to start the car and peel out of there.

Bryce leaned over and scooped up the tape. "Let's just give them what they want, for God's sake! If it's this videotape, let's just hand it over! This is Hatch's business, not ours!"

But Kyle reached past me and snatched the tape out of Bryce's grasp. "It's *my* business, too! This tape has *me* on it! Not Hatch! Not you guys! But me!"

Kyle looked desperately at Jen. "Just get us out of here!"

Outside the car, Hatch quietly informed Nick, "Things turned bad up there, tonight, Nick. Someone shot and killed Landan."

Nick looked like someone had just slapped him. He stared at Hatch in disbelief. "Shot and killed? Landan's *dead?*"

Hatch seemed pleased that he now had Nick's full attention. "I got it all down on tape. You wanna pay for a copy?"

Shaking his head, as though stunned by this turn of events, Nick rubbed his bearded chin, but Harris asked, "The camera? Did you get the camera out of there, Hatch?"

Before Hatch could answer, another loud voice shattered the relative stillness: "Get that damned kid!"

All of us looked warily down the sidewalk from where the two men had appeared moments earlier.

"Oh, good God!" I cried out.

The gunman who had killed Landan was stumbling unsteadily down the walk toward us.

"Get us out of here, Jen!" shouted Kyle.

"He's got a gun!" yelled Bryce. "Go, Jen! Go!"

As Jen started the Mustang, a number of things happened at once. The gunman staggered and fell to one knee, raising his pistol. He sighted directly on Hatch. Hatch wheeled around and stuck his head in through the back window, whispering, "Get that tape out of here, you guys! Keep it safe! I'll catch up with you later! Gotta book!"

The moment Hatch withdrew his head from the window, Nick latched onto him. "Hey!" cried Hatch as he squirmed wildly in the big man's grasp.

As Jen slammed the car into reverse and stomped on the gas, we watched Nick drag Hatch out of our path. We nearly backed over them as Jen peeled out of the parking place. She cranked the wheel and shifted into drive, and the three of us in the backseat watched as Nick and Hatch struggled in the middle of the street behind us. The two scruffy guys joined the fray, and all four of them went down in a pile.

Crack! we heard as hot lead struck the windshield of the Mustang. The kneeling gunman on the sidewalk nearly fifty feet away would have fired off another shot at the car if Harris hadn't drawn his own gun and returned fire.

"Go, Jenny!" screamed Molly. "Gun it and fly!"

And as Jen did just that, peering through the spiderweb crack in her windshield, the three of us in the backseat swiveled around to look back at the tangle of bodies in the center of the street.

"Hatch is getting away!" cried Kyle.

Nick held his own against the two men while Hatch scrambled to his feet, his suit jacket ripped down the back. In a flash of red, he sprinted for yet another alley and faded from view.

Bright fire exploded from the barrel of the gunman's pistol on our left. We saw four brilliant flashes but couldn't hear the gun's silenced shots. Fortunately, he was shooting at Harris on the opposite side of the street.

Jen took us flying down the street, and the three of us in the backseat saw Harris dive behind a parked car as hot slugs of lead shattered the vehicle's back window.

And then we were out of there.

Chapter Eleven

The tape lay on the picnic table between us. A Nebraska state senator had been murdered, and we had the irrefutable evidence in our hands.

All the way out of Omaha we'd listened to Jen rag about her damaged windshield. In fact, for the next thirty miles down I-80, she whined about the bullet that could have struck any one of us. But she couldn't seem to let go of the fact that her car had been shot. Later, when we pulled into a rest stop and piled out of the Mustang, I figured it was just Jen's way of dealing with the terror we had all experienced.

Kyle sat beside me, facing Bryce and Jen on the other side of the picnic table. I wanted to rescue him from the wrath of Bryce, to shield him from Bryce's heated glare, but I knew I wouldn't stand a chance. Bryce was totally hacked at Kyle for drawing all of us into this bizarre mess.

Bryce said, "Tell us what you and Hatch were doing, Kyle."

Kyle faced Bryce, cryptically saying, "Politics and murder!"

Jen looked up as Molly returned from using the rest room. She made room beside her on the bench and then refocused on Kyle. "Senator Landan was taking a bribe, right?"

"Way more than that," responded Kyle.

Bryce tapped the tape with his knuckles, fixing Kyle with a steady gaze. "Tell us. We're listening."

Kyle muttered, "How far I've come from where I once was."

The four of us shared a puzzled look.

Kyle sighed. Finally, he said, "Landan was opposed to too many issues. He campaigned against some same-sex union bill that was to be voted on. He also opposed that Two Twenty-One, the AIDS education program, because of some text dealing with gay issues. But he was most notorious for his fight against porn on the Internet. And so someone was paying him big bucks to back off."

Jen cleared her throat. "Back off on his fight against the AIDS program?"

Kyle shook his head. "No. The legislation against an international porn operation. To let it go dead in the water. Landan was accepting a bribe, promising not to shut down this pornography business, and vowing to refocus his agenda."

"Refocus his agenda?" said Bryce.

Kyle answered, "To sink the bribe money into his other fight, to finance his campaign to prevent Two Twenty-One from being accepted by Omaha schools."

Jen said, "So Landan would prevent this AIDS prevention program from reaching kids but allow porn to continue to spread?"

Kyle nodded. "He considered this porn thing the lesser of two evils. Landan claimed kids had a choice about whether to surf the Web for porn, but the Two Twenty-One thing would be forced down the throats of impressionable kids because the education plan would be mandatory if it was accepted in the schools."

He sighed again. "Hatch and I were hired to get a tape of Landan taking the payoff. I was supposed to get out of the room, but I didn't."

Jen whistled in disbelief. "So this video implicates you in the murder of a Nebraska senator? Who hired you to tape this thing?"

Staring at the tape before us, Kyle answered, "When I went on run to Omaha with Hatch, we stayed in a summer cottage behind Ash's mansion. Hatch told me he worked as Ash's yard boy. I only got to meet Martin Ash once in all that time. He seemed cool, but it was the director of his security outfit that actually hired us to do the taping. That big dude, Nick Riley."

Bryce placed his hand directly on top of the videotape. Kyle didn't miss the gesture. "So," said Bryce, "this Nick was planning on blackmailing Landan?"

Kyle nodded.

"Who were those other guys?" asked Jen. "Who shot Landan? You're not thinking Ash wanted Landan dead, are you? Blackmail is one thing, but murder?"

Kyle said, "Well, those other two guys, the ones that attacked Nick in the street, they're running a porn ring out of some warehouse in lower Omaha. The fat fart is Giles Davis. He might look like a Deadhead, but he's a rich man! He's involved in filming skin flicks that go all over the Internet. He's a professional pornography businessman! Believe it or not."

I looked over at Kyle, hardly believing anything I was hearing out of his mouth. "In the three weeks that you've been in Omaha, you fell in with these kind of lowlifes?"

Kyle looked away. "Landan was trying to shut down their porn trade by backing some antiporn law presented in the senate. He made enemies, not only in Omaha. Some of Landan's proposals would affect the porn trade on an international level! But the bribe was offered and he was promising to back off. So I don't know why they'd want him dead."

Jen reached across the table and gently placed her hand on Kyle's outstretched fingers. "Fell in way over your head, didn't you?"

Before Kyle could respond, Bryce said, "Let me get this straight. You and Hatch were involved in a plot to blackmail Landan, right? You went to the hotel to film him taking a bribe, correct? Then some guy comes charging in and blasts Landan away, and now *we* have the tape of the actual shooting. Are we all on the same page here?"

We all nodded. Kyle muttered, "What are we gonna do with it?"

We speculated about what we should or should not do, but we eventually ended up arguing about it. Finally, Bryce suggested we turn it over to the Omaha police, and Kyle blew up and stormed off into the surrounding shadows. I rose slowly and followed him.

Stars were out in the night sky with no city lights to spoil their dazzling brightness. Standing out there in the country, between Omaha and Lincoln, I could clearly see them sparkling in all their glory.

Walking out to the field next to the rest stop, I climbed through strands of barbed wire and moved through rows of dried cornstalks. I found myself meandering down a winding path near a small stream.

I stopped when I heard Kyle sobbing softly from somewhere ahead of me. I waited in the shadows of a lone oak tree.

My heart went out to him. I should have been angry with him for what he allowed himself to get involved in. Blackmailing a senator? Something was twisted inside of Kyle that he would stoop to this. And yet I still felt sorry for him.

After waiting patiently, I stepped out of the shadows and directly into the bright moonlight.

"What do *you* want?" Kyle asked defiantly.

"You, to come home with me, willingly," I replied.

Kyle snorted. "As if I have a choice? Besides, who will get the tape back to Hatch? He'll come looking for it, and Bryce damn well better let me have it!"

Kyle leaned back against a fence post, folding his arms over his chest defensively. I wanted so badly for him to give me a sign that he still cared about me. A deep hurt lay at the core of my heart. I was still troubled about what other things Kyle might have been involved in, and didn't deceive myself into thinking Hatch had taken Kyle in out of kindness. He had probably taken advantage of Kyle.

As I stood there, staring at Kyle, I realized there was a big difference between Hatch and me. Hatch gave gay kids a bad name. Most people who put me down because I'm gay do so because of bed hoppers like Hatch.

I wasn't attracted to Kyle just for sexual reasons. I really loved him. I had deep and strong feelings about him, and I was greatly concerned about what happened to him. I wanted to protect him, to comfort him.

I stood there, remembering the day I knew it was more than just sex between Kyle and me . . .

. . . We had been climbing out of the hot tub at his house when Kyle looked at me with this strange, haunted expression in his eyes. He placed an arm about my shoulders, solemnly saying, "Chris? I've been wanting to tell you something really serious."

I felt my heart racing. It felt really good to have Kyle's arm around me. Kyle usually wrapped his arms around me when he was trying to arouse me, yet this was a different kind of embrace.

"What is it, Kyle? Tell me what?" I asked.

For a moment Kyle looked away, too embarrassed to go on. He gave a long sigh and I could see pain in his eyes. I knew then what he wanted to say. I, too, had the same feelings, wondering if Kyle really cared about me. In my mind, I saw his face all the time. At night before falling asleep, I would have to switch my radio off because something in the sad strains of a love song really messed me up emotionally. If I listened too long, I'd end up longing to be loved and wishing for more from Kyle than sex. I would begin to cry and get this deep hurt inside. I even prayed for the day he would say, "I love you."

Standing beside the hot tub that day, I leaned forward and kissed him full on the lips. I had never done that before. As our lips touched, I felt a shiver run through me. There was something electrifying in that connection of our lips, of our faces touching, of our wet bodies locked together. It felt so good, so right. It felt like some force in the universe had brought us twisting, winding, spiraling to that very moment in time. Some power beyond us, or maybe a power inside us, drew us together in a magical way, bonding us and moving through us.

"I love you," Kyle breathed as we came up for air. "Chris Talbot, I love you. I'll love you forever."

As I stood in the moonlight, I remembered those words and wondered if what we had then was now gone.

Kyle slowly raised his hand. I thought he wanted me to take it. As I reached out to him, he casually ran his fingers through his blond hair. "You still care about me, don't you, Chris?"

"Yes," I said, barely above a whisper. "Don't play with me, Kyle. If things are over between us, then say so. I want you back in my life more than anything, but if you—"

"Here we go," he said sourly, "with the 'Together Forever' speech. Don't you get it? People don't love each other forever!"

Kyle coldly added, "Besides, I had a lot of sex while I was hanging with Hatch in the Big O. Unprotected sex. Lots of barebacking. You want me back even if I'm infected? You gonna take the chance that I might burn you?"

I had never practiced safe sex with Kyle. Neither of us ever figured we could contract HIV from each other. Kyle was telling me something startling that could very well be possible. He now might be carrying the virus. And if not HIV, if he actually had sex with a number of partners, Kyle could be infected with syphilis, gonorrhea, or even herpes.

Kyle then did something very cruel. He unzipped his jeans. "Do you still love me, Chris? You want to take the chance with me? Go ahead. Right here, right now."

I stood there staring at him, wanting to let him know that I didn't want to lose him. But as I thought of the real possibility that he might now be a carrier, I stopped myself. Was I so desperate not to lose Kyle that I would give up my life for him, risk infecting myself just to keep his love?

"How could you have allowed that, Kyle? We always talked about AIDS. You even said that only fools ever took chances by having sex with too many partners. You even talked about how condoms were such easy-to-use prevention tools. Why didn't you use them during this damned excursion into the skin trade? Why would you put yourself at such a risk?"

Kyle zipped up his jeans with one swift jerk and looked at me angrily. "Because I don't care if I live or die, Chris! I've had it with being made fun of, with having a therapist tell me how not to be gay, with my own parents being ashamed of me, with some social worker forcing me to go back to a school where I'd get bashed on a daily basis! So I just gave up! Understand that? I just wanna die. You ever been pushed so far you just wanna die?"

"Yes," I answered, looking directly into his eyes. "Not even a year ago."

He stared at me blankly. I said, "I'd always heard that suicide would send your soul to hell, that God didn't allow you to call your own checkout time. But that night, I thought it through, looking at suicide as an option to ending my struggles."

Kyle stood there, a look of disbelief in his eyes as though he thought he was the only one to feel this kind of pain.

I went on. "Remember when you taunted me about having interest in that new kid at school? For nearly two months, you talked about this kid to make me jealous. I was living in misery. Not only was I coming to terms with the fact I was gay, I was dealing with losing the one person in this world I loved. And then, that same night I heard what God thought about me."

Looking slightly confused, Kyle asked, "God?"

I nodded. "Yeah. That night, at youth group, Pastor Michael claimed that all homosexuals are doomed to hell. I figured if God condemned me anyway, then what was the use of continuing to live? I was not only totally hurt by the fact that God might be against me, but that I might be losing you as well.

"So I stole my mom's sleeping pills and I went down to the park late that night, and sat on a picnic table, the bottle of pills in one hand and your necklace in the other."

Kyle quietly asked, "The half-heart necklace I gave you?"

"Yes. I was just about to down the entire bottle of pills when something strange happened. There I was, holding half of a broken heart—knowing you had the other half—when that half-heart seemed to suddenly light up in my hand. I nearly dropped it!

"Instead, I looked up to see a falling star glaring so brilliantly green that it illuminated the necklace in my hand. I thought of it as a sign from God. He checked in on me just as I was about to check out! He didn't want me leaving the world this way. Besides, having my heart broken by you was a lot less severe than losing my soul."

My heart was breaking again, but I wasn't considering suicide as an option.

"You're weird, Chris," said Kyle. "You think way too much. If it had been me with those pills, you would be the one holding the other half of our heart necklace. Me? Hell, I'd have been dead. Just that simple."

Maybe Kyle's observation about me being weird was true because right then I thought of a Garth Brooks song titled, "If Tomorrow Never Comes." The lyrics have to do with telling those in your life that you love them in case you died today. I couldn't get that song out of my head as I faced Kyle.

Finally, I cleared my throat and said, "I love you, Kyle."

I put my hand out and touched his shoulder. "Come on, let's go home. Whatever you've got to face, I'll be there. Count on it. I am for you."

And though Kyle didn't respond warmly, he did allow me to place an arm around his shoulders and lead him back to Jen's car.

As we pulled back onto the interstate, I glanced out the rear window of the Mustang and shook my head in wonder as a bright red star went shooting through the sky. I took it as a sign that God was letting me know he was watching over us and that everything would soon be okay.

Life couldn't be that simple, though, and in the days that followed, I often thought of that red star, believing it had been an omen, warning of bad things to come.

Chapter Twelve

Jen and Molly took it upon themselves to be the mediators between Kyle and his parents when we arrived back in Lincoln. I was relieved because I didn't want to face Kyle's mom after all those things she'd said about our relationship. Part of me wanted to let her know that I cared so much about her son that I went and found him, but the other part wanted nothing to do with the self-righteous hag.

I was glad that Jen and Molly escorted Kyle up to the darkened house at three in the morning. When the porch light came on and Mr. Taylor came to the door, Bryce and I faded into the shadows beneath the trees lining the street.

"So, what do you propose we do with this?" said Bryce, holding the tape up between us.

I watched as Kyle and the girls entered the Taylor house before answering, "If we turned it in to Martin Ash, those porn guys, or even cops, we'd place Kyle in the middle of a homicide. What if he got accused of being an accessory to a murder?"

Bryce thought it over for long moments, staring down at the tape in disgust. "But if we helped cops solve a murder, wouldn't that be enough to keep Kyle out of the mix? You said the shooter wasn't even wearing a mask. If that's true, then the cops ought to be able to nail this guy and be grateful to us for helping them. After all, it was a senator who was murdered. The Omaha police ain't gonna let this die."

I couldn't be swayed that easily. I was worried about Kyle, and I couldn't see him being sent to a juvenile facility for a crime that he didn't commit. "Yeah, but what if they think Kyle was part of the plan to murder Landan? What if Hatch gets questioned and he saves himself by implicating Kyle?"

Bryce responded, "You're thinking of Kyle. That's admirable. But look around you, Chris. We're all involved in this now."

I let out a quiet sigh. I wasn't so admirable. I was thinking of Kyle, but once again I was thinking about losing him. That, in light of placing my friends in jeopardy, was surely most selfish. "Maybe we ought to do just what Kyle wanted," I finally said.

Bryce shook his head. "Let him take the tape back to Hatch? You believe that would leave us out of the loop? That Nick Riley knows we're involved. He'd want to know just how much we know. Besides, you knocked the crap out of that shooter with a fire extinguisher, remember? He ain't going to forget that Hatch and Kyle weren't the only ones in that hotel room. What if he comes looking for you?"

I hadn't thought of that. I was thinking that if Martin Ash started this thing, our troubles would end once he had a copy of the tape. Ash might deal fairly if we promised to keep our mouths shut. But those porn guys and the shooter were dangerous. They wouldn't deal fairly at all. I suddenly got a creepy feeling.

Bryce saw me looking slowly in every direction. "Come on, Chris. Don't be getting paranoid on me."

"But what if they come here to Lincoln?" I responded, staring hard at a patch of shadows near the end of the block. "What if they catch up to Hatch and he tells them how to find us?"

Shaking his head, Bryce replied, "No chance. Hatch wouldn't be that easy. He wants to make money out of this deal. More than likely, Hatch will lay low for a couple of days. Then he'll come looking for this valuable merchandise."

Yawning as he placed the tape beneath one arm, Bryce dug in his shirt pocket for his smokes.

"Damn!" he cursed as he crumpled the empty cigarette pack and tossed it in the nearby gutter. He yawned again. I was tired, too, but I really wanted to wait for Jen and Molly to see how Kyle's parents reacted to his return.

Bryce saw me stumble as I sat down on the curb. "Why don't you head home? I can wait for the girls. You look beat."

"Naw," I responded, suppressing another yawn. "I'm staying. But you can head home, if you like. We'll catch up tomorrow."

Looking relieved, Bryce said, "Sounds good to me. See you in the morning."

Before walking off down the street, he patted the tape cradled beneath his arm. "It best stay with me. Knowing you like I do—no offense—if Kyle sniveled enough, you'd give in and let him have it. Can't take that chance, Chris."

"I understand," I told him. And really, I did. Bryce was more than likely doing me a big favor.

Jen dropped Molly off at her house. She then headed toward my place four blocks away.

"So you think he'll be okay?" I asked for maybe the third time since we left Kyle with his parents.

Jen looked way too serious as she answered, "Stick by him, Chris, no matter how bad he treats you. And believe me, I know how you're feeling about now. You wanted him to come running back to you, begging for your support and forgiveness, right? But it just didn't happen, did it?"

Tears came to my eyes. Jen was blunt, but she spoke the truth.

"He's hurting too! I know he's hurt you, Chris. But if you really care about him, you'd put aside your own feelings. Besides, he's only testing you, to see if you will stick by him."

I wiped tears from my cheeks. "He wants to die," I whispered.

Jen shook her head sadly. "He's not going to get much support from those parents of his. So you have to be there for him."

"What about someone being there for me?" I said. "Do you know how much it hurt to know the things Kyle has been doing since he left home? Do you know he might be infected now? Do you know how bad it hurts when the one person you love doesn't love you back . . . anymore?"

Jen pulled up in front of my house. Shifting into park, she turned the key in the ignition switch, and the Mustang rumbled one last time before silence enveloped the two of us.

Looking over at me, she sighed heavily. "You and I, bud, are a lot alike. How many relationships have I been in since you've known me? Five or six? And what do I usually get out of them? Heartbreak! I try my damnedest to love, but it seems to always fade away. It's illusionary. I reach for it, but it evades my grasp. I hurt a lot, Chris."

I could totally relate to what Jen was telling me. "I hurt a lot, too. Maybe if I had a solid and steady relationship with someone that would never leave me or turn on me, just maybe I could accept myself."

Jen bit her bottom lip. "Maybe love shouldn't be your goal."

I looked at her, a puzzled frown on my face. "Meaning?"

"If you're always getting hurt by emotionally investing in Kyle, maybe you ought to focus on yourself. Got to love *yourself* before you can truly love someone else."

"I don't get it," I responded. "I shouldn't try loving Kyle anymore? You just said stick by him. You contradicting yourself?"

She shook back strands of her dark hair. "You just said if you had someone to love you, that maybe you could accept yourself, right? Accepting yourself—being okay with you—shouldn't depend on anyone else! Don't believe that when you find the perfect someone that all will be well within you, Chris! Be okay with you *now*.

"Once you get wrapped up in a relationship, your emotions get all twisted and the next thing you know you're living moment by moment, hopelessly addicted to that other person's gestures of affection. 'Did he say he loved me before we parted? Did he say he loved me twice or maybe ten times today? Did he hug me when he first saw me today? When I got home, did I find that he had called? What were his kind gestures today? What did he say that proved he really cares about me?' "

I sat there, a little stunned. She was a girl. How did she know I did those things? How could she possibly know that I ran through Kyle's words and actions, weighing them in my mind, to assure myself that he still cared about me?

"I do the same things, Chris," Jen said, a sad grin on her face. "I'm just as insecure. And not because I'm a lesbian, but because I'm human and probably have an attachment disorder."

"Attachment what?" I asked, unfamiliar with the words.

"I don't know how it is for straight people," she responded, "but I'm constantly needing assurance my lover still loves me. It's probably because I'm insecure with myself. Like, why would she love me?

What does she see in me? I've been dumped so many times, I've probably developed an attachment disorder. Rejection is a very traumatic thing."

"It sucks!" I declared, thinking angrily of Kyle.

"Get over it or die," stated Jen. "Harsh. But what are you going to do? Just quit living because someone quit loving you?"

I was confused. "All I'm asking for is that *someone* loves me. And it hurts so bad when I know that love has faded away. So damned bad, Jen."

She was quiet for long moments, as though digesting what I had just said. She whispered, "I know. But it's an emotional disaster waiting to happen if you don't start looking to yourself. You can't go through life dependent on someone as emotionally unstable as Kyle. It will eventually kill you. If not, your heart's going to get broken."

"But you just said—" I started to argue.

"What I said was support the boy *now* because he definitely needs your help. But do it for him, not for yourself. You know, like unconditional love. Nothing in it for you, just needing to be needed. Be there for him because he can't be there for himself. Don't depend on Kyle to fill your emotional bucket. He can't. He has too many holes in his own.

"In time, you'll be strong enough to see how much Kyle drains from you. Some people are emotional vampires. Kyle is one of them. He'll suck your soul dry if you let him. In time, you'll be strong enough to cut yourself off from the boy and move on."

I looked at her, trying to understand what she was saying, knowing she must have been through a lot of this, too. "But," I slowly said, "I don't want to cut myself off—"

"I know." She placed two fingers over my lips. "Not now. But later, down the line. He's not the one for you, Chris. You're a giver. He's a taker. Bad combination. He's a—"

"I know," I blurted, "an emotional vampire."

"Right."

I reached over and hugged Jen. She kissed me on the cheek as I drew back. We both smiled, thinking the same thing.

"Too bad," she said, "you're not my type, kiddo."

"Really," I said, winking at her as I climbed out of the car.

As Jen drove away, I whispered, "Thanks for the talk, my friend."

Then I went into my house and crashed for the night.

Chapter Thirteen

Hatch's death was a total shock to me. I knew we were in serious trouble the moment I heard about it. I knew they would be coming after us next. Whoever they were.

I was seated in the media center, typing a report for social studies, when I heard one of my fellow students loudly declare, "That's Ronnie Hatchett!"

I looked up, expecting to see Hatch standing near the media center's TV set. Instead, a picture of him was filling up the entire television screen. I sat there in stunned amazement as the reporter on the news channel barked out, "A Lincoln boy has been found murdered in the city of Omaha. It appears that Ronald A. Hatchett, a sixteen-year-old Lincoln youth, has been found dead beneath the Missouri River bridge. Police are not releasing many details, but more information should be available on the evening news. Once again, Ronald A. Hatch—"

I was standing up. The buzzing in my ears caused the newscaster's last words to fade. I felt lightheaded and thought I might faint. In fact, I didn't remember getting to my feet. I found myself reaching out to the computer table in front of me to keep from falling.

"Are you okay?" asked Mrs. Wiggert, the librarian.

I looked to the TV screen where Hatch's picture was fading and a commercial about cookies was coming on. "I don't—know," I muttered, swallowing hard and wondering if Bryce or Jen knew about this yet.

"Did you know Ronnie?" she asked.

"I don't know," I muttered again as I stumbled out of the media center. I didn't hear what she said as I headed for the main hallway.

I was halfway down the hall when I noticed some guy in a suit stepping out of the front office. I could tell just by looking at him that he wasn't a teacher. He didn't have that educator look about him. He was of medium height but built like a bouncer. His dark hair was parted down the center, swept back over his ears, and hung just above his collar. Something about the man made me think, *Out of the ordinary. Different. Not a typical citizen.*

And then I knew: He was a cop!

The moment he fixed me in his sights, I stared at him with a deer-in-the-headlights look.

Still some thirty feet down the hall, he smiled and said, "Hey there, son, could I have a word with you?"

I watched as Mr. Durban stepped out of the office to join the broad-shouldered guy. "That's him, isn't it?" I heard the man asking Durban.

Durban produced a yearbook seemingly from out of nowhere. "Yes. That's the Talbot boy. Now as to Bryce Carlile, I have his photo marked for you as well. If—"

That was all I heard as I jetted down the hallway. I careened around the corner to Second Hallway and leaped all five steps leading to the ground floor. The bathrooms were a tempting place to hide because there was a fire exit in the boy's room on this hall, but I hadn't put enough distance between myself and the cop to clear the track field beyond. So I continued, at full speed down the hallway.

"Hey!" I heard as I took a sharp left to head for the ramp leading up to the Third Hallway exit doors. But I didn't break stride. I was going to get away. This cop looked like he meant business, and if he was here on account of Ronnie being dead, I needed to find Bryce, Jen, and Molly before we all got questioned. It was only three days after the shooting of Landan in Omaha! We hadn't had time to talk about what to do with the tape, nor did we have our story straight about what we witnessed that night. I wondered how the police had gotten involved so quickly and why they were coming to talk to us.

I bolted through the hallway's exit doors and sprinted around the building to the bike racks. From there, I could clearly see into the automotive classroom's windows. Bryce was nowhere to be seen. Since he wasn't in class, I figured he'd more than likely skipped this period. If so, he'd either be hanging out at Smoker's Corner or riding around with someone.

I then noticed the dark car parked at the end of the block. A man was seated in the blue sedan and he was staring right at me. *Another cop!* I thought. *Probably the partner of the guy inside the school!*

I strolled away casually, pretending I didn't see the guy staring at me. When I made it safely to the far side of the school building, I darted off across the ballpark behind the school and headed for home. If I couldn't find Bryce and Jen, at least I knew where to find Kyle.

Kyle was moody, to say the least. He was unhappy about being back home and destined to go to juvenile court where the judge would determine his punishment for running away and skipping so many days of school. He was also being forced to return to his therapist, the one who claimed he had a choice about being gay.

"Doesn't the hag understand that saying such crap to me is like telling a cat it no longer has to be a cat if it doesn't want to be? I'm sure if she talked to a cat she would simply say, 'It's okay, you don't have to be a cat. Hell, if you want, you can choose to be a dog!' What a crock!"

Together Kyle and I walked down to the park at the end of our block. He was so overwhelmed by his own problems that when I told him about Hatch being murdered, all he did was mutter, "That stupid ass! He probably went to Giles hoping to make a deal! Greedy, trusting fool!"

Kyle was shaken up, yet he shed no tears for Hatch. I thought maybe he was just so wrapped up in his own world of hurt that he couldn't allow himself to feel any sadness.

We wandered down to the small stream at the far end of the park. As we passed the tree line, Kyle scooped up an old tire some delinquent had removed from the tire bridge at the nearby playground. He rolled the tire up against a small sapling, planted his butt on it, and stared hard at the stream for long moments.

I walked over and kneeled before him, placing a hand on his right knee. "They'll come to question us, Kyle. How those cops knew to come to the school to look for me or Bryce, I have no idea. But they'll be coming to our houses next!"

Kyle glanced down at my hand. I thought for a moment that he might brush it off, but he simply let me keep it there. I hoped he felt the support I was trying to lend him, the unconditional love that Jen spoke of.

Kyle snapped, "How did cops know to look here in Lincoln for us? It's only been a few days since Landan was shot and already cops are onto us? This doesn't make sense! Unless Hatch talked before he died."

I responded, "Whoever shot Ronnie could have beaten information out of him; could be that Hatch told them our names. But how would the cops know unless they're in contact with whoever killed Hatch?"

Kyle snorted, "Maybe they weren't real cops. Maybe they're just impersonating cops. Maybe all they want is the tape, and then they'll leave us alone."

He paused, and a wicked gleam came into his blue eyes. "Want to make some money off of this thing?"

I thought sadly, *Hatch has been murdered and Kyle is thinking of making cash off of the tape? What's wrong with his head? Doesn't he have a conscience anymore?*

"I've got a great idea," he said, smiling warmly, attempting to win me over. "You get the tape back from Bryce and you and me will travel back to Omaha and sell it to Martin Ash. He'll pay a lot for it! We'll be rich!"

I had to force myself to keep my hand on Kyle's knee after that, though I wanted to pull back and show him how appalled I was by his brilliant idea. "And what if it's Ash and his men that killed Ronnie? That Nick Riley dude seemed really angry with Hatch for trying to up the pay for the tape. Maybe Nick shot and killed Hatch. We gonna just walk right up to Ash's mansion and attempt to make a deal with a possible murderer? This is some deep shit we've stumbled into, Kyle!"

I didn't have to remove my hand after that. Kyle brushed it off of his knee and gave me an angry grimace. "What are you doing, turning into a wimp? Where's your sense of adventure?"

If I did this thing, if I followed Kyle's lead here, I just might win back his affections. I wanted that more than anything. I wanted Kyle and I to be close again, like before. I felt I'd lost him ever since he'd gone on the run, and I desperately wanted him back. But then Jen's words came back to me: *Emotional vampire. Kyle will suck your soul dry if you let him . . . in time, you'll be strong enough to cut yourself off . . . and move on.*

Oh God, things were hurting inside my chest. Call them frayed emotions or shards of a broken heart, but I felt deep pain down in my soul. I was depressed, and I wanted so badly to ease that pain by seeking comfort from Kyle. Yet in that same wounded heart, I knew Kyle couldn't really help me. Hell, he couldn't help himself, let alone comprehend how badly he'd injured me.

"No, Kyle," I told him, though I risked losing him for good, "I won't be able to get the tape. You know Bryce. He won't give it up. If those guys are real cops and they question Bryce, he'll give it to them because he thinks it's the right thing to do."

Kyle stood up. He gave the tire he'd been seated on a rough shove toward the nearby stream. As it splashed into the dirty water, he snarled, "That's just great! I'm on that tape, Chris! Me! What's gonna happen if they are cops and they believe I had something to do with Landan's shooting? Do you know what would happen to me if they locked me up in one of those detention centers? I'd become a whore for anyone who wanted to punk me! Have you thought of that?"

Indeed I had. In fact, I'd cried myself to sleep over such horrid thoughts the last two nights. I wanted to save Kyle, but I didn't know how. I looked into his angry eyes. "If I did manage to get the tape from Bryce, I'd destroy it. I wouldn't turn it over to the cops or Martin Ash or anyone . . . even if they were offering a million bucks! I'd burn it and keep you out of this mess!"

"I'd rather have the million bucks!" countered Kyle, wheeling around to walk away. I just stood there, watching him stomp through the trees up to the railroad tracks beyond the park. Unconditional love was so damned hard. How could I offer Kyle any more support when he simply pushed it aside? I reminded myself that he was going through his own personal hell, dealing with his parents, his therapist, the courts, and his own identity, but I had little to offer him now that I felt so drained myself.

I wanted to let Kyle go his own way. I was just going to turn around and walk back home. And yet I didn't. I followed him up onto the single pair of tracks and kept my distance as he balanced himself on one of the rails and began moving away.

Chapter Fourteen

The railroad bridge on the edge of town stands at least fifty feet above the river. It was named Joe's Bridge years before I was even born, in memory of some guy known as Hobo Joe who hung himself from the span. Kids had sprayed graffiti all over the sides of the bridge, and though most of the artwork faded with time, the word JOE'S was renewed each year. It stood there now, in big, bold red letters.

Kyle and I visited the bridge a lot when we were kids. It was fun throwing rocks into the river below or seeing who could send the farthest pee stream out over its rails. The bridge was out in the country, half a mile from the edge of town. It was a great place for watching the sun come up between rolling green fields far to the east. Kyle and I had often woken up early to wander out there and take in the first blood-red rays of the morning.

I watched Kyle carelessly hop from the tracks between two metal guard rails to the narrow ledge six feet below. The ledge was formed by a cement pylon that held the bridge up at its center. One step in the wrong direction and down you would plummet into the river forty feet below.

Kyle didn't seem to care. He tottered on the ledge, knowing that my heart had climbed into my mouth as I stood watching him. I dared not whisper a word. If I distracted him, I thought for sure he'd slip and go over the edge.

Grinning up at me, Kyle finally inched back away from the lip of the pylon and plopped himself down, dangling his legs over the side and leaning his back against the cement support behind him. Gazing down at the deep river, he said, "I wonder what made Hobo Joe want to die. Ever wonder that, Chris?"

Looking cautiously up and down the tracks to make sure there were no trains coming, I moved over to the side of the bridge. Looking down to where Kyle was seated, I said, "I heard he was in love with the Widow Johnson, that since he was a boy he'd loved her and begged her to marry him. When she rejected him and married another, I heard Joe started riding the rails. Rode them for nearly twenty years after that. But he always came back to check on the love of his life, just to see if maybe she'd left her husband or that maybe he'd died."

Kyle looked at the spot where Joe had tied his rope before jumping. "Widow Johnson didn't lose her husband until after Joe took his big leap. Is she still alive?"

I shook my head, watching Kyle still staring up at the wooden framework where Joe had dangled until police found his body. "Naw. She died about four years ago. I wonder how she lived with herself after reading Joe's note they found on his body. I wonder if her conscience ever bothered her."

Kyle shrugged and sent a thick stream of spit over the ledge. He watched as it slid from his lips and fell to the waters below. "Why? It wasn't her fault that she didn't love the sappy fool. Why should she feel guilty about him killing himself?"

"They were lovers at one time, Kyle. And she rejected him. Don't you know what it does to people when you tell them you no longer love them? Don't you know how bad it hurts?"

My words went right over his head. Kyle simply looked up at me and said, "How can you blame her for the guy hanging himself? Maybe he was some ugly dude anyway. Maybe she just got tired of him hanging all over her. Hell, people get tired of each other after a while, Chris. Together forever doesn't always last, you hopeful romantic."

I slowly climbed down to where Kyle sat. It was more like a cautious slide down the pylon. I had hoped Kyle would reach out and steady me as I landed on the narrow ledge, but he just sat there spitting.

I peered down at the river and shivered when I thought of slipping from my precarious position. The water was deep, but that didn't mean one couldn't get hurt by plunging into those dark depths. I'd heard that a kid had actually dived from the spot we occupied and broken his neck and drowned. I couldn't imagine jumping from that high up, let alone diving. I got the creeps just thinking about such a stupid feat.

"I wonder how long it took Hobo Joe to die," said Kyle as I sat down beside him.

I followed his gaze to the wooden framework above our heads. "Don't know. But if the rope was long enough, he more than likely broke his neck seconds after jumping."

Kyle scared me as he asked, "Do you think he died instantly when his neck snapped? Or do you think he died slowly because the rope cut off his oxygen?"

I put my hand on Kyle's leg, saying, "Don't talk this way, Kyle. Please, for me. Don't give it another thought."

Again Kyle allowed me to keep my hand on him. I hoped he was soaking up my support. "What," he asked, "if you discovered you had some rare disease and you only had months to live? Would you want to go really slow or would you want to end it all with one big jump?"

Clearing my throat, I quietly asked, "Why, Kyle? Why are you talking this way? You think because of your fooling around up there in Omaha that you now have . . . some rare disease?"

Kyle hung another glob of spit from his bottom lip. He let it slowly drip down, then peered at the spit drop spinning through empty air. "Plop!" he said as the spit hit the river below. "All it takes is one drop of infected sperm, right? One tiny cell that has the HIV virus in it, one tiny drop that can be a deadly killer once it enters your bloodstream. What do the letters stand for? Hell, I don't even remember."

Leaning closer to Kyle and hoping he didn't push me away, I told him, "HIV, human immunodeficiency virus. It's the virus that causes AIDS. Acquired means that it's not inherited, but contracted. Immune deficiency is a breakdown of the body's defense system. And syndrome means a mess of symptoms and infections."

Kyle grimaced as he said, "And there's no cure for this virus? Once you've got it, your days are numbered, right?"

I didn't want to scare him. I didn't want him to think so darkly about the fact that his unsafe sex practices might have allowed HIV to enter his system, but I had to be truthful. I cleared my throat and looked directly at him and said, "Well, without treatment, people infected with HIV will develop serious symptoms eventually. And yes, they'll die. But some people infected with HIV live for years without getting full-blown AIDS. And there's all kinds of antiretroviral drugs people with HIV take that help them live longer."

"'Full blown'?" asked Kyle, his eyes narrowed.

"When AIDS begins and you have to start fighting off opportunistic infections," I said, and felt a lump rise up in my throat, hardly able to believe we were even talking about this.

Kyle spit as far out as he could get it to fly and said, "I heard twenty-seven million people have died in Africa of AIDS. But hasn't it spread like a plague here too? How many die per year in America because they're infected?"

I answered, "Thousands of people who probably thought, 'This bastard of a virus will never get me!' People are infected through sexual contact, blood transfusions, or exchanging needles. Homosexuals and heterosexuals alike. HIV doesn't discriminate. It's like a mad demon out to rip and tear to shreds anyone it infects."

Kyle looked seriously at me as he asked, "Well, do you think this badass demon wants a piece of me?"

"I hope not," I said, squeezing his leg affectionately. "I truly hope not."

"Me, too," Kyle whispered, a sad look in his eyes.

Night had fallen by the time we made our way back to town. Neither of us had talked much on the walk back in. We merely walked side by side down the railroad tracks. I was content to be alone with Kyle—glad to have him back in my life even if he hadn't drawn me back into his emotional embrace. Kyle's musings were his own. I could only hope he was still including me somewhere in the jumbled thoughts rolling around in his head.

Kyle's harsh whisper caused me to jump in alarm: "There's someone up there watching us by the trees!"

I looked toward the shadows at the edge of the park. Slowly, I let my breath out as I scanned the entire line of trees. "I don't see anyone. You're just imagining—"

"Here they come!" he shouted as two dark figures slipped from between the trees and moved toward us at a dead run.

"Let's book!" I hollered as we both spun around to run back down the tracks. It was hard going, trying not to trip over the ties, so we leaped out from between the rails and slid down the embankment on the far side of the tracks.

"Not this way!" I heard Kyle shout.

He latched onto my arm and barely managed to keep me from slipping over the ledge in front of us. As I fought to maintain balance, I could see the reflection of silver moonlight shining back at me from the stream ten feet below.

We hastily tried to skirt the edge of the ledge, but slipped on wet grass and slid over the high embankment, dropping through empty air. A patch of thick sand cushioned our fall, and I hauled Kyle to his feet, listening to the sounds of pounding feet directly above us.

Running and leaping to clear the stream in front of us, Kyle went down with a loud splash. Thinking he would scramble out of the water to follow me, I climbed up the opposite bank, clawing my way to the top of the steep incline.

"Gotcha!" I heard behind me. Kyle cried out in pain. Glancing back, I saw two men struggling to keep him in their grasp. In the moonlight, I could clearly see Giles Davis, the stocky porn dealer from Omaha, and his massive partner, Deek.

While Deek attempted to push Kyle's head under the surface of the scummy water, Giles glared up at me, snarling, "Get your ass back down here, now!"

"Coming!" I yelled as I leaped high and stuck my right foot up before me.

I hit the heavyset dude with such force that he spun around and slammed into the dirt embankment on the opposite side of the stream. Giles Davis groaned loudly as he slid backward and into the water.

Deek peered up over Kyle's bobbing head just as I drove a fist into his nose. Crying out in pain and anger, the big, bearded guy cupped his hands to his face and stumbled away from Kyle. I leaned forward, pulling Kyle to his feet. Deek staggered in front of us, blocking our path, so we leaped over Giles and scrambled to the top of the hill, heading back toward the tracks.

"Hey!" yelled Kyle as Giles Davis, quicker than a weasel for all his bulk, grabbed him by one ankle and hauled him back down the bank. With one terrific heave, he tossed Kyle back into the water.

I had no choice but to attempt another attack. But as I charged back down the bank toward the snarling fat man, Deek came at me. I was moving too fast to avoid the massive guy and I slammed into his chest with my face. Stars exploded in front of me and steely fingers clamped onto my shoulders.

"You little maggot!" growled Deek as he spun me through the air and tossed me into the stream. I landed next to Giles. Fiery pain erupted in my side where the fat man's boot caught me. Deek latched onto my shoulders once more and he began to force me down into the dark waters. Cold water sprayed up my nose and I raised my head and gasped for air, but the monster shoved me beneath the water a second time. I thought for sure I was going to die.

"Let them go," I heard from somewhere above us. There was now a humming in my ears and my vision was blurry, but I felt Deek release me, and I crawled up the bank and away from him.

Kyle clambered up beside me, trying to put distance between himself and the two porn dealers standing in the middle of the stream. He looked up and sighed in relief as he declared, "Nick Riley!"

Nick Riley stood there like some dark-clad avenging angel. His leather jacket, his jeans, his boots, and even his leather gloves were black. And in one of these glove-covered hands, the big, blond security specialist held a pistol. A rather big gun that I figured to be a .357 Magnum. At any rate, it didn't appear as if Nick Riley was there to mess around.

I could clearly see the whiteness of his teeth as he offered the two men below a wicked grin. "What are you guys up to? Out to kill *another* kid for messing in your business? Or are you gonna be more gentle with them than you were with Hatch?"

"Piss off, Riley!" snapped Giles, glaring hatefully up at the big man.

"Yeah, stay the hell out of this!" snarled Deek as he fumbled inside his jean jacket.

Nick cocked the hammer back on his pistol. "Don't!" he said as he aimed directly at the huge bearded guy. "Leave it in its holster, Deek!"

Deek muttered angrily but lowered his massive hands to his side as he eyed the barrel of Nick's gun. Giles took a step toward us, and both Kyle and I crab-crawled the rest of the way up the bank to lay panting at Nick Riley's feet.

Riley said, "You boys are gonna have to get up and walk out of here, understand?"

Kyle nodded silently and I answered with a weak, "Yes."

As we got to our knees, Giles let out a string of foul words, then shot a murderous glare at Nick Riley. "These kids have that frickin' tape! We want it and we'll pay for it! Get it from them and get in touch! Or Martin Ash is going to have OPD banging on his door again, because inquiring minds want to know what that camcorder was all about at the scene of the crime! Understand, Nicholas?"

Nick grinned and a feral gleam came to his eyes as he replied, "I understand, Giles. I don't appreciate your threats, and I'm not happy with you about Hatch. You didn't have to kill him."

With that, Nick raised his pistol and aimed it directly at Giles. Both Giles Davis and Deek staggered back in frantic desperation, raising their hands before their faces as if that would somehow stop a .357 slug from entering their homely mugs. In their panic, they collided, slipped, and fell to their knees.

"A good position for both of you," declared Nick. "Stay that way awhile and contemplate your sins. God might forgive you, but I'm tellin' you now, if I see you slinking up behind us as we leave here, I certainly won't!"

Giles and Deek looked at Nick with hatred in their eyes. Giles growled, "Just get us that tape, Nicholas! If not, there's gonna be hell to pay!"

Nick turned to us, saying, "We're gonna walk back over to that park a couple blocks from here, and you aren't gonna run on me, right?"

Kyle and I were way out of our league. Deek and Giles might have killed us if Nick hadn't shown up. We both owed Nick Riley gratitude for his rescue. So we nodded glumly, not certain if we'd fallen from the frying pan into the fire.

Eyeing his gun one last time, I said, "We're with you. You lead and we'll follow."

"No," he firmly said, "you lead and I'll follow. Now move it!"

Kyle and I headed for the park, exchanging glances and wondering if we were going to live or die.

Chapter Fifteen

As the three of us sat down at a picnic table in the park, Nick Riley slipped his pistol into a holster beneath his jacket. He peered warily at the field separating the park from the distant train tracks, making certain that the two men weren't stalking us. After long moments, Nick turned his piercing gaze on us. "Kyle, I want no bullshit from you, okay?"

Kyle lowered his gaze and nervously asked, "Did they kill Hatch? Were they the ones who shot him?"

Nick replied, "Either they did or their associate, the man you met at the Black Lion the evening of Landan's murder. He's more callous about hurting people than those two. I'd say he did the actual shooting."

In my mind, I saw the dark-haired, bearded gunman shooting Landan. I shuddered as I thought of how I'd hit him with the lamp and the fire extinguisher.

Nick noted the fear in my eyes. "Carter Monday is his name. You don't want to mess with him. Play it smart. Maybe you won't have to."

Turning his gaze back to Kyle, Nick said, "You went in there only to film Landan taking the bribe. I had no idea Landan's last night on earth was part of someone's plan. Hatch shouldn't have been such an opportunist. I hope you're smarter than he was."

Kyle couldn't look Nick in the eye. He peeled flaking paint off the table as he said, "You want the tape, right?"

"Smart so far," replied Nick. "An hour after Hatch escaped from me that night in Omaha, he phoned . . . thought the shooting of Landan would net him heavy cash . . . told me you guys had the tape . . . wanted me to pay him off before he told me how to find you. Hatch was foolish to play such a game."

Kyle started to speak, but I opened my mouth first. "How did the cops know to come looking for me?"

A little surprised at the question, Nick asked, "And you are?"

"Chris Talbot. I was there in the other room with Hatch that night. I saw Senator Landan get shot."

"Cops have questioned you? About Landan's murder or about Hatch?"

"Neither. I ran out of school when they came. At least, I think they were cops. My principal pointed me out to this guy in the hallway and I got the hell out of there."

Nick sighed. "Cops! Within hours of identifying Hatch, we had detectives knocking on our door. Street kids told Omaha police that Hatch did gardening work for Mr. Ash. Martin played two detectives a message that Hatch left on his answering machine on Sunday, but having no knowledge about the filming of Landan, Martin had no idea what Hatch was trying to tell him. But I did. That's why I'm here. I hoped I'd get to you before the cops did."

Nick reached inside his jacket. I thought he was going to whip out his gun. Instead, he slowly withdrew a small recorder and placed it on the table between us.

"You see, security for Martin Ash is a high priority in my life. I'll do anything to help him succeed. Landan was becoming a thorn in Marty's side. I took actions to silence his sniveling. Not murder, though. I wouldn't stoop to that."

"Just blackmail!" I said, and then could have kicked myself.

Nick merely grinned. "Politics, son. Landan played the wrong game. I only meant to film him accepting a bribe then have him back off or I'd take the tape to his supporters. It's just that Landan made other enemies in his arena, preaching about porn on the Internet. Those enemies play for keeps."

He looked directly at me. "And with the business between us, we don't need porn dealers or cops interfering."

I held my hands up in a gesture of submission. "I didn't talk to anyone. I swear it! Like I said, I booked out of school like hellhounds were nipping at my heels!"

The big man studied me before saying, "Hellhounds, huh? You got a weird way of talking, kid. Good thing I believe you."

Nick pressed the button on the tape recorder. After a few seconds of static, there came a loud beep and then Martin Ash's voice with the usual "leave your name and number" spiel from an answering machine.

After another annoying beep, Hatch's voice came out of the recorder: "Mr. Ash? This is Ronnie Hatchett! Something's come up, and Kyle Taylor and I had to return to Lincoln. Sorry about the short notice, but I should be able to return to work in a few days. Please send Nick to pick me up between noon and three on Tuesday. I'll be staying with a friend, Chris Talbot. The address is 6340 Carson Street. I'd appreciate the ride back up to Omaha. If all goes as planned, I'll finish the work in the north garden by Tuesday evening. I'll see you then, Mr. Ash. Thanks."

Ronnie Hatchett's words haunted me: . . . *on Tuesday.* That was today. How could he have known he had so little time left on earth?

Kyle snapped, "Hatch actually gave out our names and told where we lived? What was he trying to prove?"

Nick narrowed his eyes as he scanned the field beyond the park. "Hatch was desperate. He was hiding out, knowing that Giles and Carter were searching for him. He phoned Martin in hopes I would know what to do with his information. I think he planned on visiting you two to retrieve the tape, but unfortunately he met up with Monday first."

Kyle glanced up at Nick. "So, you want us to hand the tape over to you? We're supposed to trust you? And if we don't? What then? You gonna do away with us? How do we know *you* didn't kill Hatch?"

Staring at Kyle, Nick appeared to be carefully considering his angry words. "Kyle, my man, you don't have to get all hard with me. I'm not your enemy. Didn't I just save you?"

Kyle asked, "Well, what are you gonna do with it once you have it? How about you just let us destroy it—"

"No!" growled Nick as he slammed a huge fist down on the table between us. "Don't even think about doing that!"

Nick's sudden anger shocked Kyle so badly he slid back on his seat, his eyes fixed on the man's tightly clenched fist.

I thought, *Whoa! This guy wants that tape in a bad way! He doesn't want cops to know about it because he wants to keep Martin Ash out of the loop. And he doesn't want those porn dealers getting hold of it because I heard Giles say something about implicating Ash in the filming. So I wonder what's up?*

I couldn't help myself. I was so curious I had to ask, "Who do you want to sell it to, Mr. Riley? Who do *you* want to make a deal with?"

Nick's massive hand closed on my right wrist so fast that I didn't know what was happening until he yanked me halfway across the table. He placed his face an inch from mine as he softly growled, "I can only be nice for so long, Chris! I have about an ounce of patience left in me! Don't push me over the edge. You won't like the results. Understand, Mr. Talbot?"

He gently lowered me back to my seat, and I saw a Jekyll-and-Hyde transformation take place as a friendly grin returned to his face. "That was my tough-guy routine. Not bad, huh? Now, seriously, boys, I'm not out to make your lives miserable. I just ask for your co-operation. Give me the tape and you'll never hear from me again. I'll even do what I can to back off Monday."

I rubbed my wrist where Nick's hand had been. I fixed him with a serious look. "We're not trying to screw with you, Mr. Riley. Honest. It's just that we don't have possession of it at this time."

Muttering beneath his breath, Nick studied the two of us for a moment before asking, "So where can we pick it up?"

I smiled then. I couldn't help myself. I was thinking of Nick Riley walking up to Bryce's house to retrieve the tape. If Bryce got his brothers involved, Nick would have his hands full. It would serve the guy right. Besides, I wanted someone to pay for all the terror I was feeling. Because of this damned videotape—that Nick Riley was responsible for—my life was turning into a living hell.

"Picking up the tape may take some time," I said, telling him the truth. "You might get hurt trying it the hard way. But if you give me time to talk my friend into handing it over—"

"Hell, too!" shouted Kyle as he surged to his feet. Slamming both palms down on the table, he glared at me. "Even if we turned the tape over to Nick, think about me being on it. Who are you going to show it to, Nick? How are you going to keep us out of this mess? I'm on that tape! And think on this, Chris: Carter Monday saw us both in that room at the Black Lion. We are eyewitnesses to the murder of Landan. Do you think we'll ever be safe from that crazy bastard?"

Nick shot to his feet and stepped away from the table, his hand slipping inside his leather jacket. I was wondering what size hole a .357 slug made in a person, when Nick withdrew his hand. Both Kyle and I looked on as the big man tossed an envelope down on the table between us. "There. A down payment. You'll get the other half when you hand me the tape."

I didn't dare move to look inside the envelope, but Kyle did. He snatched it up and opened it curiously, letting out a whistle.

"Two thousand," said Nick. "The deal goes smoothly and by the end of this night, you guys could be five thousand richer for your efforts."

I exchanged glances with Kyle. He nodded to show me Nick was telling the truth about the amount in the envelope. He opened it further and fanned through the many bills, holding them under my nose. This thing was getting deeper and deeper. And unlike me, Kyle was no longer looking for a safe way out. I could see it by the excited gleam in his eyes. He was willing now to play Nick Riley's game. I didn't know what to do. Five thousand dollars was a lot of money.

As calmly as I could, I told Nick, "We'll get the tape for you. But I can tell you, it's gonna take time. Our friend is not one to give in so easily. Give us two days, okay?"

He didn't seem pleased with the prospect of waiting that long, and for a moment I thought he was going to snatch the money out of Kyle's hands, indicating the deal was off. Instead, he looked up at the stars and gave a low, frustrated growl.

"As far as I know," Nick finally said, "those Omaha detectives don't know anything about you having the tape. If they come your way again, you tell them any story you want about why Hatch would place your names on Martin's machine. But don't mention a thing about the filming of Landan. In the meantime, I'll do what I can about keeping Giles and Deek out of your face. But I must warn you,

you're on your own when it comes to Carter Monday. He plays by his own rules, and you're in over your heads if he has you in his sights."

He started to walk out of the park. At the end of the sidewalk, he glanced back and said, "Two nights from now, I'll meet you back here. Bring me what I want and I'll give you the other payment. Okay?"

"Okay," I heard Kyle say, and wished he'd kept the mockery out of his tone. It wouldn't do us any good to piss off Nick Riley.

Chapter Sixteen

Wednesday, October 31st

Bryce was close to pummeling Kyle.

I glanced from Bryce's angry eyes to Kyle's smooth-skinned cheeks, wondering which one Bryce was going to redden with a swift punch. I didn't want Kyle to get hurt, but with all the crude names he'd just called Bryce, I knew he was pushing his luck.

The three of us had ventured to the park as the sun came up. As it was a bit nippy at the early morning hour, we all wore jackets to ward off the chill. Bryce stood before us in his black leather jacket, a beat-up old thing handed down to him by one of his brothers. He was not happy with either of us. To broach the subject about giving us the tape, I had told him about our encounters the previous night, the terror-filled moments with Giles and Deek, the rescue by Nick Riley, and the request he'd made afterward. I didn't mention the two thousand dollars I had hidden in my bedroom. I was saving that for the kicker if Bryce turned cold-hearted on us . . . as he had so far.

Kyle sat on one of those rocking horses with the huge springs coiled beneath its butt. The moment Bryce told us he would not give us the tape, he let loose with a string of foul, white-hot, four-letter words, directing them at Bryce.

I had been standing near Kyle, yet when he began his tirade I seated myself on the stone ledge surrounding the playground area, taking a neutral position.

Bryce surprised me with his calm tones. One second, he had the look of a lion in his eyes, and I truly thought he meant to punch Kyle in the mouth. However, the next, he composed himself and attempted to convince Kyle he was taking the wrong approach. "Look, those two detectives came to my house last night. Not yours. Not yet. Though you can bet they'll return. They want to know about your connection to Ronnie. They think you owed him money for drugs."

"Drugs?" I asked. "How did they come up with that?"

Bryce shook his head and shrugged his shoulders.

Kyle laughed with little humor. "Hatch was so stupid! Why did he mention our names when he called Ash?"

A puzzled frown on his face, Bryce stopped pacing as he asked, "He was involving you guys in a deal with Martin Ash?"

I explained, "Hatch was so scared of the guys after him that he called Ash for help. We think he just wanted Nick Riley to come looking for us so he could retrieve the tape. Riley thinks either Giles Davis or the assassin, a guy named Carter Monday, shot Hatch. He warned us that this Monday might be after us next."

Bryce studied me, judging whether I was being straight with him. Just as he looked away, Kyle spoke up and royally blew our chances of earning Bryce's trust. "Damn you, Bryce! Don't be so pigheaded. Just give us that tape! It's not yours. It should be mine. If anyone's gonna make cash off it, it should be me!"

Bryce didn't miss the fact that I suddenly rolled my eyes. He didn't bother even to ask Kyle, but instead fixed me in his stern gaze.

"Money? That's what this is about? You two made a deal with this Nick Riley dude? How do you know that he didn't kill Hatch?"

I replied, "We don't. But it seems if we have to trust anyone it might as well be Riley. He could have hurt us last night, but he didn't. I think he has another reason for wanting the tape."

Kyle banged on the head of his pony seat and spit angrily over his shoulder. "Yeah, he probably wants to sell it to those porn dealers and make a hell of a lot more money than we're going to make out of this deal!"

"No," I said, keeping my voice low so as to keep Bryce and Kyle earnestly listening. "I think Riley has his sights on a higher bidder."

Bryce asked, "Higher bidder? What do you mean, Chris?"

Pitching my voice lower, I said, "Maybe Riley has a gold mine in that tape. Maybe he has someone else in mind to sell it to, like people who backed Landan. Whoever supported Senator Landan wouldn't want it known he was taking a bribe, especially if it had to do with porn."

Bryce offered me a faint smile. "You've been giving this a lot of thought, haven't you, Christopher?"

I replied, "Well, what happens to Landan's causes if his supporters don't carry on his fight? Riley mentioned using the tape to blackmail Landan. These supporters probably have tons of money dumped into his antiporn campaign. Think what they might pay for that tape so they could destroy evidence of Landan taking that bribe."

Bryce pulled a cigarette from the pack in his shirt pocket. "You're starting to scare me, Chris. What kind of people do you think these might be?"

Kyle muttered, "It has to be someone really rich! Someone who'd pay more than five grand for it!"

Staring at Kyle as he lit his smoke, Bryce asked, "More than five grand for it? How did you come up with that amount?"

Knowing he'd said too much, Kyle snidely remarked, "Don't know. Hatch probably set that price or something."

Bryce blew out a huge puff of smoke, then peered curiously at me. "Hatch tried to sell that tape to Nick Riley for five thousand? Is that what I'm hearing?"

Kyle let loose with another string of obscenities. He stood up from his pony seat, looking like he might attack Bryce as he snarled, "Talk to him, Chris! Convince him it doesn't belong to him! It's me on that tape! It should be mine!"

I sighed in relief when Kyle wheeled around and stormed off down the sidewalk leading out of the park.

Bryce calmly blew out three perfect smoke rings as he watched Kyle stomp his way down the street. "Temperamental as always. I thought for a second there he was actually gonna hit me. He's really worked up about this thing, huh?"

I shrugged. "Yeah. So what are you going to do with the tape, Bryce?"

Bryce took a long, slow drag on his smoke. He narrowed his eyes as he exhaled. "What if I told you I already trashed it?"

I forced myself to remain calm as I responded, "Destroyed it? Are you serious, Bryce?"

He grinned. "That certainly would bother you. I can tell. So, tell me the truth. What's so important about this tape?"

I told him about the money we'd already received as a down payment on the five grand offered by Nick Riley. When he didn't immediately react, I thought he was getting ready to blow up on me for being so stupid as to deal with Riley. After two long drags, he asked, "Two grand is at your house? Really? Riley's coming for the tape tomorrow evening, huh?"

I couldn't tell what Bryce was thinking. However, at the mention of all that money, I thought maybe he was now intrigued at the prospect of making such a large amount of cash. But then something flickered in his eyes, and I knew I had misjudged him. Bryce was his own man. No one swayed him once he set his mind to something.

Bryce simply said, "We'll talk about this later, Chris. I want to see how you feel about things after the police talk with you. And believe me, they'll be looking you up like they did me . . . and Jen."

"Jen? The police have talked to her, too?"

Bryce nodded. "Yeah. Evidently, when that cop visited school the other day, he was focused on you and Kyle because of that message Hatch left on Ash's machine. Durban must have put us on their hit list also. Jen told them what they already knew: That we went to Omaha to bring Kyle home. They didn't mention Landan. They asked how well we knew Hatch and what kind of drugs you might be selling. Nothing about the tape."

"Drugs? Did you tell them I don't even mess with drugs?"

Bryce said, "Told them that very thing. Just play it cool when you talk to them. They're not going to be able to connect you with Hatch's murder. Those cops are just assuming this crap about drugs and money that you might have owed Hatch."

I glanced down at my wristwatch, checking the time. "We'd better get to school. I've probably got detention for skipping the rest of the day yesterday. I don't need any more added to it."

With that, Bryce and I headed for school.

Third period that Wednesday morning is when I got the call slip from the office. I figured Durban wanted to chew me out for booking out of school yesterday. He was there to meet me, but he wasn't alone.

"Chris Talbot," Mr. Durban said as he ushered me into his office, "this is Detective John Kitchen."

I sat down across from the dark-haired man seated before Durban's desk. John Kitchen of the Omaha homicide unit was the same man I'd run from in the hall yesterday. When he shook my hand, I felt like I'd been grabbed by a pro wrestler. He had one hell of a grip. He said, "Good morning, Chris. We got off to a bad start yesterday."

The man had these penetrating eyes that plastered me to my seat. I cleared my throat, asking, "Will I need a lawyer?"

Detective Kitchen offered me a friendly grin. "No, son, I just want to ask you a few questions about a friend of yours. Ronald Hatchett."

I flicked my bangs out of my eyes with a jerk of my head. "Hatch is what we called him. I heard the news yesterday that he was found murdered up in Omaha."

John Kitchen sat forward, placing an elbow on one knee, looking like a coach about to share a game plan. "Word is that you and some of your friends met Ron in Omaha on Saturday evening. Anything unusual happen on that night?

I had a hard time staring back at the guy. *Unusual?* I thought. *Hell, no. I just witnessed the murder of a state senator!*

"Well," the detective said, "I have reason to believe that you had some business transaction with Ron. Any truth to that?"

This made me angry. "No! No truth to that! I was told that you suspected we were involved in drugs. No way! Hatch? Who knows? But my friends and I don't mess with drugs!"

John Kitchen looked hard at me. "Good. But Ron indicated some connection was to take place between the two of you down here in Lincoln. He left a message with his employer, leaving your home address as a pickup point. Any idea what that was about?"

I responded, "I didn't owe Hatch anything. I certainly didn't owe him money for drugs. Like I said—"

"I know," Kitchen cut me off, "you don't mess with drugs."

Kitchen explained about the message on Ash's answering machine and assured me that any drug transactions between Ronnie and myself wouldn't implicate me in his murder.

This time I simply sighed and thought, *He knows nothing about the tape! Nothing about our connection to the murder of Landan. He's thrashing around blindly, believing this rumor about Hatch and a drug deal between us. I just need to keep my cool and I'm out of here.*

John Kitchen surprised me as he threw me a curve. "You might not do drugs, but it's not quite true about your friend."

"Who? Hatch?" I asked.

"No. Kyle Taylor. I visited him this morning. He reeked of pot and his eyes were about as red as that shirt you're wearing!"

I thought, *Kyle, you stupid ass! What other bad habits did you pick up hanging out with Hatch? Smoking dope! Next, you'll be snorting up! Where in the hell did you get it, anyway? Man, you and I are going to have a talk!*

"Look," I said, feeling like I was about to grovel, "I don't use drugs of any kind. If you think Kyle was stoned, well, that's your opinion. The truth is, neither of us owed Hatch money for drugs. We didn't go to Omaha to see Hatch. We went there because Kyle ran away from home. We last saw Hatch down in the Old Market. He was with some other kids—"

"Old Market?" questioned Kitchen. "You last saw Ron in the Old Market on Saturday evening? What time was this?"

Oh, shit! I thought, kicking my butt all over the place. *Why did I say that? The Old Market is three blocks from the Black Lion! This guy's too smart not to piece this together. I gotta be smarter than this. I gotta keep my big mouth shut!*

I forced myself to remain calm. "We left Hatch around ten or so. I don't really know."

"Did he say where he'd been? Did he seem upset? How many kids was he with? Did you know any of them?"

I raised a hand in the air. "Whoa! Rapid-fire questions don't work with me, sir. You need to understand something. I'm really sorry that Hatch is dead. But Ronnie and me, we weren't all that close. He was a bad influence on Kyle. So I'm probably not a good source of information."

Kitchen raised his brows. "Bad influence on Kyle? How so? Do you mean using drugs?"

I shook my head, thinking, *No! He talked Kyle into blackmailing a state senator! Nothing so stupid as doing drugs!*

And then I told him, "Kyle is my friend. I look out for him. He ran away. I went and brought him home. It was Hatch who gave him the idea of going on run. I'm still hacked at Hatch for that. Kyle has a mind of his own, but—"

"Kyle Taylor," said Durban, trying to shed some light on the matter, "has some social issues. He was recently referred to the courts because of attendance problems. I've never been aware that he had any sort of drug problem, though."

Social issues? I thought, disgustedly. *Oh, so that's what Kyle's problems are all about, huh? I guess that's a nice way of saying he's a gay kid who can't come to school because he'll get bashed up and down the hallways because of his . . . social issues!*

John Kitchen smiled at me. "You look out for the boy? Very noble of you, young man. We all need someone to look out for us, don't we?"

He looked so sincere that I could only nod at him as he stood up. "Well," he quietly said, "sorry to have taken your time. If there's anything else that I think of, I'll be in touch."

I was on my feet and ready to launch myself out through the door when I felt a firm hand come to rest on my shoulder. I turned to face John Kitchen. "Something else?"

Kitchen narrowed his eyes. "One last thing. Were you aware that Ron Hatchett sold himself to older men?"

Calm! I reminded myself. *Real calm! Don't look away!*

"Yes, I'd heard something to that effect," I answered. "But like I said, I didn't hang around with Hatch."

"No, but Kyle Taylor did," declared Kitchen.

I kept my mouth shut. *I will not confirm or deny,* I thought.

Detective Kitchen removed his hand from my shoulder and opened the door for me. As I stepped past him, he said, "You have an honest look about you, Chris Talbot. I sure hope you're being straight with

me. The murder of Ronald Hatchett is serious. If there's anything else
that you think of, please get in touch with me, will you?"

I took his card, pocketed it without even glancing at it, and left the
room.

Chapter Seventeen

On my walk home from school that afternoon, I planned to confront Kyle about being stoned. All of my anger melted, though, when I arrived home and found Kyle's note. It was taped to the outside of my bedroom window. I noticed it as I sat on the edge of my bed to eat an afterschool snack. My mouth full of Oreos, I nearly choked as I read the words:

> Chris,
>
> I can't do this anymore. I'm too tired of all the crap. My life sucks. I hate myself. I hate my life. I just want to die and end this misery. Remember, I loved you. Thanks for being my friend.
>
> Love,
> Kyle
>
> P.S. Maybe they'll name a bridge after me someday.

I immediately ran out to the garage to retrieve my old Trek mountain bike. Spitting mashed cookies out as I pedaled off down the driveway, I prayed I would reach Kyle before he did something stupid.

I knew where he'd be. Why else had he mentioned naming a bridge after him? He'd been so morose the other day when we talked about Hobo Joe's suicide. He'd been seriously contemplating this even then. I just didn't realize how troubled he was.

As I tore through the park and headed for the railroad tracks, I felt guilty as hell. Here I had been feeling sorry for myself because Kyle left me, ran away from me, abandoned me, betrayed me by sleeping with others, and tore my heart to pieces by not caring about me like he used to. How selfish had I been? Kyle was going through his own emotional crisis, and I was hurt about him not being there for *me*. Jen had been right: *He can't even be there for himself.*

I'm a thinker. Always have been, always will be. I can usually think my way through my problems. I might not find immediate solutions to my own depression, but I at least scope it out from various angles. It's what kept me from committing suicide the night I had seriously considered it. I just decided that no matter how badly I hurt, suicide wasn't right. Besides, no matter how sad I felt, I was more than a little curious to see if things might get better. In thinking things through, I always managed to find a shred of hope, and it kept me hanging on.

Kyle, on the other hand? The boy is not a deep thinker. Kyle doesn't dwell on his thoughts for very long. He's impulsive, big on acting before thinking. It's what caused him to run away in the first place. He didn't give it much thought, just knew that living here was no longer any good and so he ran. How wrong he had been. Living up there in Omaha hadn't been a good experience for impulsive Kyle.

I rode straight down the tracks when I reached them, taking every bump by standing up on the pedals and keeping my butt off the seat. It was rough going, but I kept my eyes locked on the outline of the bridge far ahead of me and pedaled like crazy to reach it.

Remember, I loved you, Kyle's note had read. *Thanks for being my friend.*

Always, I thought as I rode. *But please don't leave me! Not now. Not this soon. Stay around longer. God doesn't think highly of suicide. You can't call your own checkout time, Kyle. It's not up to you!*

I was crying by the time I reached the bridge. I was also badly winded from my desperate ride. Throwing my bike to one side of the tracks, I ran out onto the span, wiping tears out of my eyes to clear my vision. There was no sign of Kyle.

Slowly, I lowered myself to my knees, sucking in great gulps of air. I wondered if Kyle had been pranking me, pulling a stunt to get attention. But then I heard gravel scraping beneath his shoes and I knew where he was.

"Kyle!" I shouted as I sprang to my feet. "Kyle, I'm here!"

I ran to one side of the bridge. There he stood, directly below me on the same ledge we'd been on the day before. He had a noose around his neck, pulled up tight so that it bit into his skin. I then saw why the rope was so tight. Kyle was actually leaning out and about to step off the ledge. He heard me above him but refused to spare me even a glance. I followed the line of yellow rope to a board just below my feet. It looked rotten, and yet Kyle had tied the rope to it, with three major knots to hold it in place. I would have to work fast if I was to undo such knot work.

"Don't, Kyle!" I cried. "Just don't do this! I'm here for you. Let's talk this out, please. Kyle, you can't leave me!"

Leaning forward, Kyle gasped as the noose tightened. His words rasping out from between his quivering lips, he said, "Leave—me—alone, Chris. I—just—want—to—die."

"No, you don't," I told him as I leaned down and tried to reach the knots in the rope. "You just want the pain to end. You can't cope with how much it hurts. I know, Kyle. I know what you're feeling. But killing yourself—"

"Can't take it anymore!" he cried out, agony showing on his up-raised face. "*Won't* take it anymore!"

I looked down into his tear-filled blue eyes, realizing that once he stepped off of that ledge, Kyle would be gone from me forever. Tears ran down my face, dropping through the six feet of the space that separated us, landing on Kyle's face.

I could no longer see clearly. Still, I grappled with the rope, twisting and turning the frayed ends, trying to force them back through the tight knots.

"Please wait, Kyle. Please just listen to me. I am here for you. I always have been. Everything will be okay. I promise."

Gazing up at me, his blond hair falling past his ears and bunching up on his slender shoulders, Kyle looked like an angel as the last rays of the sunset grazed his uplifted, tear-streaked face. He looked directly into my eyes, and then . . . he stepped off of the ledge.

I cried out as I grasped frantically at the rope. But it was no use. The weight of Kyle's body had caused the rope to go taut, and I could no longer work at the knots. Leaping to my feet, I took two steps and dropped down to the ledge. Kyle hung there before me, his fingers hooked between the rope and his neck, as if at the last second, he'd had second thoughts and attempted to save himself. Even so, the rope was cutting off his air, and in moments, Kyle would pass out. His eyes were tightly closed and he struggled and kicked as he swung back and forth before me.

I heard the board above us creaking and groaning as Kyle hung suspended forty feet above the river and three feet in front of me. I leaned forward and grasped at the waistband of his jeans. My fingers scraped his leather belt and I felt myself beginning to fall. Shifting my weight, I rocked back on my heels and steadied myself on the ledge.

"God," I began to cry. "Please let me reach him. Please . . ."

The board above gave a loud *crack*. I noticed that Kyle now hung slightly lower than before. Either the rope was stretching or the board had shifted. I couldn't tell as I hastily reached out for him again. On my third try at grabbing him, I managed to latch onto one sleeve of his shirt. Bunching the fabric up in my fingers, I swung Kyle back toward the ledge. "Use your legs!" I shouted. "Get your feet back on the ledge! Help me! I can't do this alone!"

But Kyle was too far gone and didn't have the strength to lift his legs onto the ledge. I gave a terrific heave backward and banged his knees on the cement pylon. I nearly slipped and fell again as I leaned out as far as possible and stretched my free hand out toward him. My fingers grazed his shoulder, but I couldn't swing him back far enough to get a good grip.

At that point, Kyle lurched upward, using his clawed fingers and the rope as leverage. The sudden move brought him closer to me, and I grabbed him with both hands. It was not a good move. My left foot slipped off of the ledge and I spun around, losing my grip on Kyle's shirt sleeve. I started to fall forward, and with nothing but air beneath me, I reached out above Kyle's head and grabbed onto the rope with both hands.

It was our combined weight that snapped the rotting board above us. And with a sudden jolt, we hurtled down toward the rushing dark waters forty feet below.

The splash rang loudly in my ears as we struck the surface of the river. The woosh of the waves echoed around me as I began to sink into the dark depths. Opening my eyes and seeing only murky green before me, I reached out blindly for anything resembling part of Kyle. I missed him completely and started toward the surface when my hand closed around a length of rope. Holding my breath, I pulled on the rope and collided with Kyle's struggling form. Together, we fought our way to the surface, both gasping for air as our heads shot out of the water.

Kyle was so weak he started to slip back under. I saw his eyes close and the round O of his mouth as a green wave hit him. I caught him beneath his arms just before choppy water closed over his head.

I don't know how we managed to reach the rocky shore, but after drifting nearly thirty more feet, we angled over to our left and I felt solid ground beneath my feet. Kyle would have been swept back out into deeper water if I hadn't draped my arm around his chest and pulled his limp form against me. His head lolling over my shoulder, I dragged him slowly up onto the rocky shoreline, scraping my arms and hands as I tried to protect him from sharp pieces of shattered concrete and river rocks.

Kyle groaned. I gently placed him down on the bank. Looking at his face, I could see he was able to breathe again. Though his eyes remained closed, I saw his open mouth suck in air. I placed my left hand beneath his head while using my right to remove the noose from around his neck.

As I removed the rope, slipping it over his head, Kyle mumbled something I couldn't quite hear. Tossing the rope aside, I looked down at his prone form and shook my head. I was totally in a daze as I sat there, thinking of what Kyle's pitiful attempt at suicide might have resulted in.

When Kyle finally spoke, I stared down at him, tears filling my eyes once more.

He peered up at me and said, "Should have let me die, Chris. Should have let me die."

Thursday, November 1st

Jen convinced me to talk to Kyle's mom about the incident at the bridge and the one that happened two months ago when Kyle took his dad's pistol and led me on the wild chase through the grounds of the abandoned missile silos. She even promised to go with me if I worked up the nerve. It took me all afternoon that next day to plan out just what I would say so that Kyle didn't think I was betraying him when we explained to Katie Taylor how her son had seriously attempted suicide.

It took Jen and me almost another hour to work up the courage to approach the Taylor house even after we arrived. In fact, we sat on the curb out front, in the shade of a large maple tree, talking about Kyle and how he arrived at these treacherous crossroads in his life.

Jen ripped up blades of grass and placed a few between her teeth.

I said, "He's in serious trouble, Jen. He needs help. Maybe he needs to go to the hospital. Probably most definitely needs to be placed on meds. He's carrying a lot of sorrow in his soul."

Jen chewed thoughtfully on a grass blade and then blew it out of her mouth before saying, "Sorrow that's eating away at him. Coping with pain is not something Kyle knows how to do. He'd just rather push a button or take a pill or have a magic wand waved over his head . . . to make bad things go away. Life just isn't like that."

I thought of the number of reasons Kyle didn't want to go on living. Though I didn't want to verbalize them and it hurt me to even talk about them, I hesitantly said, "He's still having a hard time dealing with the fact that he's gay, that his parents won't accept him, that he'd get bashed at school, and that he's soon going to suffer the consequences of running away."

I told her more details about Kyle's confession at the rest area the night we left Omaha, about all the unprotected sex he'd had and that he feared he might now be infected with the virus.

Jen sadly shook her head. "How can you ever have sex with him again, knowing those odds? Is that why he attempted to hang himself from Joe's Bridge?"

I shrugged. "Don't know. But it crossed his mind. Wished he would have thought about the virus before he let himself go, before Hatch got him involved in . . . whatever it is they called it."

Jen glanced over her shoulder toward the Taylor house. "Maybe Kyle became *addicted* to sex. Maybe his little excursion into the skin trade has him feeling guilty about all the things he did. Kyle let himself go too far. Now he has to live with those memories, even the desires, that come with crossing the boundaries. The sex drive is a powerful thing. Anything that affects the pleasure center of a person is a very powerful force. Drugs and alcohol often create addictions. People like what they feel when using drugs or booze, and next thing you know, they want to use them to feel good all the time."

I looked over at Jen. "So, you think once Kyle got started doing things, he got addicted to them? But Kyle was never like that before. I don't know how it is for lesbians, Jen, but as for me and Kyle, sometimes it wasn't just sex between us. Sometimes we just held each other. You know, like one time, on this snowy winter morning, we just cuddled up beneath the blankets on my bed and held each other while we watched the snow fall outside my window. There was no sex, just closeness."

Jen patted me on the shoulder. "Sounds like a great way to spend a winter morning."

My eyes teared up thinking of that day last winter. I wished Kyle and I could be that close again in this lifetime.

I muttered, "I know what you're trying to say about Kyle. Maybe he does feel bad about what he did."

Jen responded, "Well, hormones sometimes rule over emotions in boys and girls—straight and gay—and that leads to being quite promiscuous."

Jen finally stood up and gently pulled me to my feet. "Even two thousand dollars richer and Kyle still feels like checking out. Or could that be another reason he doesn't want to live? The tape, him being filmed with Landan?"

I followed Jen up the sidewalk toward Kyle's front door. "Lots of things cluttering up the poor kid's mind," I said. "Life for him certainly became more difficult with his trip to Omaha. Getting involved in Hatch's scam. Delving into street prostitution. Opening a door for HIV. Coming back to a hostile environment at school, which he refuses to attend, and dealing with his parents who don't understand him. And now, dealing with the fact that I didn't let him die yesterday."

We stood, talking in front of the house for at least another thirty minutes. We then made our way onto the front porch. Jen rang the doorbell, and I prayed Katie Taylor would keep her head together for what she was about to receive.

Chapter Eighteen

Katie opened the door, offering Jen a pleasant smile. However, upon seeing me her smile was quickly replaced by a frown.

Jen asked if we could come in. Katie kept the door in her hands, barring our entrance. "Kyle's not home right now. He and his father are at juvenile court, talking to a probation officer about Kyle's terms. I'm afraid his truancies have finally caught up with him. If you'd like, you can come back later."

I started to step off the porch, but Jen grabbed my arm and kept me on task as she said, "Mrs. Taylor, we didn't actually come to see Kyle. We came to talk with you."

Katie seemed surprised. "Me? You want to speak with me?" Stepping back, she opened the door, saying, "Come in then. We'll talk in the family room."

Jen followed her down the hallway while I closed the front door. Reluctantly, I went down the hallway and into the Taylor family room. Katie offered Jen and me the couch and she sat in a puffy recliner. Jen made small talk, making comments about the drapes, the fireplace, and the pictures of Kyle plastered on the wall above the mantle.

I barely heard Katie's response. I hadn't liked the lady since she'd spoken so bluntly to my mom when Kyle first ran away. She was too damned perceptive, determining that her son was gay, trying to convince my mom that I was, too. It was none of her business. Besides, I didn't like the way she kept turning her judgmental gaze on me, as if she blamed me for her child turning out gay.

"Kyle has dug himself an awful big hole," said Katie, "skipping school. Running away from home. Refusing to adhere to our rules. And now, he's being placed on probation."

Jen nodded. "Kyle needs serious help, Mrs. Taylor."

Katie sat still, listening intently as Jen told her about Kyle's suicide attempts. Each time she said my name, Katie glanced my way. I shifted uncomfortably. Even with Jen making me sound like some kind of hero, I couldn't help but think that Katie blamed me for Kyle's jump from Joe's Bridge.

It became quiet for a long while after Jen stopped talking. Katie sat there stunned, like all the wind had been sucked out of her sails. For a moment, I felt sorry for her. We were talking about her only son, her troubled, wayward, mixed-up son. All of those pictures above the mantel depicted Kyle as a happy child: a boy in a Little League uniform, a kid coming home from a fishing expedition, a son holding a bowling trophy, a child dressed in Cub Scout blues holding up a merit badge, a little boy seated on the floor opening up Christmas presents. The pictures caught Kyle at some of his best moments. There he was, frozen in time, back when life wasn't so bad.

I gazed at those pictures, thinking, *That's all we would have had to remember Kyle by if he'd succeeded yesterday. Thank God I saw that note he left me. But what happens if I'm not there the next time? Even as I sit here with his award-winning grins and happy times plastered on the wall before me, I know Kyle will try it again. Because he's sure not happy now. And I don't know if he ever will be again.*

Katie surprised me as she said, "Thank you, Christopher. For being there for my son."

I didn't know what to say. The witch was being nice for once. I almost thought I could like the woman. Almost. But then she changed before our eyes.

Katie snapped, "It's all because of this gay thing! Kyle just hasn't been himself ever since he started this ridiculous nonsense about wanting to be a homosexual! Why can't he see what this is doing to our family? Does he want to be locked away somewhere? Didn't he take his father seriously the other evening when he threatened to send him to Orchard Glens?"

Orchard Glens? I wondered silently. *That's some sort of mental institution! They can't send Kyle to the Glens, where they'd dope him up, lock him in a room, and prod, poke, and analyze him! That would really mess him up!*

Jen tried to calm Katie down. "Depression is a mental health issue, Mrs. Taylor. Kyle is severely depressed. Have you taken him to see your family doctor lately? My mom's on some antidepressants. They really seem to help her. Maybe Kyle—"

"Kyle wouldn't be so damned depressed if he would just be normal!" snapped Katie.

I thought, *Can't she get past this crap? Can't she understand? Kyle's dealing with things out of his control, accepting the fact that he's gay, that he can't change, and that he has to deal with it for the rest of his life.*

Katie picked up a book from the table beside her chair. Holding it up like it was some sort of deadly token of evil power, she snarled, "You know what this doctor claims? He's done years of research and says it's in the genes, claiming people are born as either straight or gay, that it's not a choice! He claims a study was done showing the hypothalamus, a part of the brain that regulates sexual behavior, was smaller in homosexual men than in heterosexual men.

"He writes about the blueprint for the human structure, and he believes there's a gene that determines a person's sexual orientation, that in the genetic structure of all humans, this gene determines whether a person is straight or gay or both, as in bisexual. One tiny gene, and he believes it was placed there in the works *before* we were even born!"

Tossing the book down on the floor between us, Katie snorted, "This doctor claims that most children even know they are homosexual or lesbian at a very young age. Some when they are seven or eight years old! Can you believe that? Children shouldn't experiment, let alone have nasty thoughts at such a young age! I call it a mental problem! This doctor claims it's natural."

Jen bluntly said, "Well, there may be some truth to what he says, Mrs. Taylor. You see, I'm a lesbian. I believe, too, that I was *born* this way."

Katie's mouth actually fell open.

Jen simply continued talking. "I had my first encounter when I was nine, but I first felt strong affections for another girl when I was in the first grade. It was real confusing for me at first. All the other girls I knew had posters of male rock stars on their walls with their tight outfits and all. I could never figure out why they liked those guys so much. Me? I was always fascinated with big breasts. Call that weird, but I'm trying to be honest with you. Considering how serious your son's problem is, I'd say let's not paint pretty pictures by thinning the truth."

Katie swallowed hard. "Are you saying Kyle has been this way since he was a little boy?"

She then turned her angry gaze on me. "Have you and my son ever . . . ? Have you and Kyle been homosexuals together? Do you have this problem too?"

You witch! I wanted to scream at her. *You self-righteous, criticizing, analytical hag! We're here trying to help your son, and you turn this into an inquisition! It's none of your damned business what Kyle and I have done together! None!*

Jen saved me. "Mrs. Taylor, some kids adjust to their sexual orientation better than others. Kids in general deal with a number of problems as they grow up—drugs, alcohol, delinquency, depression, and even suicide. The suicide rate among gay and lesbian youth is much higher than among youth who are straight. Being gay isn't the problem these kids have, though. It's adjusting to being gay, finding acceptance among friends and family, or accepting themselves. How would you like to go through life not even knowing who you really are?"

Katie looked at Jen with distress in her eyes. "But don't you think Kyle would come out of his depression if he just didn't pursue this thing? Can't he just decide he doesn't want to be a homosexual? Wouldn't that be easier on all of us?" Katie sighed. "I wanted my son to marry a nice girl. I wanted grandchildren. I wanted my son to make me proud of him!"

I nearly blurted out, *And now he can't because he's gay?*

Jen smiled and said, "Sexual orientation does not determine a person's ability to make a mark, let alone make history. Socrates, Michelangelo, Leonardo da Vinci, Alexander the Great, Richard the Lion-Hearted, Shakespeare, Susan B. Anthony, and even Rosie O'Donnell! You don't believe that any of those people made their mothers proud?"

Katie looked at Jen as if she just didn't get it. "Well, if this doctor's theory about this tiny gene is correct, then there ought to be some sort of medication that can *fix* a person's sexual orientation. Maybe if Kyle is admitted to Orchard Glens they can conduct a thorough examination and determine what medications might cure his problem."

I nudged Jen with my leg. It was time to go. Katie now knew that Kyle needed serious help. I felt bad, though. Now Katie seemed even more determined to send Kyle away to the Glens. If he found out I told Katie he had jumped from the bridge, he was going to feel betrayed. I wanted to leave before Kyle came through that front door.

Jen nudged me back. She wasn't finished. "Mrs. Taylor, gays and lesbians have had to endure all kinds of treatments. Prostitution therapy was once used, in hopes of turning 'inverted men' on to cogender sexual desire. Marriage therapy was used, thinking that when presented with the option of courting and marriage, the 'deviant' would naturally go 'straight.' Castration and removal of the ovaries were tried, because doctors believed that if homosexuality was hereditary it couldn't be passed on. Hypnosis, psychoanalysis, and hormone therapy—"

"And did any of these treatments work?" blurted Katie, as if maybe she might suggest one for Kyle.

Jen said, "I wasn't finished yet, Mrs. Taylor. Please listen."

Katie closed her mouth but glared at Jen as she continued.

"Radiation treatments, because they were believed to reduce homosexual urges brought on by glandular hyperactivity. Even lobotomies were performed, where doctors cut certain fibers in the front of the brain to eliminate homosexual drives. And no, none of these treatments cured or changed sexual orientation."

Katie looked lost. Jen had just given her way too much to think about. The lady was sailing through uncharted waters.

Jen quietly said, "It would help Kyle a lot if you would just come to terms with him being gay. Maybe—"

"But I don't want my son to be gay!" growled Katie.

Jen said, "I know. But now that you know he is, *accepting* him would help him pull through this terrible time he's going through. Kyle needs our help, not our anger, not our criticism, nor our judgment. Help. He's a lost, lonely boy caught up in a mixed-up situation."

For a minute there I thought Jen was going to tell Katie about the taping in Omaha. But she went nowhere near that as she directed Katie's attention to the photos above the mantel. "He's still your son. If you're having trouble with the gay part, then think about Kyle's depression. That's a mental health issue. It's something—"

"So is being gay!" snapped Katie. "It's a mental illness! Kyle needs help in combating his urges to be—"

"Not according to the Mental Health Association," countered Jen, sounding like a lawyer. "Homosexuality is no longer classified as a mental illness. But depression is, and like I was trying to tell you, Mrs. Taylor, depression can be helped by medication, diet, vitamins, and maybe a little understanding. Does that make sense to you?"

Before Katie could respond, Jen stood up. I quickly followed her as she started for the door. "Thanks for listening, Mrs. Taylor. Chris and I have to go now. But if you'd like, we'd be glad to talk with Kyle later. I'm sure you'll tell him we stopped by. I just hope you use a little tact in telling him why. We don't want him to feel like we turned against him . . . too."

As she opened the front door, Jen added, "We only wanted to help."

I followed Jen out the door, closing it behind us as we left Katie alone with her troubled, self-centered thoughts.

Chapter Nineteen

Bryce phoned my house shortly after our meeting with Katie Taylor. Jen and I were still frustrated about Katie's attitude. When I answered the phone in the kitchen, I was a bit testy. "Yeah."

"Hello . . . is usually what I expect to hear on the other end of the line," said Bryce.

I offered, "Sorry. Just had a rough time. Tell you about it later."

Bryce asked, "You still on for this meeting tonight?"

"With Nick Riley? Yeah. But not if I don't have a tape to give him."

Bryce surprised me. "I'll go along with this on one condition."

I waited, not certain if I should talk or simply listen.

Bryce waited, too, certain that he had my undivided attention. "You still have the two grand, right? Well, here's the way this is going to go down. You with me so far?"

I nodded.

"I can't hear you, Christopher."

"I'm listening, Bryce."

"Bring me four hundred dollars of the cash you have stashed."

"Four hundred? Why?"

Bryce cleared his throat. He said, "Deal's off if you're gonna be an ass, Chris. I've got my reasons. Come on over around eight, and we'll go to your meeting at the park together. Okay?"

"Eight," I answered. "With four hundred dollars. I got it, Bryce. See you then."

On the walk over to Bryce's place, seven blocks from my house, Jen and I speculated as to why Bryce was now cooperating. I figured Bryce didn't want us to fall into deeper trouble with Nick Riley or Giles Davis. Jen was certain that Bryce wasn't motivated by the money. He had told her that the tape shouldn't have been produced, that Landan, victim of a blackmail scheme gone horribly bad, was now dead, and it was totally wrong to make money off of such a tragedy. We both remembered that Bryce had suggested we turn the tape over to the police, but even so, he had backed away from that idea when we all agreed that doing so might implicate Kyle as an accessory to murder. Jen and I concluded that Bryce probably figured that since Riley had initiated the filming, he would know what to do with the tape, and we would then no longer be responsible for what happened to it once he had it.

Bryce met us at the door when we arrived. He ushered us in and offered us seats in the family room. Jen took the sofa. I plopped down in a recliner to one side of the large-screen TV.

"Kyle joining us?" asked Bryce, slipping on his faded jean jacket.

I'd thought about calling him, but I knew by now his mom had probably confronted him about the incident at Joe's Bridge. I explained the situation to Bryce, telling him about yesterday. Bryce gave me a long look. When I finished by telling him about both of Kyle's suicide attempts, he offered me a sympathetic look. "You went through hell then. Sorry, Chris. Kyle really needs help."

I felt tears beginning to form in my eyes. Since the situation at the bridge, I'd tried to block out my feelings. I loved Kyle. His suicide attempt hurt me deeply. I was still not dealing well with the fact that he would have left me behind with no regard for what his death would do to me.

Bryce noticed my tears and quickly changed the subject. "Got the four hundred?" he asked, holding out his hand.

While Jen peered at him curiously, I dug in my pocket for the four folded bills. Jen asked, "For what, Bryce?"

Snatching the money out of my hand, Bryce smirked and said, "Security deposit."

He moved off down the front hallway and disappeared from sight. Minutes later, he reappeared and said, "Let's get moving."

As the three of us started down the front steps, Bryce eyed Jen. "You sure you want to be involved in this?"

"No. I'm not. But someone has to watch out for you two. That a problem?"

Bryce told her it wasn't, and we headed for the park.

Bryce, Jen, and I were just entering the dark field next to the park when Kyle sprang up from the tall weeds near the edge of the field, a pistol gripped in both hands.

"Where the hell you think you're going?" he snarled.

The three of us clumsily collided as we eyed the pistol.

Kyle angrily declared, "You guys were going to make a deal without me and get the money for yourselves!"

Bryce focused on the gun in Kyle's grasp. "Get that out of my face or I'll—"

"Shut up!" ordered Kyle. Bryce stood perfectly still as Kyle placed the tip of the barrel against Bryce's left cheek. I thought Kyle was actually going to shove the gun barrel up Bryce's left nostril.

Jen softly asked, "Kyle, what's wrong with you?"

Kyle ignored her as he used one thumb to cock the hammer of the pistol. "Got the tape? Hand it over now, Bryce!"

I stepped closer, saying, "Kyle, we were heading to the park to meet Riley, but we weren't doing it behind your back. It's not like that at all."

"What's it like, then?" he shouted, keeping the gun barrel pressed to Bryce's cheek.

"Take this gun off of my face," demanded Bryce, "and we'll tell you what it's like . . . Kyle."

Kyle stood up on his tiptoes, keeping the pistol level with Bryce's face. He coldly hissed, "No!"

To which Bryce snapped, "Yes!"

With lightning-quick movements, Bryce latched onto Kyle's left wrist and spun him around, taking him to the ground. Kyle groaned loudly. Bryce rapidly whipped his arm back and forth and the pistol went flying out of Kyle's grasp. Bryce yanked him to his feet and doubled up a fist to pummel him.

I knew Kyle had it coming, that there was nothing I could say to convince Bryce not to punch him out for his stupidity. It was Jen who saved Kyle from getting the worst beating of his life. She scooped the gun up, saying, "It's only a damned BB gun, Bryce!"

Bryce drew Kyle close and harshly snarled, "Dumb ass!" He sent Kyle sprawling with a tremendous heave.

Kyle landed at my feet. I kneeled down to check on him. "You okay?" I asked, placing a hand on his shoulder.

Immediately shrugging off my hand, Kyle sat up. Still bent on trouble, he glared at Bryce. "You got the tape or don't you?"

Taking the BB pistol out of Jen's hands, Bryce peered down at Kyle. He tossed the pistol over his shoulder, and we all watched it spin crazily through the air and fall to the street, where it broke into several pieces.

The black metal flew in all directions, and Kyle struggled to rise, yelling, "Damn you!"

Bryce grabbed the front of Kyle's jacket and flung him back to the ground. I thought he was pulling out a weapon of his own as he whipped something long and black out of the inner pocket of his jean jacket. He growled, "*This* what you're so worked up about, you stupid little peckerwood?"

Bryce held the videotape up between them. Kyle tried to snatch it out of his hands. Turning away from him, Bryce said, "No. This stays with me until the deal is done."

Slowly, he placed the tape back inside his jacket pocket. "And you? Do what you want. Either come with us or go home. After that stupid stunt, I don't really care!"

I helped Kyle to his feet, keeping hold of him so he wouldn't pursue the matter any further. I was relieved when he stayed behind as Bryce and Jen moved on toward the park. I knew if Kyle pushed Bryce any further, he was going to get clocked.

"Damn him!" whispered Kyle, peering at his broken pistol out in the street.

"Kyle, that wasn't cool," I told him.

"And going behind my back was?" he countered, convinced that we had plotted against him. "What was I supposed to think when I called over to your house and your old lady said you were over at Bryce's? Did you think I forgot about our meeting with Nick Riley?"

I shook my head and placed a hand on his shoulder. "No, Kyle. But what happened yesterday . . . I just didn't think you needed to be bothered with—"

"Yesterday? Oh, that? Yeah, right! Let's not talk about it!"

He let me keep my hand on his shoulder. I think he needed to know that I hadn't turned against him. Yesterday he had wanted to die. Tonight he was already putting that behind him in hopes of making cash on the trade with Nick Riley. The kid was so messed up.

As we crossed the walkway into the park, I whispered, "Better tell Bryce you're sorry."

Bryce and Jen turned as we approached, both looking warily at Kyle. Kyle grinned sheepishly at Bryce and lamely offered an apology. "Sorry."

Nodding silently at Kyle, Bryce directed our attention to the lone figure seated at the table inside the shelter nearly thirty yards away.

"Riley?" I asked, peering hard into the shadowy depths of the shelter.

"Don't know," replied Bryce. He lightly tapped Kyle on the shoulder. "For your stunt I ought to send you up there by yourself to find out."

Kyle responded, "If I still had my gun—that someone broke—I'd walk right up to the guy."

Jen shook her head, her eyes narrowing. "I don't know, you guys. I don't like this. We're all pretty isolated here. If he wanted to, he could gun us down and simply take the tape."

Bryce gave her a serious look. "If you want, Jen, please go home. I don't like *any* of this. But someone has to get these guys out of this deal. You don't have to be involved."

She shrugged and said, "Oh, hell, what are friends for?"

With that, the four of us began the long, slow walk up to the man seated in the shelter.

Chapter Twenty

Nick Riley watched us approaching. He appeared calm and cool, but as we drew nearer I could see he had a wary look in his piercing green eyes. I think he suspected that we had set him up for those Omaha detectives as we joined him at the picnic table in the park shelter.

Bryce spoke in even tones. "Mr. Riley, are we here to do business or simply get scammed?"

Nick grinned. "Aren't we the cocky one? You must be the kid playing the heavy with the tape. I'm here to do business and then be gone. How about you?"

Bryce withdrew the tape from inside his jean jacket. "Not that it's any of my business, but why is this worth so much to you?"

With a soft chuckle, Nick replied, "You got that right, kid. It's *not* your business. Matters regarding this tape are above your head. The less you know about this, the better."

Kyle stepped up beside Bryce. "What are you going to do with this, Nick? Is there any way you can use the tape and somehow edit me out? Will I be blamed in any way for Senator Landan's murder?"

Nick turned his gaze upon Kyle. "Not sure, Kyle. You and Landan shouldn't have been in that room together. I'll see it for myself and then decide what can or cannot be cut."

I spoke up then, telling Nick about the entire filming session and exactly what Hatch and I witnessed from the adjacent room. I explained that Kyle had been face down on the bed when the shooting took place, that he really didn't get a good look at Carter Monday.

"No mask or nothing to conceal his features, huh?" questioned Nick. "You and Hatch saw him?"

"Yes," I answered. "I guess, as far as live witnesses go, I'm the only one."

Nick nodded sagely. "Any of you others see this tape? Any of you can identify Monday?"

Bryce tapped the tape with the knuckles of his free hand. "Yeah. I watched it. Why?"

Nick Riley offered us a broad grin. "Well, contrary to what you might believe about me, I'm not a bad guy. Not bad like Monday and Giles Davis. I'm actually working for a greater good, and I'm definitely going to use that tape. Thing is, I'm working out how to keep you folks out of the works. The people I'm dealing with won't be the problem. However, Carter and Giles are another matter."

Snap came from somewhere in the shadows beneath the pine trees thirty feet from the shelter where we stood.

The four of us peered in that direction. Nick shot to his feet, his features grim.

I was about to assure him that we hadn't set him up when a dark figure materialized from between the bushes to our left. The man was tall and broad-shouldered and he held a long-barreled pistol in his right hand. The damned thing had a silencer on the end of its barrel, the same type that Carter Monday had used when he shot Senator Landan. I looked directly into Monday's angry eyes.

"Sit back down!" commanded Carter Monday, pointing his pistol directly at Nick Riley. "Sit down and slowly remove that three fifty-seven from your shoulder holster. You so much as make me think you might shoot me, I'll kill one of these kids, Nicholas!"

I saw the look of hatred that Nick shot at Monday. I also saw him look our way with sympathy in his eyes. "Sorry, kids. I didn't think anyone followed me. I must be slipping."

Nick then fixed Monday with his steely-eyed gaze. "My gun is coming out now, and I'll slowly place it on the table. Just don't do something foolish, Carter. These kids don't have to get hurt."

"That will be entirely up to you," growled Monday. He kept his pistol trained on Nick as he watched him place his gun on the table. Monday then aimed his gun at Bryce, snarling, "You there, hand me that tape!"

Bryce had this fierce, tigerlike look in his eyes as he faced Monday. He seemed prepared to launch himself at the guy instead of complying.

Monday didn't appreciate Bryce's defiant look. He slowly raised his gun and aimed it at Kyle. "Give me the tape or pretty boy gets one in the face! Don't screw with me, kid!"

Click sounded so loudly from a row of bushes to our right that we all flinched in alarm.

"Backup has arrived," whispered Bryce, grinning at me with a confident smirk on his face.

Suddenly, Bryce's two brothers appeared, one stepping from between the bushes near the park shelter, the other moving out from beside the bathrooms twenty feet away. Both were armed with shotguns.

Jason and Chad Carlile were huge, both bikers with bad reputations. Bryce once went to a party where four jocks roughed him up. Bryce went straight home. Neither Jason or Chad liked the fact that their little brother had been tromped by jocks, so they rode their bikes over to the party house. I was glad I wasn't one of those four jocks. Later, cops couldn't prove it was the Carlile brothers who put those four guys in a world of hurt, but everyone else around the city knew who sent those guys to the hospital that night. No one messed with Bryce after that.

I knew then why Bryce had wanted the four hundred dollars. I was greatly relieved that Jason and Chad were there to save us, but if their hot tempers flared, I knew we were not going to leave that park without some sort of bloody shootout taking place.

Tall, with long, blond hair and a full reddish beard, Jason came casually down the sidewalk from the bathrooms. He held his .12 gauge at his side, pointed at Carter Monday. Monday kept his pistol leveled at Kyle, his head swiveling back and forth as he sized up the two large bikers.

Chad, his dark hair pulled back in a tight ponytail, shouldered his shotgun. He appeared ready to open fire as he approached the shelter, looking first at Monday and then at Nick still seated at the table.

"You need to drop that gun, mister," said Jason, still moving steadily toward Carter Monday.

Nick Riley chuckled softly.

Everyone looked in his direction, wondering what he found so amusing.

"You look like you're about to fill your drawers," Nick told Monday. "If I were you, I'd drop your gun. In the Gulf, I witnessed what a scatter gun does at close range. You best comply, Carter."

Monday hesitated a bit too long. Jason slammed the barrel of his shotgun down on Monday's wrist.

Monday hissed in pain as the pistol flew from his grasp. "You son of a bitch!"

"Be nice!" warned Jason as the pistol clattered on the sidewalk at his feet. He swung his gun barrel up and held the muzzle an inch from Monday's chest.

Chad stepped into the shelter, his gun leveled at Nick Riley. "This the one supposed to pay you?"

Bryce stepped closer to the table, offering Nick a smug grin. He told Chad, "Yeah. This is the guy from Omaha."

Bryce slowly placed the tape on the edge of the table.

I was totally surprised when Bryce scooped up Nick's .357 Magnum. I thought he was going way too far if he actually aimed it at Riley, but Bryce was smarter than that. He simply opened the chamber and removed all six rather large bullets. He tossed the cartridges out into the shadows and then gently placed the big pistol back in front of Riley.

"Wouldn't want anyone to lose their tempers here tonight," said Bryce as he looked down at Nick Riley.

"I'm cool." Nick smiled up at Bryce. "As long as we play fair, nothing has to get out of control."

Nick eyed the tape and slowly held up his right hand. "Tell your man with the gauge that I'm going to slowly reach into my left front pocket and draw out an envelope, okay?"

Chad sneered at Nick as he stepped closer to the table. "I got ears! I also got my finger on this trigger! Any sign that you're drawing a piece, and you'll take a direct hit to the chest!"

Nick locked gazes with Chad. At that moment, I was glad Chad had a gun. If not, I think Nick would have been all over him.

"I've got the three right here," Nick assured Bryce. "My end of the deal hasn't changed. Tell the tough guy to point his gun in another direction. I've no reason to cause trouble."

A puzzled frown on his face, Chad asked, "Three? Only three hundred? You said a grand, Bryce. This guy trying to rip you off?"

I saw Bryce roll his eyes.

Nick addressed Chad directly, saying, "I'm not ripping anyone off! We make this trade without any problems, and you guys all end up walking away with the other three thousand as I promised. Now, point that gun in another direction or—"

"*Three thousand?*" blurted Jason, keeping his shotgun leveled at Carter Monday, but now peering angrily at Bryce. "You tryin' to scam us, bro? What was all this talk about *one* thousand? And what's this about the *other* three grand?"

Bryce looked uncomfortable as he faced his older brother. He shrugged and said, "You guys were going to walk away with a thousand all total, so what's the problem?"

Silently, I grinned. Bryce hadn't been honest with his brothers. Somehow, he had got them to help by forking over four hundred dollars. Not that I wasn't greatly pleased that he had done so, but I wondered if he'd told them about the contents of the tape and how much Riley was planning on paying us.

Nick finally caught on to what had gone down. He chuckled softly.

"What's so damned funny?" snapped Chad, placing the muzzle of his shotgun only a foot away from Nick's face.

Eyeing the gun warily, yet forcing himself to maintain a smile, Nick responded, "Money does strange things to people. Who can you trust?"

It was Carter Monday who threw the wrench in the gears as he said, "You were paying three grand for that tape, Riley? Hell, I'd be willing to pay much more than that!"

At this, Jason and Chad studied Monday as if seeing the man for the first time. Only I noticed Nick shake his head, then slowly lower it so that his chin rested on his upraised hands.

Jason towered over Carter by about six inches. He looked capable of tearing the guy apart with his bare hands, yet he kept his gun on him as he questioned, "You scammin' us? Or do you propose to pay bigger bucks for that damned tape?"

Carter glanced down at Jason's gun. Slowly then, he raised his eyes and said, "I'll pay ten grand if you're willing to deal."

"Judas Priest!" blurted Chad, taking his eyes off Nick long enough to exchange questioning looks with Jason. "What kind of deal has our little bro got us into? We gonna thank him later or kick his butt for lying to us in the first place?"

Jason pushed his gun against Monday's chest. "Ten thousand dollars? Are you serious?"

Bryce lowered his gaze, refusing to look at his brothers as he quietly pleaded, "Don't, you guys. This isn't right. This is the guy that actually shot the senator. The tape needs to go to Nick, not to this lowlife murderer."

Jason and Chad exchanged confused looks, but eventually both fixed Bryce with an angry glare. "Okay, Bryce," said Jason between gritted teeth, "since you weren't honest with us about the amount this Riley was paying, how do you expect us to trust you on this? For all we know, both of these scum might have been involved in that damned shooting. So who cares who gets this tape as long we make a mint off of it?"

I had to admire Bryce for his tenacity. "I lied to get your help, but believe me, you guys, don't trust that sadistic psycho!"

Bryce pointed directly at Carter Monday.

"Stupid ass!" spat Monday, glaring hatefully at Bryce.

Ignoring the murderous gleam in Monday's dark eyes, Bryce went on to say, "In fact, if you guys let Riley walk away with the tape now, we'll let you have the entire five grand. Deal?"

At this, Kyle stammered, "Wh—wha—what? Are you serious, Bryce? You can't give them our money! My money! That's not your call!"

Jason shook back long, shaggy hair from his bearded face. "No," he sternly said, ignoring Kyle and looking at Bryce. "No deal. Personally, I like the sound of ten better than five. But we probably got a problem."

Keeping his gun barrel against Monday's chest, Jason fixed the murderer with a serious look. "You offering us cash?" the big biker asked.

Carter Monday kept eye contact with Jason as he replied, "Exactly. But I don't walk around with that sort of cash on me. I can make certain arrangements."

His mind preoccupied by thoughts of getting rich, Chad took his eyes off of Nick as he asked, "What sort of arrangements?"

It was then that Nick Riley made his move. Quick as a snake, he reached up and latched onto the barrel of Chad's .12 gauge. As he did, he smoothly rose to his feet and cleared the space between him and the pony-tailed biker. Even as Nick attempted to wrench the gun out of Chad's grasp, Chad frantically clawed at the stock and his fingers grazed the trigger. The roar of the shotgun sounded like thunder in the close confines of the shelter.

Ka-blam!

Chapter Twenty-One

Chad gaped up at the basketball-sized hole he'd just blown in the roof of the shelter, and Nick spun around and elbowed him in the face. Without a sound, Chad crumpled and fell to the ground.

Ripping the .12 gauge out of Chad's grasp, Nick leaped over the table, placing himself directly in front of Jason and Monday. Jason viciously jabbed the barrel of his gun at Nick's face, but Nick blocked the jab with the butt of the gun he held. Wielding the shotgun like a staff, he repeatedly slammed the stock against Jason's barrel, and with a swift downward chop, sent Jason's gun spinning out of his grasp. Jason dove for it, but Nick swung the butt of the gun up against Jason's chest, forcing him back into Carter Monday. Both Monday and Jason went crashing to the ground, curses exploding from their lips.

"Jesus!" gasped Kyle, peering in wonder at Nick.

Working the pump on the shotgun with one hand, Nick ejected the spent casing. With a swift upward jerk, he sent another shell up into the chamber. He took the shotgun in both hands, swung it to his side, and aimed it at Carter Monday, who was scrambling across the grass and reaching for his pistol.

"Not a good idea, Carter," declared Nick.

Monday froze. He leered up at Nick, then dropped back onto his butt with a loud sigh of defeat.

"No!" I cried out even as Chad rushed Nick from behind.

Chad body-slammed Nick, and the two went down, grappling for possession of the shotgun. In their violent struggle, the gun went off again.

The blast of fiery pellets shattered one of the lights hanging from a pole above the park shelter. Glass rained down and a purple glow appeared where the light had been. In the eerie light, I saw Jason scrambling to his feet and heading toward Nick and Chad, still locked in their struggle.

Sirens wailed from somewhere in the distance, and Bryce shouted, "Someone's called the cops!"

Jen hauled me to one side as Chad, Nick, and Jason came flying in my direction.

I was impressed. Nick Riley was a real brawler. He had thrown the shotgun aside and was now unlocking every hold Jason and Chad were attempting to put on him. Slipping free of their grappling hands, Nick launched himself at Jason. He hammered him upside the head half a dozen times before the big biker dropped. Chad got in a few good punches, clipping Nick in the jaw, but it didn't seem to phase him. Nick merely blocked three more wild swings, then delivered a straight-armed thrust, sending the palm of his right hand into Chad's solar plexus. Chad flew off his feet and sprawled on his back with a loud groan.

As Nick surveyed the damage he had done, Carter Monday scooped up his pistol by its long barrel and slammed the butt down on Nick's head. I heard the *crack* that followed, then watched as Nick Riley dropped to one knee, swaying dizzily as he fought to maintain balance.

Bryce threw himself directly at Monday, sending him flying toward Jen and me. Neither of us could move fast enough, and with Bryce pummeling Monday, the four of us went sprawling in the dirt.

Throwing Bryce to one side with a vicious heave, Monday sprang to his feet. He reversed his hold on his pistol, taking the gun in a two-fisted grip. He then pointed it down at the back of Nick's head.

Police sirens sounded again. This time, they were closer. Only seconds away.

Nick Riley would have died. I'm sure of it. Carter Monday pulled back the hammer of his pistol and with a vicious gleam in his dark eyes shoved the muzzle against Nick's head, when suddenly there came a noise from behind us.

"Get back here, kid!" screamed Monday as he glanced over one shoulder to see Kyle darting away from the park shelter.

Only after Monday started to run after him did I realize what Kyle must have taken with him.

Bryce figured it out, too. "The tape! Kyle's got the tape!"

"He'll kill him!" cried Jen as she took off running right behind Monday.

"What's she trying to prove?" yelled Bryce. "He'll kill them both!"

Six blocks down the street, the cherries of a police cruiser lit up the night. Cops would be at the park in the next few seconds. We had to get out of there.

Bryce knew we only had moments to spare. He watched Jen moving off across the shadowy lawn stretching away into the park. He looked back at his brothers struggling to get to their feet. Torn, Bryce looked directly into my eyes.

"Here!" he said, scooping up one of the shotguns. "Go help Jen and Kyle! I gotta get these two out of here! Go, Chris! Run like hell!"

Nearly getting my front teeth knocked out as Bryce heaved the shotgun at me, I grabbed the gun in both hands.

"Go!" shouted Bryce as he shoved me toward the sidewalk leading deeper into the park. "Just get out of here, Chris!"

I stumbled forward, glancing at Nick now struggling to rise. Instead of angry like I expected him to be, his eyes held sadness. He closed them and slowly shook his head. Then I was racing across the grass and into deeper shadows.

Kyle was seated on the railroad tracks by the time I caught up to him. He was hunched over, holding his flannel shirtsleeve to his bloody nose.

Winded from my long run across the park and the field beyond, I approached him, breathing heavily. "You okay? Where's Jen?"

Kyle peered over his bloody sleeve, his eyes straying to the shotgun in my grasp. Flicking on the safety beside the trigger guard, I pushed on a button beneath the slide mechanism. The metallic click of the opening chamber echoed across the field as I worked the pump on the gun.

Both of us watched as a spent shell casing went flying into the darkness. Not certain that I had accomplished anything more than that as I slid the pump back into place, I looked down at the shotgun, wondering whether it was now loaded.

"Where's Jen?" I asked, looking worriedly in all directions.

Kyle mumbled something.

"What?" I asked, stepping up beside him and wondering where Carter Monday had gone.

"On the other side of the tracks," said Kyle, slowly lowering his arm from his face.

Glancing down at the blood trailing from his left nostril, I asked, "Is she—she okay? Is Jen okay?"

Through his tears, Kyle offered me a grin. "She saved my life. She kicked that psycho right in the nuts!"

I couldn't figure how Kyle could be smiling at a time like this, but I knew he was probably in a state of shock. "Where's she at? And where did Monday go?"

Before Kyle could answer me, more sirens sounded from the park nearly three blocks away. We looked toward the tall pines standing on the edge of the park, and both of us cursed, for those trees blocked our view. All we could see from where we sat were red and blue lights flashing in the vicinity of the park entrance. There was no way to tell what had happened at the shelter area. Nick Riley and Bryce and his brothers were on their own.

"Here I am, Chris," whispered Jen as she came up the slope on the opposite side of the tracks. As she joined us, I could see she carried something dark in her hands.

"My God, Jen, are you okay?" I asked, looking her over to make sure she wasn't bleeding from any bullet holes.

She saw the shotgun and smiled. "Coming to rescue us, were you?"

Searching the darkness surrounding us, I held the gun out to my side. "Maybe. If I even knew whether the thing was loaded! Where's the creep?"

Kyle dabbed at his nose with his shirtsleeve. "He tackled me right down there, down the hill before the tracks. Slapped the crap out of me and then ripped the tape out of my hands."

Jen placed the dark object she held beside Kyle. She bent forward, her hands on her knees, to examine Kyle's nose. "Slapped you? He hit you with all the force of a freight train! I thought he killed you the way you flew through the air!"

"He would have, if not for you playing the hero, Jen," said Kyle, shaking his head in disbelief. "Should have seen her, Chris. She went after him like a mad cat! Clawed his face, pulled his hair, kicked him, punched him, poked him right in the eye! But the best was when she kicked him right in the jewels!"

I stared incredulously at Jen. She hadn't seen Carter Monday the night he gunned down Senator Landan. She hadn't seen the crazed look in his eyes when he threw Hatch through that two-way mirror, nor the murderous glare he gave us when he was about to shoot us in that elevator. No, Jen hadn't seen him the way I had. It was probably just as well.

"So," I was almost afraid to ask, "where's he at now?"

Jen answered, "Ran away with the tape. A cop turned his beam down this way as he crossed the tracks on Mormon Street. He must have been racing to the park, but his spotlight shone right down here at us. I ducked between the tracks and Monday dove for cover on the other side there."

I looked down the tracks to the east where Mormon Street crossed the rails nearly two blocks away.

Jen grimaced and examined her knuckles. "When I first hit him, Monday and I slipped and fell down the bank over there. Something flew out of his hands and went sailing almost into the creek. It was his gun, Chris."

She reached down and scooped it up. "He didn't strike me back because he was too busy trying to keep hold of the tape and his gun at the same time. After I sent his gun flying, he latched onto that tape with both hands. I didn't give him a chance to hit me back because at that point I turned lethal!"

Cradling the shotgun so that the muzzle was pointed away from Jen and Kyle, I leaned down to a get a better look at the pistol Jen held. It sure looked like the same gun Monday had killed Landan with. I gave a low whistle. "We lose the tape only to end up with the murder weapon? What if he's coming back for it?"

At this, Jen and Kyle hastily joined me as I skidded down the rocky slope leading away from the tracks. The three of us ran to the edge of the eastern field adjacent to the park, all the time wondering if we were going to be cut off by Carter Monday or spotted by the cops still at the shelter in the park.

We encountered no one as we left the field, yet we didn't stop running until we hit the sidewalk leading into the residential area three blocks from the park entrance. Once there, we headed to my place.

Chapter Twenty-Two

Seated in my fort within the branches of an oak tree at the center of my backyard, we whispered quietly, fearful that raising our voices would bring hell our way in a hurry. Carter Monday was still out there in the night somewhere. So, too, were the cops.

Jen lit candles and stuck them in the mouths of empty wine bottles scattered on an old crate table, and we sat watching as the flickering light cast eerie shadows on the wall before us.

Monday's pistol lay on a table in the corner, and I had the shotgun propped against the wall beside me. I had carefully worked the mechanism beneath the barrel, ejecting three shells. The hole it had made in the shelter roof was amazingly big, and I didn't want the gun to fall over and blast a hole in anything else.

Finally I asked, "What are we going to do about *that* thing?"

Jen looked at the pistol and shrugged. "Not sure. If it's the same gun that killed Landan, then it might be a good thing for that Detective Kitchen to have."

"No!" protested Kyle, taking two steps toward the gun in the far corner. "This thing is over with now! Don't you see? Monday will destroy that tape. It's evidence of him shooting Landan. He'll just want to burn it. And as far as his gun goes, we don't know if this is the gun he used to shoot Landan with. If it's not, Monday won't bother to come looking for it."

I waited tensely as Kyle moved closer to the gun.

"Okay, say you're right about the tape," said Jen, her eyes straying to the pistol. "Say Monday destroys it, erases evidence that you were up in that hotel room, Kyle. But what about Chris? Chris is an eyewitness. So was Hatch, and look what happened to him! It's time to turn things over to the police!"

Kyle snorted, "How are we gonna explain how we came up with that pistol?"

I stood up and walked over to the table. Kyle watched me as I picked up the pistol, carefully removed the clip, and made sure there wasn't a cartridge in the chamber. "This looks like the same gun he used on Landan. If it is, Monday will be wanting it back. It places us in a hell of a position."

Kyle looked imploringly at me. "Chris, you can't involve the police. Once that tape is destroyed, things will be okay."

"Okay?" I snapped, surprising Kyle with my intensity. "Things have not been *okay* ever since you ran away to Omaha! We saw a man get killed, remember? None of this is okay! We need to do something to make this right."

Jen agreed. "Turning this over to Detective Kitchen would be smart. He could arrest Monday and clear up a murder."

Kyle countered, "And I might be arrested as an accomplice to murder! Do either of you want to see that happen?"

Before we could answer him, the front door of the tree house swung inward. Jen let out a startled yelp and leaped backward. A shadow appeared in the doorway. Kyle cursed and scrambled off the bed, reaching for the unloaded shotgun. I simply stood staring in fear, holding the now unloaded pistol in my shaking hands.

"Good to see you all alive!" declared Bryce, moving through the door and pulling it closed behind him.

"God!" cried Jen, stepping forward and giving Bryce a hug. "Scared me spitless, you fool!"

Bryce slowly removed himself from Jen's embrace. He forced a smile as he said, "Should have seen your face, Jen! All of you! It was definitely a Kodak moment!"

We all looked at him, relief on our faces.

Looking at his brother's shotgun, Bryce said, "I wondered if I'd ever see that again. But what's that?" He pointed at the pistol I had placed on the bed. "You guys starting a collection?"

Jen explained to him how we ended up with Monday's gun, downplaying her part in rescuing Kyle, but Kyle was quick to boast about her deeds. When she finished, I asked Bryce about the outcome at the park. I was especially concerned about Nick Riley. He hadn't looked so good after Monday struck him, and I was hoping he hadn't been arrested.

Bryce put his hand up to slow me down as the questions came pouring out of my mouth. "Whoa, hoss. Slow it down some." He gave us all a sly smirk. "Jason and Chad made it out of the park by way of the ball field just as three cruisers screeched up to the park entrance. I stayed behind to help Riley."

Bryce became animated as he retold the story. "The cops were about a block from the shelter, searching the park with their flashlights. I told Riley we ought to run toward the field, but he shook his head and said he didn't feel much like running on account of that whack he took to the head. He scooped up his gun, slipped it into his shoulder holster, and grabbed me by the collar. He led me over to the bathrooms and boosted me up onto the roof. Then he reaches up and does this perfect pullover, and slips onto the roof beside me. And we just stayed up there, hidden, until the cops went away."

Kyle gave Bryce a puzzled frown. "He ain't mad that the deal went south? He was willing to help you even though you screwed up his plans to get the tape?"

Bryce grinned.

Kyle became irritated. "What's so damned funny? Didn't you hear what we said? Monday got the tape! Our deal with Riley is off! Don't you understand?"

Bryce totally surprised all of us then. "Riley's deal is still on. I had a long talk with Riley after the cops left. He's coming back to Lincoln on Saturday night."

"For what?" I finally said. "How you planning to make a trade with Nick if Monday stole the tape?"

We looked at Bryce in amazement as he explained, "Monday didn't actually get the tape. I wasn't sure how much we could trust Nick Riley, so I switched tapes before we went to the park. I thought he was going to scam us, so I replaced it with another one."

We looked at Bryce in total disbelief as he said, "About this time right now, Monday is probably in a furious rage. *South Park* is all he's going to see on that tape!"

He then laughed, and did a perfect imitation of Cartman as he asked, "Got any Cheesy Poofs?"

After the four of us split up that Thursday evening, I waited at my bedroom window. Bryce had agreed to take Monday's pistol into his possession. I didn't want Kyle sneaking back over to take it, so I remained at my window, watching until Jason drove Bryce back over to retrieve the pistol and Chad's shotgun.

When they left, I drifted off to sleep . . . only to be awakened by a soft rapping on my bedroom window.

Fearful that Monday might be staring back at me, I hesitantly pulled back the shades to peer out.

"Chris!" wept Kyle when he saw my startled face. "Chris, let me in! Please, we've got to talk!"

Breathing a sigh of relief, I slid my window screen up so that Kyle could crawl through. We'd done this before on more than one occasion, and Kyle usually ended up spending the rest of the night at my place afterward.

Kyle slipped through my window, and the lava lamp beside my bed illuminated his tear-streaked face. He huddled against the pillows of my bed, softly weeping.

"What's wrong?" I quietly asked, sitting down opposite him in the center of the bed.

Kyle was dressed in a sweatshirt, blue jeans, and tennies. I noticed the shirt was ripped down the front, and the laces of his shoes were untied and dangling. It appeared he'd left home in quite a hurry.

Kyle stared directly at me and said, "My parents are sending me to Orchard Glens, Chris! They want me to be evaluated!"

Guilty! I thought. *It's my fault! If Jen and I hadn't told Katie about the incident at the bridge this wouldn't be happening.*

He leaned back against my pillows and cried some more. I removed his shoes and then kneeled before him so that I could hug him. I was relieved. Kyle didn't resist. He simply melted in my embrace and cried more tears on my bare shoulder.

"They—they—think that I need—need—help. The courts want to put me on probation and someone told them about me jumping off of Joe's Bridge. They think I need serious psychological help."

Kyle hugged me tightly. "I need to get as far away from here as I can, to take the money that Nick gave us and run! I ain't letting them lock me in no mental hospital. No way in hell!"

I joined him against the pillows, situating myself so that I could hold him in my arms. Kyle scooted his legs beneath my covers and leaned against me. I thought I might have a chance to talk sense into him.

"Kyle, you need help to . . . come out of this depression. You need—"

"Not the Glens! For God's sake! Do you know what they'll do to me out there?"

"Kyle, things are serious when you try to take yourself out. You crossed a line. And I'm sorry, but I told your mom about the bridge. I had to. I didn't want to take the chance that you'd finish what you started when I wasn't there to save you. I care about you, Kyle."

His reaction surprised me. "Good. Good, Chris. I'm really glad you do. I need you to care. I'm so damned screwed up!"

He hugged me hard and cried some more. I gently patted him on the shoulder and lightly kissed the side of his face. "You're carrying around a load of sadness. If you don't find a way to get rid of it, you're gonna be hurting worse. I know the Glens sound bad, but what do you expect your parents to do?"

Kyle started to sit up, saying, "Oh, now you want me to go there too?"

It didn't take much pressure on my part to keep him from pulling away. I softly said, "No. I don't want to see you locked up anywhere. If I could, I'd talk my folks into letting you live with us, but you know that wouldn't work. Our parents—neither of our parents—understand us."

Kyle placed his left cheek against my chest, his hair spreading out over my shoulder. "You mean about being . . . ? Do your folks know you're gay?"

Not like yours do, I wanted to say. *They have no reason to except for your big-mouthed mom!*

However, all I could whisper back was, "I don't know what they think about me. They know that you and I are close, but whether they suspect anything else, I just don't know."

Kyle surprised me then by saying, "You could probably tell your mom you were, and she'd be cool about it. I wish to God my mom was cool like yours."

I peered down at his face in the amber glow of the lava lamp. "Why do you think my mom would be okay with it?"

"Because she really loves you. You can tell about things like that. She never puts you down. I've never even heard your mom nag at you. She cares about you and would accept you no matter what. God, why can't my parents be the same? Don't they realize how hard this is? I didn't choose to be a homosexual, Chris. And I can't change it. Why do they think the Glens can?"

I lightly kissed the back of his head. "No, the Glens can't change your sexual orientation. But look what everyone's reaction to your orientation has done to you. You can't even accept yourself! You want to die, but why? Because you're gay or because you're so sad? Do you even know?"

Chapter Twenty-Three

Still clinging to me as if I could make all the bad stuff go away, Kyle answered, "No."

I seriously thought about going and waking up my mom. What Kyle had said about her made me think I could get her to help us. If Kyle's parents hadn't set up an appointment yet, my mom might convince them to give Kyle a little more time. Maybe then I could bring him back from wherever he'd gone in his troubled, mixed-up head.

I was about to tell him of my plan when Kyle's mind switched gears quite suddenly. One moment, he was allowing me to comfort him, and the next he wanted something else from me.

Kyle's hand slipped beneath the covers. When I began to remove his probing fingers, he became more insistent. "Come on," he urgently whispered. "I need it, Christopher!"

I sighed in frustration, not understanding how he could be so consumed by sorrow and then suddenly want to fulfill his sexual desires. I wanted only to comfort him, but Kyle had moved to another level. He slipped out of his clothes in a matter of seconds. It didn't take him much longer to remove my boxers. One thing led to another then, and a few minutes later, Kyle quietly begged, "Go for it, Chris. Go down on me!"

I was about to, but then suddenly I stopped.

What am I doing? I thought. *What if he has HIV? He had sex with so many people in Omaha; any one of them could have been a carrier. All I would have to do is let one drop of his sperm pass into my system and I could be infected. But what are the odds? He was only up there in the O for three weeks. How many sex partners did he have in that time? Could he have contracted it from just a few partners? I don't want to hurt his feelings, but he's got to know there's a good possibility—*

"Chris!" he hissed, becoming more demanding. "What are you do-ing?"

I wrapped my hand around him then, and said, "Giving you the best hand job you've ever had!"

After we were done, Kyle turned on his side and stared at me.

I knew what he was thinking. At first, I was afraid to look in his eyes. But then I thought, *This is my life he is willing to place in danger! I haven't slept with others, practicing unsafe sex! I wouldn't be that desperate! And here he is making me feel guilty!*

"Why?" he softly asked.

I shrugged and didn't know what to say.

"You're afraid to have sex with me, aren't you, Chris?"

Closing my eyes and feeling tears building up behind my lids, I asked, "Would you take a chance with me if you thought I might be . . . burning?"

Patting me on the shoulder, Kyle adjusted the sheets around us, saying, "It's okay. I understand, Chris. Really I do."

He was actually hurt. I was surprised. It made me want to take away his hurt. I almost slid back down to . . . and then I realized what he was doing.

"No, Kyle! I don't think you do understand. HIV is a serious thing. You're not going to make me feel bad because I have sense enough to be cautious. Unprotected sex is wrong. Giving yourself to one person after another, not knowing if they're burning or not, that's like hav-ing a death wish!"

Kyle smirked. "Now you get it! We all got to go somehow."

I shocked Kyle when I reached over and took his head in my hands, and none too gently drew his face toward mine. "Dying of AIDS is no way to leave this world! It's so preventable, too! You might have a death wish, because you're feeling sorry for yourself and you want to give up, but if you contracted the virus you'll be so damned sorry! AIDS is not how you want to die, Kyle!"

Kyle stared back at me, stunned by my intensity. Slowly, he pulled my hands away, curled up on his side, and whispered, "So, is this how sex is going to be with us from now on?"

I was about to say something about condoms, but Kyle beat me to it. "I suppose now you're going to lecture me about using rubbers. Besides, who told you someone can get it from just sucking someone? Doesn't it only spread during butt sex?"

I said, "Kyle, it's spread by exchanging fluids—semen—in the butt, in the mouth, in the vagina. It spreads from homosexuals and heterosexuals. HIV is like a demon who doesn't care what your orientation is!"

"What about if you did me and then stopped just before I came?" he seriously asked. "What if I did you and pulled out just before I—"

"It doesn't matter," I tried explaining. "There's pre-cum that could be carrying the virus just like the whole load. All it takes is one tiny drop. It's that powerful, like some deadly assassin. Once that drop enters your system, there could be an incubation period that lasts for a few years, but eventually you develop symptoms—full-blown AIDS—and then you die."

Slowly, Kyle closed his eyes, laying his head on my pillows. "So I might really have it, huh?"

I pulled the sheet and blankets up so that we could both cover up and answered, "Don't know. Maybe we should get tested."

Kyle muttered, "My parents would be thrilled about that."

As I lay down beside him, Kyle said, "If I did get tested, say they find me clean, like no HIV or nothing, then would you be willing to—"

I placed my head beside his on the pillows as I told him the hard truth. "It's not that simple, Kyle. There's like this window period. If someone is exposed and infected, ninety-nine percent of the time they'll test positive for HIV antibodies within six months of the last exposure, sometimes within only three months. But they might not even show up if you were tested, because it hasn't been all that long since you had unprotected sex. You could be a carrier and not even know it."

"Not fair," he whispered, "totally unfair."

"But the truth," I softly answered, feeling his head settling in closer to mine.

"Unfair," was the last thing I heard before I fell asleep.

Friday, November 2nd

Jen and I sat watching MTV on the muted television in her bedroom. "Bummed?" she gently asked.

I sat sprawled in a beanbag chair on the floor while she sat in a huge recliner next to her bed. After taking a sip of my pop, I muttered, "More like crushed. I can't help thinking about it, Jen."

Earlier that morning, Kyle had been escorted out of my house by the police. His parents had arrived a little after eight, desperate in their search for him. It seemed they discovered his open bedroom window and a hastily scrawled note telling them he hated them, that they could go to hell. He even left a P.S. on the note, telling them he'd see them there one day if he ever succeeded at suicide.

I told Jen, "It was really embarrassing. My mom came bursting into my room! Fortunately, she had the sense to close my bedroom door behind her when she discovered I wasn't sleeping alone. I could hear Kyle's parents in the front room, talking to my dad, but my mind didn't register what was happening until my mom calmly told me Katie and Jack were there searching for Kyle.

"Mom looked over at Kyle, standing in one corner of my room, fumbling with his clothes. She didn't say anything to either of us about being in bed together. I guess she was still in shock, trying to figure out why two fourteen-year-old boys were sharing a single bed, especially when Kyle slipped out from between the sheets . . . naked."

Thinking back on it, I slumped farther down in Jen's beanbag chair. Shaking my head to clear it of unwanted thoughts, even blinking to edit out the vision of my mom's hurt look as she and I joined the Taylors and my dad in the living room. It didn't seem to help though. I sank further into the chair and pressed my fingers to my temples.

"Want some aspirin?" Jen asked with concern.

"Don't think that would ease the pain I'm feeling in my heart," I told her.

I finished my story. "The moment my mom and I walked out of my bedroom, Kyle barricaded himself in my room. He shoved two dressers against the door, screaming at his parents to get the hell away from him, swearing he'd kill himself if they carried out their plans to admit him to the Glens. It took four cops to get him out of my room! One cut off Kyle's escape route by posting himself in my backyard, and the other three broke down my door, smashing wood and heaving dressers aside. Kyle didn't go down easily. He fought like a cornered wildcat, cussing at the top of his lungs, kicking, hitting, and even biting as they placed him in cuffs and leg restraints.

"The last thing I remember is Kyle staring at me as they drove him away in the cop car. His sad-eyed, desperate look will remain with me forever, Jen."

"Try to think about the good that will come out of this," urged Jen in gentle tones. "Maybe they'll get Kyle's depression under control. Maybe they'll find the right medication to help Kyle get it together. We both know he needs help in a bad way. He wasn't going to get it by continuing as he had been. Probation wouldn't have cured much for Kyle. He would have still refused to go to school, which would have placed him in more trouble with the courts. He might have ended up going on the run again."

I sipped slowly at my pop, knowing Jen spoke the truth. "But I can't help feeling sorry for him, Jen. He'll be so lonely locked up out there, so sad and hurting."

"He'd be hurting out here, as well," stated Jen.

She got up from the bed then and kneeled down in front of me. Taking me by both shoulders, she pulled me close and gave me a hug. As she let go, I noticed she wasn't wearing her braided wristband. A ring of paler flesh showed where the bracelet had been for the past several weeks, since she and Molly had started going together. Jen didn't miss much. She saw where my eyes traveled.

Tapping her wrist with two fingers, she forced a smile. "We broke up this morning. Molly found she was more attracted to boys than girls. Though it didn't lessen the blow, at least she was nice, telling me she would remember our lesbian fling until the day she died. *Lesbian fling?* I guess she could have dumped me without any explanation like Cindy did. Molly still wants to be friends. I love her too much to just be her . . . friend. I have to cut myself off from her so it doesn't eat me up."

Holding back tears, Jen returned to the bed.

This morning? I thought. Jen had been hurting about this sudden loss in her life and I hadn't even known about it. I felt really guilty, sitting there whining. I lost Kyle due to circumstances out of our control. Jen lost Molly because Molly no longer loved her. That had to hurt. And hurt badly.

I recalled that just last night she had saved Kyle's life by launching herself at Carter Monday. I was impressed. Jen suffered, too. She was more than likely just as depressed as Kyle, and yet instead of walking around contemplating suicide, she was still committed to helping her friends out of the terrible trouble they had fallen into.

"I'll get over it," she muttered softly.

"And I'll be there for you," I promised, forcing myself to smile.

Jen responded, "Thanks, Christopher. I can always count on you."

She took the TV off mute and for a while we sat and listened to tunes on MTV. Neither of us felt much like talking anymore and so we just enjoyed each other's company. After a time, the phone rang. Jen answered and gave a soft chuckle.

Pulling the phone away from her mouth, she whispered to me, "Bryce skipped today, too. I figured that. Last night was way too late for all of us."

Jen and Bryce talked for a bit and I returned to watching TV. When I overheard her telling Bryce about Kyle being taken away, I got up and went to the kitchen for another pop.

Chapter Twenty-Four

In Jen's kitchen, I was just closing the fridge when my eyes were drawn to a magnet on the cabinet near the back door. One moment, I was reading that magnet message, a prayer about not giving up no matter how hard life becomes. A moment later, my eyes were drawn to the window in the back door, and I stared straight into the eyes of a man peering through the window at me!

"Holy Jesus!" I shouted, dropping my opened pop on the kitchen floor.

I literally crashed into Jen as I hastily exited the kitchen. We both fell to the living room floor in a tangle of arms and legs.

"A—man—man," I sputtered, pointing to the kitchen.

Scrambling to her feet, Jen started for the kitchen. "A man in the kitchen?"

"No. He was peeking in the window!"

Crossing the room to the door, Jen stepped over my pool of spilled pop. She unlocked the door and jerked it open. Scanning the backyard, she said, "Nothing. No one to be seen, Chris. You sure you saw someone?"

I swallowed hard, thinking how stupid I probably seemed to her. Besides, in all those horror shows we watched together over the years, who ever heard of the bad guy creeping around in the middle of the afternoon? All the scary, creepy scenes always happened at night.

Jen closed the door and grinned as she began cleaning up my pop with a rag from the sink. "You're way too stressed out. Maybe you need a nap. Bryce is on his way over. You can lay down on the couch until he gets here."

I went to the back door, warily peering outside. I was stressed about Kyle, but I wasn't seeing things. Some strange-looking guy had been peering in the window at me. The backyard, though, was empty.

But then the thick shrubs lining Jen's yard swayed crazily and went still. It appeared that someone had just pushed their way through the shrubbery. A second later, Jen's huge black cat came bolting out of the bushes, hissing and spitting.

"Jen? Something's up with Sabbath!"

She came up off her hands and knees, tossing the dishrag toward the sink. Shoving me aside to get to the back porch, she snarled, "Someone hurts that cat and there'll be hell to pay!"

Sabbath spun around and faced the thick shrubs. By the time Jen and I reached him, he was meowing in high-pitched war cries as if another feline had invaded his territory.

Jen kneeled down beside the ferocious cat. Noting his bristling fur and his glazed, demonic eyes, I stopped her from placing her hand on Sabbath's head, knowing how explosive cats are when they're torqued off. Jen withdrew her hand and attempted to soothe the cat. "What's wrong, boy? What's up with you, Sabbath? You got a scrapper cornered in there?"

"No," I said, "someone just booted him out of there! He came flying out as if he'd been kicked!"

Jen peered hard through the shrubs, straining to get a glimpse of whoever might have hurt her cat.

Then we heard a car start from somewhere down the alley, beyond the rows of shrubbery lining the yard. With a muttered curse, Jen hurtled into the bushes, literally clawing her way through the tightly clustered vines. I noticed thorns on some of those tough, fibrous vines, and decided to run to the gate at the center of the yard.

Jen and I met up in the middle of the alley just as a light brown sedan went squealing away down the street beyond.

"Too weird!" gasped Jen.

"For sure!" I agreed.

When we returned to the yard, Sabbath was seated on the porch, his back hunched but somewhat calmer. Jen scooped him up, examining him for injuries. Finding none, she cradled the big cat in both arms and started for the back door.

"Hey, look at this!" she loudly exclaimed as she saw the small card pinned to the door. "What's this about?"

I stepped up and removed the card from the door. It read:

> You are in grave danger! If you would like help in your troubles, please call the number below. I assure you, I only want to help you.
>
> Sincerely, a Friend.
> (555) 366-3995

Jen and I went back into the house. I said, "Okay, now what's up? Who goes sneaking around, peeping in houses in the middle of the day, leaving behind notes?"

"I don't know," replied Jen, putting Sabbath on the kitchen table. "But with the trouble we've found since traveling to Omaha, I'd say a friend would be good about now."

Jen and I were not too happy about the bruise we saw on Bryce's face when he came to Jen's house an hour later. Bryce, however, downplayed the purple flesh beneath his right eye, claiming he had it coming for not being totally straight with his brothers when he involved them as bodyguards in our scheme. He never did tell us which one had hit him, though.

A little later, seated at our favorite downtown hangout, The Coffee House, Bryce asked us, "Did you guys see the news broadcast last night on channel seven?"

Both Jen and I shook our heads.

"It was the latest on Landan," Bryce said. "They claimed he was gunned down after he was lured to that hotel room, campaigning against porn. The news announcer explained that Landan was pursuing funds to support his antiporn crusade, making him sound heroic about dying in the line of duty."

Jen took a drink of her mocha. When she set her cup down, she said, "This whole thing centers around money, doesn't it? Who would Riley be wanting to sell this tape to?"

"Powerful players," answered Bryce. He swigged his pop and belched loudly. Jen shot him an irritated look.

"Exactly," she said. "Someone who was backing Landan wants his cause to continue. They certainly don't want that tape of Landan accepting a bribe to hit the media."

Bryce agreed. He said, "When you gonna call that number the dude left on that card? I say, let's phone the number and find out who else is involved in this thing."

Removing the card from the right front pocket of her jeans, Jen told us she was troubled that the man had come to her house of all places. She was wishing she'd had nothing to do with this chaotic mess. Bryce, however, who was now part of the secret dealings involved in the entire affair, assured us that everything was going to be fine.

"While we waited for the cops to leave last night," Bryce explained, "Nick told me he was once a special ops guy, a SEAL or something. He actually became Ash's chief of security after being shot over in the Gulf War. After that injury, he retired and turned to security work."

Special ops or SEAL, I still looked at Riley as nothing more than a heartless mercenary. I said, "You talk as if he's some sort of hero. He's not, Bryce. The man's a cutthroat just like all the rest of the players in this mess!"

Bryce declared, "Well, we're making the right move by handing the tape over to Nick tomorrow night. He's gonna ride his hog up to Lincoln and meet me and my brothers out at the Woods."

"What?" I asked. "He's gonna trust your brothers after they tried to thrash him at the park?"

Bryce removed a cigarette from the upper right pocket of his jean jacket. "Yeah. As long as Nick pays them the three grand, like he swore he would before leaving the park last night, there shouldn't be any trouble between them."

"Famous last words," responded Jen.

Silver light flooded the entire park as the moon rose full in the sky. It was an awesome sight. Even Bryce was impressed.

"Cool!" he commented as we sat at the center of the park on a battered picnic table.

I nodded in agreement. "Kind of like magic, huh?"

Mist was rising from the stream at the edge of the field beyond the park. It reminded me of a ghostly battlefield. Whorls of curling mist drifted lazily above the dew-speckled grass and I imagined elven warriors riding their white steeds out of a magical portal and onto the field. One massive wave of the translucent fog rose up like an ethereal dragon behind the elven riders. I was so into the scene playing in my head that I almost told Bryce. Almost. But I didn't. He just didn't have the imagination that I did. Poor kid. It must have been awfully boring in his head.

"Sorry about Kyle," said Bryce, flicking away the last smoke in his pack.

We'd both been sitting there for two hours. The sun had gone down long ago and Jen had drifted off toward home, telling us she was going to be grounded when she arrived; skipping school just to catch up on sleep wasn't an excuse her mom would buy.

I quickly changed the subject, not wanting to talk about Kyle. "So, Bryce, what did you do with the tape? You've royally hacked off Jen by not telling her where you've hidden it."

Crumpling up his empty cigarette pack, Bryce asked, "What if that Detective Kitchen comes back to snoop? What if he finally finds out about the making of the video starring the late Senator Landan and Kyle? Wouldn't it be best if you and Jen didn't know where the tape was?"

I shrugged. "What if something happens to you before Riley returns to claim the thing? Who will know how to find it then?"

Giving me a puzzled frown, Bryce asked, "Something happens to me? Like what? So far, I don't have creepy guys peeking in my windows."

"That you know of, anyway," I shot back.

Bryce made a sour face. "You trying to scare me, Christopher? Once Nick has that tape, guys like Monday and Giles Davis will fade away. They'll have to deal with Nick then."

I peered up at the stars, hoping to see one blaze a trail through the sky. I suddenly wished I had that tape in my hands. I wanted so badly to destroy it, to erase any evidence that Kyle was up in that hotel room, involved in this scheme.

It was then that Bryce finally confided in me, saying, "Remember what Riley and Kyle were talking about last night over there at the shelter, about editing Kyle out of the tape?"

I nodded, uncertain as to where he was heading with this.

"Well, I had that done. In fact, the new version lacks the first five minutes. It now shows just the back of Kyle's head so that you can't even tell who he is, laying there with his face buried in that pillow."

I stared at him in disbelief. "You edited the tape? How? Where?"

Bryce grinned. "Kyle won't be incriminated by the new version. Besides, all Riley wants is to get Landan accepting a bribe. He still gets that, just not the face shots of the boy."

He must have totally trusted me at that point, because he finally revealed where he'd hidden the tape. "I took it to Kenneth B. the Third."

"Nerd-boy?" I responded. Though it was not a nice title, one that you didn't use in Kenneth's presence, everyone at school knew him by that name. Kenneth Braxton was a computer freak, a camera buff, an audio tech, and an electronics genius. Every kid on our side of town visited Kenneth when they wanted a bumping system installed in their vehicles. Kenneth had ways to make bass sound like real thunder. His talents were amazing.

Bryce stated, "Kenny did a fine job of editing the material. He also dubbed the tape and made me three extra copies."

I shook my head. "Ken isn't afraid to get involved with such matters? He'd more than likely have a coronary if someone like Monday visited him. Did you let him know the risks involved?"

Bryce got up from the table to stretch. "The big boy knows only that he'll be guardian of the dubbed product for the next few days. I made the other tapes in case something else goes wrong on Saturday. Just to be safe."

Suddenly, Bryce froze. He peered out toward the floating blankets of fog, looking like he'd just seen a ghost. "Someone's out there!" he whispered.

I spun around on the table and quickly scanned the thick, white mist. At first, I could see only the swelling patterns of fog. Then I spotted a large, manlike shape stalking stealthily through the ethereal formations, moving slowly in our direction.

"Let's book!" urged Bryce, grabbing me by the arm and yanking me off the table.

We both ran down the sidewalk winding its way out of the park. Behind us, we could hear solid, heavy feet rapidly pounding the ground. The loud thumping changed quite suddenly as the runner left the grassy field and started down the sidewalk.

Bryce and I didn't even bother to glance back as we exited the park. We just continued to run, making our way down the street toward my house. When we got there, completely breathless from our desperate run, we slipped around behind the house and headed directly toward the tree house.

Up there in the relative safety of my fort, Bryce and I collapsed and sat there a long while speculating who might have been chasing after us.

I wondered how much more suspense and terror I could handle.

Chapter Twenty-Five

I was not expecting anyone to be awake when I entered the house a few hours after Bryce left the tree house shortly after midnight.

As I tiptoed down the hallway toward my room, I noticed a light was on in the family room. I was about to go investigate when I heard a noise coming from my bedroom.

A second later I discovered my mom seated at my desk in one corner of my room. As I entered, she slowly turned in her seat. Her eyes were red and I could tell she'd been crying. Before her on the desk was the letter Kyle had written before he went to the bridge to jump. I thought I'd thrown it away. Evidently, it had been lost in the messiness I called my room. I stood there for long moments trying to recall what words incriminated me, what Kyle had written that revealed the truth about our relationship.

Finally, my mom said, "Kyle's note. I found it when I was changing your sheets. He writes that he loves you. What exactly does he mean by that, Chris?"

My face turned red then as I remembered this morning when Mom caught us in bed together. I thought, *What has she been thinking all day long? Has she told Dad? Is this a secret that will be kept between us? Was Kyle right? Can I really confide in my mom? Does she really love me that much that she will accept me without judging me, without outright rejecting me? Or will she send me off to Orchard Glens to get me straightened out?*

"Christopher?" she softly said. "I need you to tell me."

I moved to my bed. I sat down. This wasn't going to be easy. Sighing, I peered into her eyes. "What do you need to know, Mom?"

I noticed for maybe the first time in my life just how pretty my mom's eyes were. I mean, you can know a person for an awful long time and never realize certain things about him or her. I guess I'd never had to look really long into her blue eyes before. But now, I kept my eyes fixed on her. Funny. Eye contact is a weird thing. But at that moment, I couldn't seem to look away from my mom. She looked so sad, and yet she also had this look of compassion in her eyes.

Softly, she said, "Katie spoke with me after Kyle ran away. She told me she suspected Kyle was a homosexual. She strongly suggested that you and Kyle had some sort of relationship. I told her it was only a strong friendship. Was I wrong, Chris?"

I swallowed hard, placing my hands in my lap. Somehow, I felt like a little boy again, sitting and getting a talking-to because I was in trouble for pulling some prank Mom disapproved of. I looked down at my shoes as I removed them by using my toes and heels. Even that technique reminded me of when I was a kid, when Mom used to get on my case for breaking down my heels.

Mom said, "Katie also told me about the detective's visit. She told me the man suspected you and Kyle of being involved in some drug exchange with that boy who was killed in Omaha. Katie admitted that she thought Kyle might be using drugs. But me? Do you know what I did, Chris?"

Then I found out why she hadn't mentioned Detective Kitchen before as she explained, "After receiving confirmation from your principal about this detective questioning you at school, without my permission, I phoned Omaha. I had some fairly strong words with this detective. I told him I was certain you didn't have a drug problem, that you would not have been involved in any kind of drug exchange."

Thanks for the vote of confidence, Mom, I thought. It felt good to know that she believed the best of me.

"Was I wrong?" she bluntly asked me. "I mean, what am I to think when I hear these things and then walk in here this morning to find . . ."

Her words trailed off. She acted as if I might throw her a lifeline, help sort this thing out, explain why I was sharing my bed with Kyle.

"Is it drugs? Is that why you and Kyle were in bed together? I mean, if it is, then maybe you need counseling."

"No," I responded. "No, Mom. I don't use drugs. You were right about that. Kyle might dabble here and there, but I don't. I won't. Ever."

Mom blew out her breath in little intervals, not certain where to go with the conversation. She wanted to blame my sleeping with Kyle on drugs, as though that would explain my behavior. I wished I could confess to that and tell her that drugs reduced me to sharing my bed with another boy. I wasn't going to lie to her, though. I couldn't.

As though giving up on a difficult game of chess, I sighed and said, "Okay. I'll tell you how it is."

I thought of all the letters I'd read on the Internet from other kids who had come out. Some of those letters had been so bizarre.

One mom told her son it was her fault that he was gay. She blamed herself because she smoked a lot of pot when she was pregnant with him.

One grandmother blamed her daughter because her granddaughter was a lesbian. The wise and elderly matriarch of the family claimed if the mother hadn't dressed the little girl in blue jeans and T-shirts instead of dresses, she would have not been so *boyish*.

Some family members refused to attend a family gathering for fear of eating with the same utensils that their gay relative had used. They claimed they were afraid of contracting AIDS or some other sexually transmitted disease.

The strangest letter was from a boy who claimed he was once caught masturbating by his father and the pictures he had in front of him were from a male stripper magazine. The boy's father thought he would "cure" his son, and so he went out and rented him X-rated videos of heterosexuals. The boy was forced to watch the videos on a daily basis and actually promise his dad he'd never fantasize about men again.

I had read those letters, often thinking how brave some of those kids had been as they told people they loved (and feared to lose) that they were gay. I never once contemplated following their example. I didn't think I'd ever have to. I thought I would simply grow up, keep my sexual orientation to myself, and then one day move out on my own where I could live my life privately. If I never married a woman, well then, my mom and dad would just have to think what they wanted to.

But now, here was my mom asking me the dreaded question. I didn't know how those other kids worked up the nerve or what motivated them. I only knew I was terrified of what her reaction was going to be.

Quietly, my mom said, "Tell me, Christopher. If it's true about what Katie said, I have the right to know."

I thought, *Damn! What do you mean* you *have the right to know? It's been* me *that's had to live with this all of my life! It's been me that's had to struggle with the fact that I am gay! Not you! Me! So, tell me, Mom, what about* my *rights?*

She said, "I'm your mother. If anyone needs to support you, then I have the right to. I'll be damned if I condemn you for it. I believe Katie and Jack have taken the wrong approach with Kyle. He's going through his own crisis and all they can think about is, 'Why is this happening to us?' I'm not taking that attitude, Chris. I'm here for you now, and if now is not the time you want to talk, then I'll still be here for you later. If you're too embarrassed about this—choice—decision—orientation—whatever you call it—I'll not pry."

She smiled a sad smile that didn't quite reach her eyes as she added, "And I certainly won't talk to your father about it until you're sure you're ready. It's not something that he'll deal with lightly."

Before I could say anything, either proclaiming my innocence or admitting she had discovered the truth about me, she came over to me and embraced me. Breaking away just as quickly, she kissed me on the forehead.

"You're my son, Christopher, and I love you no matter what," she declared with a sincere look in her eyes.

Mom started to leave the room, but I cleared my throat and she turned back around to face me, her eyebrows raised inquisitively.

I told her, "Kyle was right about you. He said you'd accept me because you loved me."

Tears started down her cheeks then, and I almost couldn't continue. I forced the words out of my mouth. "I'm gay, Mom. It's not something that I wanted, but I am and I can't change it. I'm just trying to deal with it and live with it on a day-to-day basis. I'm sorry."

She moved back to me in three quick strides, taking my chin in her hands very gently. "Don't you dare apologize for who you are. There's nothing to be sorry about. If you're gay, then so be it, Chris. It's just a fact of our lives, one that we'll deal with together. Nothing changes between us."

I nodded but remained silent. Running her hand through my hair, she said, "Now, get some sleep. You've had a long day. You didn't do a very good job getting to school today, but I excused you when they called. I didn't tell them about Kyle's episode this morning, though. I simply told them we had a family problem to deal with. So you shouldn't have to serve any detention time on Monday."

"Thanks," I offered, staring up at her in amazement that she was being so cool about my confession. Her only son just told her he was gay, and she was already casually moving on, going on with life as usual. I loved her for that. Kyle might have been messed up, but he had certainly read my mom right.

"Chris?" she said as she moved toward my door. "I'm sure you're worried about Kyle. But I believe he's in the right place. He'll get the help he needs at Orchard Glens. And as soon as they give approval, I'll take you out to visit him. Sound good to you?"

She stood just outside of my room then, half in shadow and half in the light. I could see a bit of sadness still lingering in her eyes, but she was doing a good job of keeping things light between us. Maybe she was disappointed, heartbroken about her son being gay, but she wasn't going to show it, because she just wasn't that selfish.

I said, "Yeah, I'm worried about Kyle. But he's made so many wrong choices lately, I just don't know how I can help him anymore."

Mom responded, "Kyle might have not made the best choices lately, but he did make *one* good choice."

Mom smiled as I gave her a puzzled frown. "He did? What choice was that?"

She blew me a kiss and said, "He chose you to be his friend."

Tears rolled freely down my face then, but she didn't see them. She had already started down the hall, not even aware of how good her compliment made me feel. I cried for a good long time after she left my room. I wept for my loss of Kyle, but I also wept because it touched me deeply to know that my own mother was okay with who I was. I thought it very ironic. Here I'd been struggling for nearly four years to accept my own gayness, and within the first few moments after I told my mom, she seemed to be okay with it.

Life sometimes has its little surprises. And this was a good one.

Chapter Twenty-Six

Saturday, November 3rd

That next night, I went out to my refuge in the tree in my backyard shortly after dinner. Dad and Mom had been really quiet throughout the meal. Earlier, I had heard Mom talking to Katie Taylor on the phone. She started out in friendly tones, asking how Kyle was getting along at the Glens. But then she went rigid and took the phone in the kitchen, leaving me staring at the TV in the den, wondering in silent agony what the news could be.

At dinner, Mom was friendly toward me, yet I could tell something was bothering her. Dad ate two heaping plates as usual, but he kept glancing out of the corner of his eye at Mom. I wanted so badly to ask what Katie had said about Kyle. But I knew better than to mention Kyle in front of my dad. I was certain Mom had kept her word and not told Dad about my admission of being gay. And yet I didn't want to complicate things and bring Kyle into our dinner conversation.

I had even attempted a lame joke. "So," I said, sloshing my cherry Kool-Aid around in my frosted mug, "this horse and cow walked up to the bar and ordered drinks. The bartender looked at his two customers and asked, 'Hey, why the long faces?'"

Dad snorted a little. Mom smiled. Neither one laughed, though.

I tried another one on them: "This skeleton walked up to the bar and ordered a drink. The bartender handed him a beer and a mop!"

Dad muttered, "Funny. Real knee-slappers, Christopher."

Mom gave a lame laugh and continued to eat her pork chop.

After that somber meal, I badly needed the cool night air and the solitude of my tree fort. Still not knowing what Katie had related to Mom about Kyle, I had a terrible fear roiling around in my gut. Peering out the tree fort's window and looking to the fading sun on the distant horizon, I tried to put the worry beast to rest.

There has always been something about sunsets for me. I think they're spectacular. In watching them, I somehow connect with God. I mean, all the dazzling colors blending and evolving into so many shades causes me to feel like there's a power beyond me, beyond this world, some force that's out there keeping watch on us. I don't hear, "Luke, may the Force be with you!" or anything mystical like that, but I do get this comfort from the colorful closing of the day. It touches me deeply. It's what I call a connecting experience.

Take a hawk, for instance. When I see a hawk winging its way across the blue skies, I feel a *connection* to it. I feel a soaring sensation inside me, like I can actually feel the winds beneath me, the turns and twists of the hawk as it performs its graceful maneuvers. I'm *there* with that majestic creature. I feel all *lifted* inside, like some unseen threads have connected me to that soaring air acrobat.

It's the same with sunsets. I feel invisible threads connecting me to that impressive display along the western horizon . . . and to God that's beyond.

Getting up off the bed tucked away in one corner of my tree haven, I went to the window to get a better view. Cool breezes rippled through the long strands of my hair. I took a deep breath, sucking in the crispness of early November air. Autumn, my favorite season. All the trees wearing scarlet and orange overcoats. Cold drafts of sharp, clean air. Woodsmoke drifting from fireplace chimneys. And sunsets. In autumn, sunsets were the greatest.

I sat there, looking at the skies long after the sun went down. Slowly, the stars came out and the moon began to rise. I was just stepping away from the window when a flicker of movement caught my eye. Looking down toward the pine trees just beyond my backyard, I could clearly see the cherry of a cigarette glowing bright against the blackness of those shadowy depths.

My heart skipped a beat and my breath caught in my throat. The sight of someone out there, watching me, startled the hell out of me.

Involuntarily, I stepped back from the window. I could still see the dark outline of a tall figure beneath the pines. The cherry at mouth level glowed a bright shade of red, and a ghostly cloud of smoke drifted away from the silent, ominous being.

Oh, hell, I thought, tiny sparks of terror flashing through my head and threatening to ignite a roaring blaze. *Not now! Not when we were so close to getting ourselves out of this jam! Bryce is handing the tape over to Nick tonight. This thing will end then. Just leave me alone! I have nothing for you, anyway!*

The tall, dark specter raised his arm. I thought maybe he had just aimed a gun at me. If he had a silencer on his weapon, I knew I wouldn't even hear the shot. I'd get struck by hot lead and be dead before I even knew what hit me. But the stranger's arm blurred suddenly, and the red ember of his cherry went twirling away through the air. Like a firefly in flight, the burning spark whizzed out over the lawn and dropped down among sparkling grass blades. There, it soaked up silver droplets of moisture and died.

I had watched the cherry far too long. When I looked to the spot where I expected to see the mysterious stranger still standing, he was not there. He had moved.

I totally freaked, searching frantically to locate him. My eyes darted everywhere. I had just stepped closer to the window to get a clearer view of the yard when I heard the whisper of sound from somewhere below me.

It was the unmistakable sound of shoe leather scraping on the boards leading directly up into my fort. Someone was climbing those boards nailed into the trunk of the oak tree.

Quickly, I moved to the door, hastily slipping the bolt lock into place. *He'll have to make quite a bit of noise,* I thought, *to break down that barrier. He'll have to wake the damned dead! And everyone in the entire neighborhood!*

Yet the moment I slid the knob on the bolt into place with a loud *click,* I heard wicked laughter.

"That won't save you!" a voice hissed, its maliciousness leaking between the boards of my fortress.

I heard myself gasp, "What do you want?"

The groans of the climbing boards echoed up into my ears. I could also hear harsh and heavy breathing.

"What the hell do you want?" I demanded to know.

"I want you . . . dead!" came the cold reply.

Dead? my thoughts screamed.

And then it struck me like a sharp slap in the face: *It's Carter Monday! He said the very same words to Senator Landan that night in the Black Lion! And two seconds later, Landan was. Dead. Monday's one cold-hearted bastard! I need help. I need help in a bad way!*

"Shouldn't have screwed with me, kid!" he growled as he reached the last board and drew even with the door.

He tested it, shoving against the barrier. Cursing bitterly, he hammered a fist on the door and I nearly whizzed in my jeans.

Monday banged again. I knew that if he positioned himself just right, he could raise both feet level with the door. Three or four powerful kicks, and he'd batter down the only thing protecting me from his wrath.

I scrambled onto the bed and hastily squeezed out through the window. Reaching up to a slender branch, I grasped it with both hands. Hanging suspended some thirty feet off the ground, I swung back and forth, building momentum for a leap to another branch some four feet below me.

Monday banged on the door with renewed intensity, growling like a berserk demon. I could imagine him actually frothing at the mouth and gnashing his teeth. He wanted me in a bad way.

I swung out, released my hold, and dropped with heart-stopping speed to the wider branch below. I landed on my stomach, clawing like a spastic cat to keep from sliding off the rough bark and plummeting twenty feet to the yard below.

Again Monday slammed something hard against my tree fort's door. It sounded like thunder. It sounded like Monday was using his hard-soled shoes to savagely kick the hell out of the door. I hoped the loud racket brought all of my neighbors running to see what the commotion was. At least I hoped Mom or Dad heard the noise and called the cops when they spotted the maniac up in their tree, trying to kill their dearly beloved son.

But even as I scrambled down through myriad branches, I also realized by the time any cops arrived, I'd already be a victim. Maybe my parents, too, if they interfered in this business between us.

My sweaty fingers slipped from the last branch I tried to grasp, and the next thing I knew I was sprawled flat on my stomach on the ground, gasping for air.

Monday heard me crash to the ground. He stopped assaulting the door and fixed me in his sights from twenty feet above. As I struggled to get to my feet, he grinned wickedly and began to quickly climb down the boards nailed to the tree.

I felt like I was in one of those terrible dreams where I couldn't move fast enough, like time had slipped into slow-mo and I was trying to run for my life with lead boots on my feet. While I set my sights on the back porch forty feet away and tried to run, Carter Monday shimmied down the tree like a gibbon monkey.

I was halfway to the porch when I felt his clawlike hands graze my shoulders. Instinctively, I dove, tucked, and rolled like a gymnast.

Monday cursed angrily and ran past me. Tearing up patches of grass as he wheeled around, he was back in my face in seconds. I had nowhere to go but down. This time he anticipated my dive to the ground and brought his knee up to catch me in the center of my chest.

I went up fast, sailing backward with the painful blow. When I landed before him on my back, Monday sneered and came for me again.

I rolled sideways, looking like some damned idiot playing pigs-in-a-blanket, but I was slipping into a state of blind panic.

A click echoed throughout the backyard as Monday produced a lock-blade knife seemingly from thin air. I knew then that I was not long for this world. One savage swipe, one wicked plunge, one direct and powerful jab with those six inches of cold steel, and I would be standing before the throne.

Monday lunged forward, the knife extended before him. I was almost to my knees when I heard the wind whistling just above my head. He missed! But that was only his first attempt. With his second swipe, I knew he would pierce me. In fact, on his second attempt he would have buried that knife in the center of my chest if not for the unexpected—yet timely—arrival of my dad.

Crack! Dad brutally struck Carter Monday's wrist with an aluminum bat he had retrieved from the garage.

Monday screamed in pain, and as his knife went sailing out of his grasp, he doubled over and cradled his broken wrist to his chest.

Dad raised the bat for another strike, but Mom hollered from the back porch, "I called nine-one-one! The police are on their way! You two, get up here, now!"

Slinging the bat over his shoulder like a player walking up to the plate, Dad latched onto me with his free hand and headed me very quickly up to the porch and into the house.

Mom slammed the door closed behind the three of us, and slid both locks into place. Dad immediately switched off the kitchen lights and took a wary peek out the kitchen window.

"Get away from that window, John!" Mom shouted. "He might have a gun! He might—"

"No," Dad told us both as he leaned over the kitchen sink and continued to peer out the window. "He's running away! I think I hurt him pretty badly. He's almost to the trees near the alley!"

Mom and I joined him at the sink. The three of us watched the dark figure cradling his wrist against his chest and zigzagging his way out of our yard. Moments later, and even in the shadows of the darkened kitchen, I could feel both of my parents watching me. And I sighed, partly in relief, partly in grief. Because I knew I was going to have a hell of a lot of explaining to do.

Chapter Twenty-Seven

A short while later, I explained to two police officers that I didn't have any idea who my psychotic attacker had been. While I talked and one of the cops took notes, I kept glancing at Mom and Dad. Both were shooting these weird looks at each other, more than a little upset about the strange events that had gone on in our backyard. Both knew there was more to this knife-wielding nutcase than I was letting on.

After the cops left, I set my sights on the hallway leading to my room. As I got up off the couch, I said, "Thanks, Dad. You saved my life."

My dad nodded solemnly, yet managed to offer me a slight smile. "What are dads for?"

"Yeah, really," I responded, then turned to leave the den.

Mom, however, decided she'd had enough of my falsehoods.

"Chris?" she asked in a firm voice. "Did you *really* have an altercation with that man like you told the officers? Did you *really* almost collide with him as you rode your bike through the park? Did he *really* call you all those foul names and did you *really* flip him the bird, like you told the officers? Or is there something we should know?"

I thought my story gave the "psychotic man" all the motive he needed to exact his revenge on the mouthy kid who nearly ran into him with his bike at the park. I really thought I had done a good storytelling job on such short notice. My mom wasn't to be fooled that easily, though. And she didn't deserve to be lied to. Not a second time, anyway. I just didn't know where to begin.

"Can we talk about this in the morning?" I asked, giving her the weariest look I could muster.

Mom looked at Dad. Dad looked at me, shrugging as if he couldn't make up his mind. "I suppose we could all use a good night's rest. That was quite the ordeal."

"Extremely stressful," I added, shaking my head as if I still couldn't believe what I'd endured, that I couldn't quite grasp why I was still alive.

Mom stood up from her chair. I thought I had gone too far with my theatrics, but I had misjudged her. She simply walked up and lightly kissed me on the forehead. "Until morning, then. Good night, Christopher."

"Good night, Mom," I responded as I hugged her. "And Dad? Thanks again for saving my life."

Sunday, November 4th

Fretting for the first thirty minutes of that next morning, I lay in bed, trying to decide where I should begin my story when I went down to breakfast. I was certain my tale about the Landan tape was going to go off like a bomb the moment I told my parents about it.

But at breakfast, Mom and Dad didn't even bring up the events of the previous night. They had something far more troubling on their minds. I was just working up the nerve to say, "It all started when I witnessed the murder of a Nebraska state senator," when Mom spoke first.

"Chris, I'm afraid we have some rather distressing news to tell you about . . . Kyle."

He's dead! was my first thought. My stomach turned queasy and a lump arose in my throat. I fought to keep tears out of my eyes. *Kyle succeeded at killing himself with a sheet or a razor blade or by taking sleeping pills! Kyle is gone!*

I sat in stunned silence, knowing by her tone that I wasn't going to handle this very well. I knew Dad was looking directly at me, but I didn't care. If Kyle had committed suicide, I was going to lose it in front of both of my parents. Mom would understand. Dad would be a little confused. Later, I would give Mom permission to tell Dad how it was between the two of us.

Dad took over, which surprised me. He touched Mom's hand and she nodded at him as she got up to get more coffee. Dad said, "It seems they ran some tests on Kyle at the Glens. Kyle tested positive for HIV, Chris. Doctors believe he is infected with the virus. Katie phoned your mother last night to inform her. We wanted to tell you last night, but didn't know how to break it to you after the chaotic mess we all went through."

He then paused, took a sip of his coffee, and said, "Chris? I need to ask you something."

I wanted to melt where I sat, to become a gelatinous liquid that would seep down over the sides of the chair and soak through the linoleum floor. I knew what was coming next, and I couldn't face my dad as he asked me the dreaded question.

I knew then that Mom had told him. I couldn't blame her. This matter was just too serious. I had trusted her with my secret, and she had promised not to reveal it to Dad until I was ready. But circumstances had spiraled out of her control. One part of me wanted to be mad at her for betraying my trust. But another part of me felt sorry for her. Only two days ago I told her I was gay, and now she had to fear for my life. She probably had attempted to draw Dad into our corner by confiding in him, hoping that he'd offer his support in light of this tragic news.

"Did you and Kyle ever . . ." and that's as much as he could say. He stopped himself, trying not to let disgust show on his face. He knew that I knew what he wanted to ask. Neither of us could look each other in the eye. Both of us looked down at our cereal bowls.

Finally, to my utter relief, Mom stepped in. Pouring herself a cup of coffee and then walking back over to the counter, she said, "Chris, we've set up an appointment for you with Dr. Gandahar. He specializes in viral infections and sexually transmitted diseases. The doctor at the Glens actually phoned this Gandahar and set things in motion. You and I will visit his clinic next week."

Replacing the coffee pot on its warmer, she said, "I know how much you enjoy going to a doctor, but at least you'll get to skip four periods of school. I'll pick you up shortly before lunch. Maybe we'll grab a bite to eat somewhere. Maybe we'll swing by the Emerald for burgers and fries."

Good ol' Mom, I thought, *trying to make this as painless as possible. Nice touch, too.*

The Emerald was one of my favorite places to eat. I knew she was trying to keep this whole thing as low-key as possible. But I felt so damned guilty. Eating at the Emerald would be a reward. I didn't deserve anything good coming my way. She was taking me in to get me checked because I had had sex with another boy. And not just once or twice like it was an experiment or something. Kyle and I had had numerous encounters; many climaxes together, by hand, orally, and anally.

My mom was taking me to a doctor to determine whether my sexual practices had infected me with a deadly virus. I didn't deserve her grace, her mercy, or her kind gesture.

I no longer wanted to melt in my chair and seep through the floor. I now wanted to leap up from the table and run far away from my dad's accusatory looks, far away from my mom's sad-eyed stare. I wanted to pat one of my dad's slumped shoulders, tell him I'm sorry because I'll never be the son that he'll be proud of, to fiercely embrace my mom, begging her to forgive me for putting her through such stress and sorrow.

I started to leap up when Mom placed a hand on my shoulder. "Chris, we love you. We are—both—here for you. You're not going through any of this by yourself. I—"

She stopped, and both Dad and I looked up to her standing there beside me, tears streaming down her face. She could say no more, overwhelmed by emotion. She was trying not to cry, but it was no use. Tears were coming anyway. Her lips quivered. A small sob escaped from somewhere deep within her chest. The hand on my shoulder rose and she wiped at her cheeks.

I couldn't bear to see any more of her pain.

When I got up, I didn't leap. I simply pulled myself out of my chair and started for the hallway and my room. Glancing once more at my dad, I felt even worse. He just looked at me with defeat in his eyes. The same eyes darted quickly to Mom as if he now blamed me for her shaking shoulders, her tear-streaked face, and the sobs that began spilling out now like a dam had burst inside of her. Though he said nothing, I could clearly hear the words he wanted to madly scream at me: *See what your playing around with another boy has done to your mother?*

But he said nothing, and I went to my room and avoided looking at myself in my bathroom mirror.

Monday, November 5th

I felt like a total ass. Dealing with the grief, shock, disbelief, and sorrow of my parents left me disappointed in myself, at my failure to be the wonderful son they always believed I was. And the fear didn't sink in until that next day in school.

Anxiously surfing the Web in the media center, searching for any information I could find about AIDS, I overheard Billy Martin whisper, "I screwed the wheels off of Martha Keller last night!"

I tried to ignore the snide remarks from Gary Owens (who sat behind me, taking up most of his seat with his ample bulk). But the two boys carried on their exchange, and I overheard all about Billy's *screwing* and Martha's *wheels* for quite some time as I continued to check out numerous sites.

And then something Billy said struck a nerve in me and hit me like a Titan missile. Billy chuckled, "And she thought I was wearing a rubber all that time!"

Kyle has HIV! a voice roared in my mind. *Doctors did tests. He tested positive! Kyle's infected with the human immunodeficiency virus. Kyle has a virus that there is no cure for. Sooner or later, Kyle is going to die!*

Billy's comment about rubbers brought to mind the last conversation Kyle and I had about sex, the other night in my room, when he wanted me to go down on him. I almost did him the pleasure. But I recalled Kyle sharing his fears with me the night of our ride back from Omaha, confessing that he'd had many potentially dangerous sexual encounters without any protection. I did him by hand, to be safe. And then we talked about sex in the future and using condoms.

I tried to think straight, forcing myself to read the words before me on the Internet site:

Bodily fluids are exchanged during oral and anal sex. The virus, known as the human immunodeficiency virus, travels in cum and blood. It can enter a person's system and then hide itself in blood cells. It can get passed from one person to another by shooting sperm in someone's mouth, rectum, or vagina. Large amounts, tiny drops, it doesn't matter. All it takes is a tiny bit of the microscopic virus, and it's in. And there's no way to get it out once it's in!

Reading those facts, I tried to recall when Kyle and I last had intercourse or gave each other a blow job.

Was it a week before he ran away? I wondered. *We didn't get much alone time together after Kyle got expelled from school that first time. We did that thing between our legs, but no sperm passed between us. I didn't give him head, but I think he did me. Yeah, that's right. But after that, he was too stressed just dealing with all the pressure of his parents and his therapist, and finally he ran away. So I can honestly say, the last time Kyle and I had sex (unsafe, anyway) was nearly a month ago.*

I was sort of relieved, because I didn't have sex with Kyle after we brought him home from Omaha. The hand job was the only encounter we'd had. *Can't get AIDS from jacking someone off unless there's a cut on your hand,* I thought.

But then I shuddered. I thought of how close I'd come to being manipulated by Kyle the other night in my room. Even knowing that he'd had all those unprotected sexual encounters while he was on the run, even knowing he had been at a high risk of contracting the virus from any of his partners, even knowing that he might burn me, I almost gave in. It would have been so easy to do in my state of mind. I wanted desperately to know if he still loved me, and I wanted so badly to prove my love for him. I could have given in, but I didn't.

But even then, I wondered to myself, *Does that mean I passed the test? Does that mean Kyle contracted the virus only while he was in Omaha? Am I safe? Or was Kyle carrying the virus from an encounter he had long ago in Lincoln? He's cheated on me several times, maybe even with Hatch.*

As I sat there in the media room, wondering if I was going to live or die, I heard Billy Martin giggle and say, "And she thought I was wearing a Trojan!"

Poor Martha, I thought, feeling her pain. *She had sex with bucktoothed Billy there, probably believing him when he told her he was wearing protection. Maybe she didn't look. Maybe she didn't feel. Maybe in the heat of the moment, she just let him insert himself and believed he had on a condom. Now, poor girl runs the chance of either becoming pregnant or contracting HIV.*

I thought of Billy's choice of words, especially the word *Trojan,* a popular brand of condom. I thought of the HIV virus, of how much like a Trojan horse it is. The Trojan horse was the giant, hollow horse filled with Greek soldiers and left at the gates to the city of Troy. The people of Troy foolishly took the horse inside their gates. While they partied that night, the Greek soldiers climbed out of the horse and opened the gates of the city, letting in their entire army. Then they looted and burned the city and returned home with their queen, leaving their enemies in a pile of ashes.

Even as I heard that story for the first time, I wondered how stupid the soldiers of Troy must have been. Taking a wooden horse inside their city? Partying even while the giant horse sat within their fortress, oblivious to the fact that their enemies were hiding inside it? And then getting their brains bashed and their city burned because of their stupidity?

Bunch of morons! I thought when our history teacher, Ms. Luke, told us the legendary story.

But Ms. Luke went on to explain another angle on the whole Trojan horse affair. She told us that the writer of the story may very well have been using figurative language while readers took his meaning to be literal. Ms. Luke was convinced that the real Trojan horse was actually a deceitful, cunning, manipulating *man* who wormed his way into the good graces of the leaders of Troy. She explained that once this trickster or false friend won his way past guards and securely locked city gates, he let his fellow Greek soldiers in. Thus, he accomplished what an entire army had been trying to do throughout the Trojan Wars: destroy the city of Troy.

Chapter Twenty-Eight

After school that day, unaware of Kyle's test results and of the research I was conducting on the Net, Bryce heard my theory on the entire AIDS subject as he walked up behind me in the media center.

"HIV," I declared, as I turned in my seat, spoiling his chance to sneak up on me, "is just like a damned Trojan horse! We fool ourselves by having unprotected sex, and the enemy gets inside our fortress, and a royal war breaks out!"

I pointed to the screen of the monitor before me, and as he looked over my shoulder, we both read:

> The HIV germ becomes surrounded by white blood cells, and is attacked and broken apart. The white blood cells then call for the B cells to come to the scene of the battle. B cells produce protein which surrounds the HIV germs. This protein signals the BIG GUNS: the Killer T cells.

Bryce glanced at me, flicking his shaggy, dark bangs out of his eyes, yet remained silent. We continued to read the information on the monitor:

> These T cells are also known as Sentinels. Their mission is to sit and wait for a virus or germ to enter a body's system. These T cells recognize invaders and call on other blood cells to kill them. When the battle is over, some T cells go to sleep until the immune system is attacked by the same enemy again. They serve as the immune system's memory. These T cells are called "resting memory cells" because they store a record of the germs they encounter, and they must survive for a long time. Otherwise we would catch the same diseases over and over.

I looked over my shoulder at Bryce and said, "Now comes the Trojan horse, because HIV has learned how to secretly attach itself to these T cells, then insert its own genetic information inside the T cell's nucleus. See?"

With a deep furrow in his brow, Bryce viewed the screen again as we read the information on the Internet site:

HIV DNA stitches itself into the T cell's own DNA. Reprogrammed, the T cells become an HIV factory, producing the proteins and things that form new viruses. Soon, the cell dies from the infection or is killed by the immune system. But some infected cells survive and before beginning to produce HIV, they return to their resting state, storing HIV's genetic information.

Bryce remarked, "Tricky little bastards, huh?"

I nodded. "Yes. Because resting T cells look normal, the immune system and AIDS drugs won't even attack them! The cells can live for years, loaded but asleep. But when the cells awaken to combat their foes, they start churning out HIV. So, HIV is like a Trojan horse, and it cunningly, stealthily infiltrates the immune system!"

After my fact-filled lesson about AIDS, I expected a little more than Bryce's offhand comment. He smirked and asked, "And your *point* in all of this ranting?"

It royally pissed me off. I spun around, sprang out of my chair, grabbed the front of his leather jacket, and snarled, "My point is that the virus that causes AIDS is one devious, cunning, dangerous bastard with the intelligence of an alien being!"

We stood alone before the rows of computers in the media center. Bryce looked silently down at my hands gripping ample amounts of his leather jacket. I stood shaking like a leaf in an autumn gale as I knew I was going to get pummeled senseless for my insolence.

Bryce, however, didn't hit me. He merely glanced down at my hands, hooked like claws to his leather jacket. Then, very slowly, he lifted his eyes to meet my own.

"Very convincing, Chris," he quietly said. "I have no doubt you believe what you're saying. But would you please release me before I knock you flat on your ass?"

I let go of him, then dropped to my knees and started crying.

I thought for sure Bryce would run to distance himself from the sobbing idiot sprawled before him. But he didn't.

I suddenly felt Bryce's strong hands coming to rest on both of my quivering shoulders. A moment later and he was kneeling beside me, his arm across my back as he drew me closer to him. "What's wrong, Chris?" he softly asked.

Bryce's concern touched me deeply, and I wept like a hopeless, lost child as he tried to comfort me.

I'll never forget the look of confusion on Bryce's face as I tearfully muttered, "I think I'm going to die."

Bryce, still worried about me after I had broken down in front of him, decided to hang out with me at my house. I had sobbed my way through an explanation for my actions, telling him that Kyle had tested positive for HIV, that I couldn't be sure when Kyle had contracted the virus. We both knew, without saying it, that I could be carrying the virus, too.

Bryce and I were watching TV in the den when Jen came to the front door. Just before opening the door, Bryce asked me, "Does Jen know yet?"

"No," I replied. "Let's not talk about it, okay? I'll tell her in my own time."

The moment Jen stepped into the house, she looked directly at Bryce and evenly stated, "Nick Riley didn't show up Saturday night at the Woods, did he? He did not come to get the tape."

Bryce responded, "No. I've been trying to contact you guys since Saturday night, but my brothers grounded me to the house and from the phone. Jason and Chad are pissed that they didn't get to collect three thousand more dollars."

He added, "Something isn't right. This was way too important for Nick to just space off. Maybe he's dead like Hatch. Maybe Monday got to him or Giles or Deek or someone else."

I had their undivided attention then as I told them about my encounter with Monday in my backyard late Saturday night.

Jen shook her head in amazement, looking at me as if it was an act of God that I was still alive.

Bryce muttered, "This has all gone far enough. It ends here. We've lost Nick Riley as the solution to our problem. I believe Nick is dead. It's time we took care of matters before all of us suffer consequences like Hatch and, quite possibly, Nick."

Jen readily agreed. She launched into her campaign to bring us both over to her way of thinking on what to do with the tape. Jen slipped the little white card out of her pocket, the same card we'd found taped to her back door. Jen said, "I called this number and contacted our wannabe friend. Remember the lady we ran into at the Black Lion that night in Omaha, the one who got us past hotel security and invited us to the Forum?"

Bryce and I nodded silently.

Jen said, "Her name is Cora Jackson. She's a private investigator. The man at my back door was her partner. He's been keeping an eye on us for the past week. He didn't want to scare us by directly approaching us, so he placed the card on my door to see if we would respond. Cora Jackson wants to help us."

I felt a little hollow spot in the pit of my stomach. "Help us with what? The tape? Monday's gun?"

Jen told us, "Cora is representing a group of people who invested lots of money in Landan's campaign. She's been investigating Landan for the past year. Her 'people' financed Landan as he waged his war on same-sex unions, pornography, and a gay and lesbian curriculum designed for parochial and public schools. Her people have assigned her the task of finding out why Landan was murdered that night."

"Good for her," I said. "But what does this have to do with us?"

Sighing, Jen said, "Cora said we all need a haven in this storm. She knows we're just a bunch of kids who got involved way over our heads. She exchanged bits of info with that Detective Kitchen. That's how she found out who we—Hatch's friends—were. She told me she suspected some sort of scam was going down in the Lion that night. Then she mentioned the mysterious, empty camcorder."

Jen admitted, "I told her about Hatch's scam. I told her about us just trying to rescue Kyle. Then I told her the entire story about Landan and Kyle, Carter Monday bursting into that room, and the shooting that followed. I told Cora we got it all on tape."

I let her words sink in for a moment before asking, "But what about Bryce's deal with Nick? Does Cora know about Martin Ash's *noninvolvement* in this situation? Did you tell her about our troubles with Giles Davis and Monday? Did you tell her about the five thousand Nick is offering for the tape?"

"Shh!" Jen urged. "No. I told her nothing more than the fact we had a tape of Landan's murder and quite possibly Monday's gun. I agreed to meet with her."

I was surprised and Jen was totally relieved when Bryce didn't offer any stubborn protest. He simply shrugged his shoulders and asked, "So, when does she want to meet with you?"

Jen replied, "In the morning."

Tuesday, November 6th

The next morning, Bryce and I met Jen at her house. Within two hours after Jen phoned Cora Jackson, she and Detective Kitchen showed up at Jen's place. Both cop and private investigator were pleased that we gave them our full cooperation, explaining in detail how we ended up with Monday's pistol and a tape of Senator Landan's murder.

Thinking that we were going to be in major trouble, even though we were finally doing the right thing, the three of us were relieved when Detective Kitchen let us off with a light scolding for not asking for his help sooner. He agreed to talk with our parents, explaining our involvement in the entire affair before taking Bryce to his house to retrieve the gun and the tape.

At the end of that night, I felt like we had closed a chapter on a memorable event in our young lives. After all, how many kids can say they were actually involved in solving the murder of a Nebraska state senator?

My mom and dad took the hit pretty well. Cora Jackson and John Kitchen both explained in a fairly calm manner that we had stumbled into affairs at the Black Lion that night in Omaha. Both Cora and Kitchen thought it was admirable that we had gone there to retrieve Kyle, and they tried to keep Mom and Dad focused on the final results of the ordeal rather than on the fact that we had kept the evidence for so long. Neither one mentioned that we nearly suffered serious consequences for our reluctance to turn things over to authorities when we should have.

Mom and Dad were fairly calm. I thought they might ground me for being so sneaky about things, especially the fact that I had lied to them about the night Carter Monday attacked me. But to my relief, they were both really cool about the entire matter. Mom was more concerned about whether I had been having any nightmares about witnessing Landan getting shot. Dad expressed the same concerns, but he was also pretty hard on Detective Kitchen, saying, "You damn well better catch this creep before he comes back here to give us any more grief!"

Before Kitchen and Cora Jackson left, they assured my parents that Monday would soon be apprehended. Kitchen even gave us his home phone number, telling us we could call him anytime to check on the status of the manhunt for Monday. Cora told us that she doubted very much if Monday would venture to Lincoln, that he would go to ground in Omaha.

After the two left, Mom wanted me to head to bed, but I talked her into letting me stay up so that I could call Jen and Bryce after Cora and Kitchen had visited their houses also.

Thirty minutes later, Jen phoned to tell me how her mom had taken the news. Jen was not her usual talkative self. She told me her mom was still in shock over the news Cora and Kitchen had shared. Jen even said that after the two had left, her mom had walked her down the hallway to her room and tucked her in bed like she did when she was a little girl. Then Jen got all emotional on me, saying that was a real cool thing for her mom to do, that she hadn't given her that kind of attention for a long, long time. Before I hung up, Jen wept a little and then said, "Hell of an ordeal for a bunch of kids, huh, Christopher? Glad it's all over."

Jen's words were still rolling around inside my head when I heard the knock on the front door.

Chapter Twenty-Nine

By the time I reached the living room, Dad had retrieved the baseball bat from the hall closet. He stood to one side of the door, giving Mom the go-ahead only after he took a defensive stance with the bat raised over one shoulder. Mom peered out the peephole on the front door and whispered, "John, turn on the porch light! All I can see are shadows out there!"

I looked at my parents in amazement. "Really, you guys! You don't think a cold-blooded psycho like Monday would just walk up to our front door in the middle of the night and knock, do you?"

Reaching for the light switch, Dad said, "Never can tell! He'll have hell to pay if he thinks he's getting in here, though!"

A moment later, Mom sighed in relief. "It's Bryce," she said, undoing the bolt lock and pulling the door open.

It was past midnight, but both of my parents were cool with the fact that Bryce stood there on our front steps. Better him than Carter Monday. Mom ushered him in and Dad looked rather sheepish as he lowered the bat and stepped past Bryce to relock the door.

Mom asked Bryce if he wanted anything to drink. When he politely told her no, both Mom and Dad seemed to know that Bryce was troubled and they had sense enough to back off so we could talk in private.

Mom said, "If you boys need anything, let us know."

She placed a hand on Dad's arm and led him down the hallway to their room, saying, "Come on, slugger."

In my room, Bryce collapsed on my beanbag chair and sat all hunched up in a black leather jacket that was way too large for him.

"Well," he muttered, "we're out of the woods with the cops in regards to the Landan murder, but I'm in deep weeds with my brothers!"

He slipped out of the extra-large jacket, tossing it on the floor between us. "Oh, crap! Had to swoop out of my place so fast, I actually snagged Jason's jacket instead of mine! I'll pay for that mistake, too!"

I looked to the worry creases around Bryce's eyes and said, "You gave Kitchen the tape and the gun, right?"

Slowly nodding, Bryce blew out a powerful breath and miserably declared, "Yes, I did. My mom about had a coronary when Kitchen and Cora Jackson told her all about Landan's murder! Even with Jase and Chad cussing up a storm and telling Kitchen he needed a warrant to search our house, my mom demanded that I cooperate with Kitchen. I had no choice but to give him the tape and the gun."

I really felt sorry for Bryce. His brothers certainly had to see that he had no choice in the matter, that the money they thought they were going to make off of the deal with Nick Riley was not as important as turning in evidence of a murder. But as Bryce explained, Jason and Chad hated cops, and both were more angry with him for cooperating with Detective Kitchen than for blowing their deal with Riley.

"And both of them wanted to kick my butt right after that Kitchen dude left my house," he muttered. "Now I wish more than ever that Nick would have showed up Saturday night."

I sat down on the bed opposite Bryce, watching him sink even lower in my beanbag chair. "Yes, Nick's disappearance is about as mysterious as this whole damned thing. It just proves we were in way over our heads, Bryce. It was time to turn it over to the authorities. Your brothers will see it that way, too, once Kitchen nails Monday and the murder gets plastered all over the papers."

Bryce shrugged. "If I live that long. I can't go home tonight, that's for sure."

I said, "I'm sure my mom will be cool with you staying here tonight. After I explain your situation, she'll be bringing you milk and cookies."

Looking quite relieved, Bryce responded, "Yeah, your mom's cool that way. I'll even sleep on the floor. Wouldn't want to kick you out of your own bed."

"Naw," I said, "you're the guest. You get the bed. I'll be just fine once I smash that beanbag flat."

Two hours later, after winding down from a long talk in the shadows of my room, Bryce and I concluded by speculating about what would probably happen in the next several weeks.

He told me he had given Detective Kitchen the edited version of the tape. It wasn't really necessary to protect Kyle anymore, since we had all been straight with Kitchen, but Bryce didn't want to involve Kenneth, who still had the original. And so he gave Kitchen the one tape he had in his possession. This tape, while not showing Kyle's face, would still reveal that Monday had gunned down Landan in cold blood. It would definitely incriminate Carter Monday.

Bryce had then brought up something I hadn't considered. If Monday was eventually arrested, Kyle and I both would have to appear as material witnesses during the trial. This scared the hell out of me, because in all likelihood, it was going to be revealed just what Senator Landan was doing in that hotel room. And if there was some sinister power out there who didn't want the public to know about Landan's bribe taking, then Kyle and I might be in danger once more.

I shared my fears with Bryce.

He laughed and told me I had a wild imagination. But when I brought up the disappearance of Nick Riley, Bryce got all quiet. His long silence confirmed that I had made a valid point.

To distract me from worrying myself to death about being silenced before I testified about Landan in court, Bryce looked down at me from his place on my bed. "Glad your mom let me stay the night. This will give Jase and Chad time to cool down."

Scrunched up in my beanbag chair, wrapped up in a cocoon of three blankets, I peered up at him, trying to see his features in the shadows of my darkened bedroom. "You really think they'd pummel you just for cooperating with a cop?"

"Oh, yeah," replied Bryce. "They can be pretty heartless sometimes."

Not wanting to talk about his irrational brothers, Bryce said, "Remind me to thank your mom in the morning."

"Don't worry about it," I told him. "That's just the way she is."

Then Bryce totally surprised me. "Yeah, Jen told me she was pretty cool. She told me about the night you told her you were . . . you know . . . that you were . . ."

"Gay?" I said.

"Yeah," answered Bryce. "Jen said your mom accepted you still and that she had your back in regard to your . . ."

"Orientation?" I supplied.

"Uh-huh." Bryce fell silent for long moments before asking, "How's your dad taking it?"

I didn't answer him right away. His question sort of had me at a loss. Finally, I muttered, "He's sort of like your brothers, heartless about the entire subject."

Sprawled on my bed, Bryce rose up on one elbow to look down at me. "You mean he's *beaten* on you because of it?"

"No," I answered. "But his silence about the thing is sometimes just as cruel. I guess it's what he doesn't say that bothers me the most."

"Bummer, Chris. Sorry I brought him up."

"Yeah. Me, too," I responded.

I turned over, wrapped my blankets more tightly around my shoulders, and nestled my head deeply into my pillow.

Bryce fluffed out his pillows and pulled the covers up around his own shoulders, saying, "People can be so mean at times."

Just the way he said this made me want to cry. Bryce sounded so much like a little kid with that statement. Growing up among his tough biker brothers hadn't been easy. Thinking they were making up for the dad they had all lost due to a tragic motorcycle accident, Jason and Chad often played the heavies with their younger brother. Jen and I were both upset when Bryce showed up after our incident in the park between Monday and Nick. The bruise on Bryce's face had been caused by a fairly powerful punch delivered by one of his brothers. Yet Bryce seemed to take it all in stride. Physical altercations were commonplace over at the Carlile residence, and for Bryce to think that my father was anything like his brothers made me actually want to defend my dad.

He wasn't being mean on purpose, not like Jason or Chad when they punched Bryce. He was just having a difficult time dealing with who I was. It was harder for him, I think, than it was for my mom. He was, after all, a man. A big and masculine man who wanted his only son to grow up and be just like him, a chip off the old block. When I was born, he probably figured I would grow up to carry on the family name, to be another link in the endless generations of the Talbot line, to have a son of my own. But now what? Now that my dad knew I was gay, how could he dream about such things anymore?

I'd told Bryce my dad was heartless, but that wasn't really fair. He hadn't ever hit me. He hadn't gotten in my face like Kyle's dad had when he learned his own son was gay. No, he hadn't ever mentioned my sexual orientation. But he was disappointed in me. I could tell. There was a big valley of silence between us, and it had all started when my dad learned about the relationship between Kyle and me. And like I told Bryce, that silence from my dad caused a pain all its own.

"Good night, Chris," came softly from Bryce. "At least I'm still on your side."

I pretended to be asleep, not trusting myself to respond for fear my voice would crack. Before long, Bryce was sleeping soundly, and I lay there talking to God again. My prayer was all screwed up, because one moment I was thanking him for having people like Bryce, Jen, and Mom in my life, and the next I was pitching a beef about why Dad hadn't accepted me.

As I drifted off to sleep, I wondered if God ever got tired of me bitching all the time.

That following week, the media went above and beyond the call of duty with their coverage on the "recovery of the murder weapon" and the "key piece of evidence" in the murder of Senator Landan. It was big news. Front-page stuff. Aired on both television and radio. A Nebraska state senator involved in a conspiracy and then mysteriously assassinated? It was just too good for most journalists to pass up.

Due to such coverage, the story about Landan trying to quash the AIDS education program was a real pebble in the pond. And when it was learned that Landan had been accepting a bribe in favor of the pornography industry, the ripple effect spread in ever-widening circles.

Our social studies teachers at school made the story the main topic of current events. When it became public that part of the bribe taking that Landan was involved in had something to do with the AIDS prevention program, our health teacher brought up the story to fuel discussions using the "Landan murder" to spark off lively talks about the AIDS epidemic, safe-sex practices, and the spread of sexually transmitted diseases. Not one kid left Old Man Hefner's class without the letters S-T-D burned into his or her brain. And in science class, Mr. Drury drilled us over and over on all the many viruses that threatened life as we knew it on planet earth.

Jen and Bryce wanted so badly to tell other students the major role we had played in the entire Landan affair, but Kenneth Braxton, the Nerd-boy, warned the three of us to keep a low profile. He was convincing in his argument that some "higher power" had been behind Landan in this cause, and he was certain that whoever these supporters were, they wouldn't be our friends.

In fact, Kenneth told us, "They probably want you dead, just like that Carter Monday guy wanted Landan. Remember? Just like he said on the tape?"

So we told no one at school about the tape or the gun. Only our parents and, of course, Bryce's brothers knew the whole story. At least the news coverage served to mellow out Jason and Chad. They no longer wanted to punch their little brother for deceiving them and involving them in the entire affair. But they did bring up the topic that had been haunting Bryce since he'd turned the tape and gun over to Detective Kitchen. Both of them wanted to know: *What happened to that Nick Riley dude?*

Bryce confided in Jen and me that he firmly believed Nick had been wiped out just like Hatch had been. It was one more reason for us to follow Kenneth's advice about keeping a low profile.

Yeah, it would have been great to see the look on people's faces at school when we told them how we had been there at the Black Lion on the evening Landan had been shot—how I actually witnessed the murder—the escape from the shootout in the Old Market—the stalking by Giles and Deek—the exciting conclusion of our misadventures when my dad saved me from Monday in my backyard—but the three of us decided it was way too risky.

"Besides," Jen had laughed, "who would believe us?"

The only negative thing to come out of Bryce relinquishing the evidence related to the Landan murder was the e-mail I received toward the end of that first week.

It came from Kyle.

He had not adapted well to the environment at Orchard Glens. According to reports my mom received from Katie Taylor, Kyle had been abusive to staff and disruptive among other clients. He had been locked down numerous times and lost all of his points, and therefore was denied visits by anyone but his parents. He was, however, allowed to use a computer to send e-mails to both Jen and me.

Kyle's e-mail to me was so full of bitterness that I imagined the keyboard had been smoking when he'd furiously hammered away at the keys to send it.

He called me a "Judas," claiming I had betrayed him by turning the tape and the gun over to Detective Kitchen. He even accused all of us of getting a reward from Crime Stoppers, saying we had probably spent all of the money so he couldn't collect his share. It was a pitiful, scathing rebuke. I read his e-mail twice before knowing how I should respond.

Kyle's words hurt. I understood he was in his own world of pain, and there was no way to explain to him how much danger I had been in when I was attacked by Monday, that we had no choice left in the matter regarding the tape. So, I simply e-mailed him back with one single word: *Sorry.*

Chapter Thirty

One good thing to come out of the media blowing Senator Landan's murder out of proportion was the coverage that was given to Senator Martin Ash. Reporters and common folk alike wanted to know what lay at the heart of the controversy between these two Nebraska senators. So news crews flocked to the state capitol when Senator Ash appeared there to speak out about AIDS. He spent several days reading from a long list of those who have died of the virus in America, listing doctors, lawyers, teachers, parents, artists, authors, and many others. Ash conveyed that AIDS education is the key element in the battle against this enemy that has stolen and destroyed some of our most valuable resources. "It, too," Ash claimed, "is part of a terrorist network that must be destroyed."

Jen, Bryce, and I actually drove down to the capitol building in downtown Lincoln to hear Ash speak. His presentation was dramatic, and his words on educating teens about prevention were quite powerful. We tried to push our way through the crowds to speak directly with the senator afterward, but the entire round chamber of the capitol building was crammed full of people, either supporting Ash or opposing him.

As the three of us withdrew from the masses, Bryce complained, "Damn! I just wanted to ask the guy if he knew what happened to Nick."

Jen glanced back at the long-haired senator. "I wanted to tell him he's doing a great job by standing his ground and pursuing this education matter. More kids need to know about AIDS."

A voice startled the three of us as we turned to leave: "Well, if it isn't my three friends from Lincoln!"

We turned to face Cora Jackson. The investigator greeted us with a pleasant smile. "Never know where you guys might show up. It's good to see you again."

Jen responded, "Hello, Ms. Jackson. Nice to see you, too."

The older lady nodded in Senator Ash's direction and asked, "Supporters of his, or are you part of the opposition?"

"Oh, we're for the man," answered Jen. "What he's doing needs to be done."

Cora smiled. "I'm glad that you support him, since you three are partly responsible for Martin Ash being here today."

She grinned at our confused looks. "Care for some coffee?"

A short while later, Cora Jackson bought us all mochas at The Coffee House.

Cora had our undivided attention the moment she declared, "What I am about to tell you must be kept in the strictest confidence. Is that understood?"

The three of us quickly peered around the room to make certain there weren't any sinister people aiming guns at us from beneath their tables.

Cora sensed we were on edge. She smiled warmly. "You have nothing to fear from me."

Jen cut to the chase by saying, "No, but this thing isn't over with yet, is it?"

Cora took a moment to sip from her latte. Casually, she placed her cup back on its saucer, and said, "With your efforts to rescue your runaway friend at the Black Lion the night Landan was shot, you actually prevented a second murder from taking place, one that might have had global consequences. Had you not caused the commotion that you did when Monday discovered the camcorder in that room, he might very well have accomplished *both* of his assignments that evening."

Bryce poured an ample amount of sugar into his mocha. "What are you saying? Global consequences? Both assignments? Can you speak a little more plainly?"

Cora Jackson nodded. "Monday was hired that night to take out not only Landan but also . . . Senator Martin Ash."

The three of us exchanged stunned looks. But Bryce still didn't trust Cora. "How do you know this for a fact?" he bluntly asked her.

Scooping up her coffee cup, Cora took a sip. She then answered, "Reliable information. I was hired by a powerful group of men from several denominations who believe Martin Ash's 'Gay Agenda' is terribly wrong. The Alliance, as they call themselves, believe it is their Christian duty to silence Ash, to oppose the homosexuality that he openly promotes. They hired me to find dirt on Ash to mount a character assassination campaign against him."

Jen asked, "For real? Who would be involved in such a thing?"

"Men who are convinced they are right," stated Cora.

She took a sip of her latte and watched to gauge our reaction. "The Alliance is a secret religious unit formed by those who believe gays and lesbians are a blight upon the Church. They are a power, with money, influence, and ties to churches, schools, and politics. They have set themselves against all who believe the way Martin Ash does."

Jen and I were trying to absorb what we were hearing, but Bryce said, "The Alliance, huh? So they hired you to tear down Ash by digging into his past? And?"

Cora smiled at Bryce. "My investigation turned up nothing to indicate that Martin Ash was corrupt. Ash is a successful AIDS activist who has raised thousands of dollars for extensive research into the virus. With his support of educational programs, he's made the entire world more aware of the epidemic we face. But Ash has also proposed same-sex unions and rights for gays and lesbians. He knows the law. He also knows his Bible. It makes him a major threat to a unit such as the Alliance. They believe Ash is determined to tear down the family structure in America."

Jen looked disgusted. "What about divorce rates? Spouse abuse? Child abuse? Broken homes? Alcoholism? Wouldn't it be better for these men of God to put their efforts into preventing such things that do tear down the family structure, rather than target Ash? In the Bible, there are six main scriptures that mention homosexuality, and three hundred and sixty-six regarding heterosexual relationships! Maybe there's a reason for that! Maybe heterosexuals need more guidance than homosexuals do!"

Cora seemed to think Jen's remark was humorous. She said, "Good point, but the Alliance—and those like them—have taken those few scriptures out of context to alienate gays and lesbians who believe in the very same God that they do. They've deceived themselves into believing they have godly authority to condemn those who don't believe the way they do."

Bryce responded, "Sort of like those terrorists who killed so many people at the World Trade Center, taking their own Bible out of context about killing their enemies. In speech class, Mr. Fellers talked about how religious interpretations can really screw some people up."

Cora said, "Very true. And in regard to the matter of sexual orientation, a lot of religious zealots have served to turn away those who need God the most. Ash has been working to repair such damage most of his life."

Stirring her dab of whipped cream into her mocha, Jen said, "The Alliance found Ash to be a danger, and they wanted him shot and killed? And these men believe they are Christians?"

Slightly shaking her head, Cora said, "Not so fast there. The Alliance wanted me to help with a character assassination of Ash, to investigate Landan accepting the bribe on the pornography issue. But they did not authorize that Landan and Ash be murdered. However, since they were Landan's financial supporters and openly opposed Ash, they are under investigation by Detective Kitchen. I believe, though, they are innocent of the charges of murder or attempted murder."

"Why?" asked Jen. "Just because they are Christians?"

"No," answered Cora. "Because of what Nick Riley told me yesterday."

Bryce sat his coffee cup down on his saucer with a loud *click*. "Nick is alive? But why didn't he show up to retrieve the tape?"

Cora finished off her latte. "Alive and well! And actually causing the Alliance—and some other agency—more problems than Senator Ash!"

Noting our puzzled looks, she explained, "There is another power out there, possibly religious or political, but definitely very sinister. Nick calls it the Entity. He claims it sent Monday to murder Landan and Ash, and that it would like to see Nick himself vanish from the face of the earth."

Bryce asked, "Because he works for a gay senator?"

Raising her brows, Cora informed us, "No investigation has yet determined that Martin Ash is gay. But as to Nick, there's no question about his orientation."

At this, Bryce actually choked on his coffee. He coughed and spluttered, "He's—he's gay? But he told me he was a soldier—a special ops marine—who fought in the Gulf!"

"And highly decorated," declared Cora. "It's probably why he's caused so much controversy this past week. He didn't meet with you kids to retrieve the tape because he was called upon to testify at a special hearing in Washington."

Jen and I exchanged glances. Both of us were amused that this dose of reality had evidently shattered Bryce's stereotypical concept that all gay men were effeminate.

Jen asked, "Special hearing?"

Cora answered, "A committee investigating Nick's discharge from the military. Nick's claim is they awarded him medals for killing two men while serving his country, yet discharged him for loving one."

Jen asked, "'Don't ask, don't tell' didn't apply to Nick?"

Cora said, "More complicated than that. After Nick returned from the Gulf War—where he was wounded after killing two enemies in combat—he was awarded citations and offered a promising career as a military analyst."

Pausing for a moment to see if we were following, Cora explained, "Many veterans of the Gulf War were just then speaking out, instigating investigations into the chemicals they were exposed to during their service. Nick became a spokesman for one particular group, partly because they were fellow vets, partly for personal reasons.

"Unrelated to the military cause, Nick's partner did not qualify for financial aid to receive treatment to combat the virus—HIV—he'd contracted, and Nick attempted to bring the man's plight to some-one's attention.

"In doing so, Nick raised many questions about viruses, lethal chemicals, and germ warfare. His arguments were sound regarding the chemicals Gulf War veterans had been exposed to, but he also argued that not enough was being done in regard to the AIDS epidemic. Shortly after this fiery speech, Nick believes he was targeted by a covert operations group, the Entity."

At this point, Jen couldn't help herself as she said, "You are telling us some wicked stuff, Cora Jackson!"

"Shhh!" came from Bryce. "I want to hear the rest of this!"

"So do I," admitted Jen. "But is this true? Is someone out there really that evil?"

Cora answered, "Nick Riley believes so. After his presentation to a board of inquiry, someone moved to destroy him. He was exposed as a homosexual desperately seeking financial aid for the treatment of his lover dying of AIDS. It finished him as a spokesman for his fellow vets on the chemical exposure issue and ended his career in the military. Because of this allegation, Nick was conveniently discharged."

Chapter Thirty-One

After all the info Cora had shared with us, Bryce had been reluctant to accept her offer of a ride back to Jen's Mustang near the state capitol. We were all spooked pretty badly. *The Alliance. The Entity. Devious folks working behind the scenes.* But Jen and I trusted Cora, and to save face, Bryce rode along to watch our backs.

Cora dropped us off—safely—near Jen's Mustang. The investigator then leaned over and gently took hold of Bryce's wrist as he climbed out of her car. "You have the right attitude about all of this," she softly said.

As she released Bryce's wrist, she told the three of us, "I didn't invite you to coffee to frighten you. I simply wanted to let you know what you had *really* been involved in. You had a right to know. I truly believe that—for you three—it's over. You saved Martin Ash's life, turned in evidence related to Senator Landan's murder, and in turn set the media hounds to barking, providing the coverage Ash needed to continue his crusade."

I bent down to peer inside Cora's car, asking, "But won't this Entity be mad at us for helping Senator Ash? And what about when Monday is arrested? Won't Kyle and I have to testify at his trial? Won't they want to silence us?"

Cora answered, "According to Nick, there won't be a trial. Landan's crusade against porn and Ash's crusade for AIDS education placed both men in the sights of the Entity. Landan and Ash were both supposed to be eliminated, leaving a trail that led to the Alliance. Monday, Giles Davis, and Deek failed at their assigned task. They won't live long enough to be arrested or to . . . testify. But as to you kids?"

We listened intently to her last words on the subject: "You are beneath their consideration. You don't know enough about any of this scheme to be a threat. So, Nick believes you're free and clear, and he wanted you to know that."

As Cora prepared to drive away, Jen stepped closer to her car. Cora shifted into drive, then braked when she noted Jen's inquisitive gaze. "Yes? One last thing?"

Looking uncomfortable, Jen hesitantly said, "Uh, about Nick's—friend—partner—lover? Is he . . . ?"

"Yes," answered Cora. "He passed a year ago."

"Sad," remarked Jen as Cora let up on her brake.

"Very sad," responded Cora as she slowly pulled away from the three of us standing on the curb.

Wednesday, November 14th

That next morning before school, I walked into the middle of a discussion between my mom and dad. They were having coffee in our glassed-in porch, and I had been reaching into the fridge in the nearby kitchen when I overheard Dad say, "They're both going through hell! Katie has been going to church, praying that Kyle will change. She's even contacted some religious group that specializes in reparative therapy. Poor Jack has been doing his damnedest to keep Katie focused on the new problem: the HIV thing. Jack's hired a lawyer to fight his insurance company. They refuse to pay health care benefits to keep Kyle in therapy at the Glens. His HIV is not covered, nor is some treatment program that costs nearly forty thousand dollars!"

Mom said, "Yes, I've been reading about clinics in other states where they give patients many types of antiretroviral drugs that have proven to be fairly effective. But these programs are expensive. Jack and Katie could never afford to send Kyle to such a place."

Dad muttered something under his breath and then said, "Besides, all their money will go down the tubes if Kyle can't change his preferences. These treatments might stave off the AIDS from spreading or whatever it does, but will it help Kyle to stop being gay?"

"That's not the point, John!" declared Mom in firm tones.

Dad was silenced by Mom's words for a moment. He stammered, "Wha—what—I—I meant was . . ."

That's when I looked in on them from the doorway of the kitchen, saying, "No, Mom. Don't get on his case. In a way, he's just asking a question. I think I can answer it for him."

I locked eyes with my dad and said, "No, Dad. Nothing will stop Kyle from being gay. He was born this way. He will die this way. He will live with who he is until then. Money and treatments won't change him. It's like—like the color of his hair or eyes. It's all part of his makeup, who he is as an individual, who he was destined to be. Gay. Homosexual. No power in the world can—or will—change that. Do you understand?"

Even as I said it, Dad knew I was no longer talking about Kyle. He stared at me silently for long moments. I would have been more comfortable if I had seen annoyance or hostility in his eyes, but neither were there. He just looked confused, like a man washed up on a beach after a shipwreck, trying his best to determine where he was and how he was going to survive.

I repeated my last question: "Do you understand?"

He blinked several times and muttered, "I think so."

I started to walk back into the kitchen then, thinking now was not the time to deal with the issue. But I stopped and turned back around to face both of them.

Mom looked at me. Dad still had that lost look in his eyes.

I looked at Mom. "I've been wondering about something ever since the night Carter Monday attacked me in the backyard. Did Dad know *before* or *after* that attack about why Katie Taylor phoned you earlier that night? You know, about Kyle testing positive? About Kyle . . . and me?"

I paused, looking from one face to the other before asking, "*Before* or *after,* you know, when Dad came rushing out there wielding a baseball bat to save me?"

"Before," answered Mom, already knowing where I was going with this line of thought. "Yes, Chris. He risked his own life to save you even with that knowledge."

I nodded and then looked at my dad and said, "Thanks, Dad."

He couldn't respond. He opened his mouth, yet no words could he speak, for tears were slowly spilling down his cheeks. It stung him that badly that I even doubted his love.

And though uncertain he could see me through his tear-blurred vision, I offered him a smile and passed through the kitchen, fighting back tears of my own.

Wednesday, November 21st

Two days before I was to be tested for the virus, I ventured out on a quest to help Kyle, who already carried it.

After I told Bryce and Jen of my plan, the two readily joined me. Before leaving Lincoln, Bryce visited Kenneth Braxton to retrieve the item I requested, and Jen provided the services of her Mustang and her wild driving to take us to Omaha.

It was noon as we pulled up to Saint Patrick's Cathedral in lower east Omaha, the place where Cora Jackson assured us we would find Martin Ash at this particular time of the day.

As we approached Nick Riley and two other security guards stationed near a black car parked before the massive church, I could clearly see the look of surprise on Nick's face.

He smiled broadly and gave a quiet chuckle. "Well, if it's not my friends from Lincoln! Sorry we couldn't have seen our deal to the end, but as things turned out, you guys did all right without me. We might have caused certain powers a little more grief had we played it through my way, but I had more pressing matters to see to. And you guys? You did the right thing, under the circumstances."

The big man stuck out his hand. Jen returned his smile and promptly shook his outstretched hand. Not wanting to be rude, I also placed my hand within his massive grasp. But Bryce eyed Nick rather coolly and kept both of his hands stuck deep inside his pockets. Nick accepted his gesture without offense.

"What brings you to our neck of the woods?" Nick asked, missing nothing as I slowly withdrew the tape from the inside pocket of my jacket.

I said, "I need to see Senator Ash. It's really important, Nick."

Nick eyed the black case in my hands. "May I assume that's the 'original' version of Senator Landan's last night on earth? If so, it's a little too late to make a deal. Detective Kitchen is still investigating the matter and doing just fine with the tape you guys provided him. Sorry, kids. We're all a little out of the loop on this matter now."

Bryce couldn't help but ask, "You're not in trouble for placing that camcorder in that room to film Landan taking a bribe?"

Shaking his head, Nick replied, "I'm a security specialist. My job is to protect my employer. No crime in setting up surveillance for security purposes. Giles Davis set the stage for two senators to be gunned down that night. I just happened to foil his plans by shuffling things about a bit."

I said, "You're talking about those envelopes, right? Kyle was instructed to pass them both—the red and the blue—to Landan and Ash. But you had already instructed Kyle that he was not to pass any invitation on to Senator Ash, right?"

Scratching thoughtfully at his red-gold beard, Nick responded, "Not sure where this is going, but, yes. Giles hired Kyle to pass information on to both senators. One invitation to lure Landan to that room. Another that would have placed Martin in a secluded location in the hotel to meet with a supposed 'wealthy contributor' interested in his AIDS cause. Little did Giles know that Kyle already worked for me.

"Cora Jackson explained to you that your ruckus with Monday prevented him from gunning down Martin, didn't she? Because I'm certain Monday would have finished his business with Landan and then proceeded downstairs to finish off Martin. That is, if you hadn't knocked him senseless with that fire extinguisher!"

Nick gave us a fierce grin. "You do deserve credit for the little diversion you provided that evening. But really, kids, credit is all you're gonna get for your acts of bravery."

I lowered my gaze, and flatly stated, "I didn't go in that room because I was brave. I went in there to get my friend. Because he needed my help. That's why I'm here now."

A little surprised at my serious tones, Nick raised his brows. "Kyle? Is he in some sort of trouble again?"

I reached into my jacket pocket and handed Nick the wad of bills he had given us as down payment for the tape. "Here," I said. "This is yours. Could I see Senator Ash, now?"

Taking the money, Nick answered, "Martin's busy. This is his God time. Confession of sins. Offering of prayers. Reflecting on past mistakes. Sighting on future goals. Doubt very much he would wish to be disturbed. Of course, you can speak with him when he is finished. Why don't we go across the street to that fountain shop and I'll buy us all some sodas?"

Nick placed the money in his jacket pocket as he stepped off the curb. Bryce and Jen followed him. The three all stopped, though, when I stood rooted to the sidewalk. I refused to meet their gazes as I focused on the stone steps leading up to the massive cathedral doors.

I declared, "What I need to talk with Martin Ash about has a lot to do with God."

Chapter Thirty-Two

Martin Ash offered me a puzzled look as I walked down the aisle to where he was kneeling before a huge statue of Jesus.

I introduced myself, but he already knew who I was and what I had accomplished that night at the Black Lion, explaining that Nick had shared the details with him.

He politely asked, "How can I help you?"

I handed him the tape. As he took it, he sat in a wooden pew and asked me to join him. I sat down, telling him that if he would view the tape he would see the original version of what had taken place that evening, the part Kyle Taylor had played, how he had been stuck in the room with Landan, been struck by Monday, and had to lay there while Landan was gunned down.

I told him, "So, you see, if Kyle wouldn't have screwed up and been stuck in that room, I wouldn't have gone in there to get him. And Monday wouldn't have even come after us. He would have shot Landan, and then maybe made his way downstairs to shoot you. So, if it wasn't for Kyle . . ."

Then it all came spilling out. I told Martin Ash about my life, about how Kyle's life was intertwined with mine. And though I blushed at some points and hesitated at others, I told him about experimenting on camp outs when we were younger. I told him about feeling deep affection for Kyle, crying myself to sleep at night, and stressing over whether he loved me back. I also told him that I knew without a doubt that both Kyle and I were gay.

Martin opened his mouth to comment, but I pushed ahead with my story, launching into details about Kyle's erection in gym class, about his parents and school officials assuming the worst of him, about his therapy sessions, about why he ran away, and why I went searching for him. Then I told Martin about all the weird events that happened just before Landan was shot that evening in Omaha.

I concluded my long-winded speech with the suicide attempt by Kyle, his admission to Orchard Glens, and the blood test that revealed Kyle was HIV positive.

When at last I fell silent, Martin quietly asked, "Have you been tested yet?"

"No," I answered, trying hard to meet his earnest gaze. "That happens on Friday."

For long moments, Martin simply stared up at the statue of Jesus, and just when I thought he was listening to some voice that I couldn't hear, he asked, "And you tell me all of this because?"

"Because . . . Kyle needs help," I firmly stated. I wanted to say more, to tell him how the insurance company wouldn't cover the cost of the treatment Kyle's dad had looked into. I wanted to tell him that I'd been on the Internet myself, thoroughly researching treatments, and had learned that not one but a combination of drugs worked best in helping people with the virus stay alive longer. I wanted to tell him that at least Jack, Kyle's dad, had taken the right approach. He was looking into what would help Kyle control this virus, which was far better than Katie's attempt to locate a group that offered reparative therapy to change Kyle's sexual orientation.

But I could say no more. I could only softly weep.

Martin handed me a package of tissues, and he sat in silence until I put my sorrow away and got hold of myself. After blowing my nose, and sounding like some damned goose, I managed to force a sad grin as I said, "Thanks for listening. I just needed you to know these things."

Nodding thoughtfully, Martin stood up and walked me to the double doors of the cathedral. Just before opening one of the massive oak doors, he tapped the tape he held. "I'll take a look at this, Chris. I'll also say a prayer for Kyle. On Friday, I'll say one for you as well."

Sunlight streamed in through the open door then, and I left Saint Patrick's feeling a little better for getting all of that off of my chest.

Friday, November 23rd

Dr. Gandahar was actually a pretty cool guy. When I first shook hands with the pudgy, balding, soft-spoken doctor from India, I thought, *Oh, my lord, I'm gonna have to talk about my sex life with this overweight quack who probably believes that even masturbation is a sin!*

But I was wrong. I'd judged the man before he even spoke. All of my preconceived notions about the doctor—who specialized in sexually transmitted diseases and viral infections—were wrong. I found that out after his brief introduction and his gentle handshake.

Taking a seat on the couch in his office instead of in the chair behind his enormous desk, he said, "Well, Christopher, we may have a problem, right?"

I had to reposition myself in the chair between the couch and his desk, swiveling around to face him. "A problem? You've got test results back that fast? You trying to tell me I've got it?"

Dr. Gandahar smiled warmly. "Slow down and take a deep breath, son. I know how you are dreading to find out the results of your blood test. My associates are working in the lab as we speak. I know nothing yet. What I meant to say is, with the *possibility* that you might be infected with HIV, we—you and I—have before us a problem."

I fiddled with the cotton ball in the hollow of my arm where a nurse had taken blood earlier.

"How is that *your* problem?" I asked.

Gandahar looked directly at me with his piercing brown eyes. "If you'll have me, I am now your doctor. You'll not face this alone. Together we will discover whether you have contracted this virus."

Why should you care? I almost spat, yet the warmth, compassion, and lack of condemnation in his eyes spoke volumes to me about what the guy was trying to say.

"Christopher," he asked, "what do you believe about the afterlife?"

Whoa! Majorly to the point! I thought, not certain I liked his line of questioning. *He's convinced I'm dying already! He's trying to prepare me for the worst. He wants to know if I believe I'll go to heaven or hell. He knows I have it. That's why he wants to know how I feel about . . . death!*

"Or do you even believe," Dr. Gandahar asked, "that a person has a soul? Do you think that life is just some cosmic accident, or do you feel that all life has been preordained by a divine creator? Will you sleep the sleep of the dead for all eternity, or will your soul be taken to a higher level, welcomed by a loving being or judged by a god of wrath? What, Christopher, do you believe in?"

I didn't hesitate—which surprised me—as I answered, "I believe in God."

Under most circumstances, if someone knew I was gay or that I might have AIDS because I had sex with another boy—actually had anal sex or performed oral sex—I would have felt foolish even mentioning that I still believed in God.

I mean, if I proclaimed I had a belief system to anyone, and they know the real truth about who I am, I figure they would simply judge and condemn me as abnormal and far outside the grace, mercy, or love of God. But for some reason, either because of the feelings of acceptance Gandahar offered me or because I was about to face my own mortality, I felt okay with telling it true.

"I believe in God," I said once more. "I'm not sure where I stand with him. But I don't reject him or doubt his existence. I really believe that he is out there. And as far as my soul goes, well, I don't really know where it will eventually end up."

The dark-skinned, pudgy doctor leaned forward and lightly tapped my knee. "That is good!" he declared, his eyes lighting up as though I'd just revealed the truth of the ages to him. "Good that you have a system of belief! Everyone needs to build their castle on rock, not on sand. Otherwise, when it storms, the waves come in and wash the foundation away."

I said, "Huh? Rock? Sand? Castle? Guess I don't get it."

Gandahar laughed. "So sorry. I'm speaking of a parable." He explained, "It is something Jesus of Nazareth once shared. He said, 'Build your castle—your life—your beliefs—your entire existence—on rock,' meaning something solid, something definite. 'Do not build your castle on sand, which shifts, which sinks, which breaks apart and easily gets swept away.'

"If one goes through life believing in nothing or is at odds with what he believes in, that person is very *alone* in this world. That is a tragedy. Believing in God—a power beyond—a source of life—a force of love—a divine being watching over you, that is a good, solid thing, a belief that builds your castle on rock."

I nodded, trying not to appear too dumb. "Oh, now I get what you're saying."

"Good," he responded, his eyes lighting up again. "But what is this uncertainty you feel about your soul?"

I felt my face getting all red as I said, "Well, the things I do. The reason I'm here at your office. Like the sex I had . . . with Kyle."

He nodded slowly. "You are uncertain about your soul then because of your . . . sexual activities or . . . your sexual orientation?"

"Both," I admitted, feeling like he was trying to pull some enormous weight off of my shoulders. "I have never been certain that God looks kindly at me because of who and what I am. I—"

"*Who* and *what* you are," he told me, "is your sexual orientation. There are three areas of sexuality. One is behavior, acting out, what we do with sex, body stuff. Two is identity, who we see ourselves to be, mind stuff. And three is orientation, who we are at the very core of our being, internal stuff."

"Yeah. I know," I muttered, trying not to sound disrespectful. "But along with my orientation, there's the matter of sex—"

"Your sexual activities," he supplied, but not unkindly. "Can you have one without the other?"

I looked at him with no immediate answer coming to my lips. *So, what's he saying? I'm gay and therefore I'm bound to have gay sex? My orientation is gay. It's natural that I have gay sex. Or is he saying that I should have controlled myself better?*

"So," he asked, "you are gay and have had, as you say, 'gay sex,' but does that fact place you at odds with God? Do you feel that those facts are strikes against you in terms of where your soul will eventually end up?"

I sighed. "That's one thing in my life I've never quite figured out. I've never totally forgiven God for making me gay. So I don't know if he even looks down on me too kindly."

Gandahar rubbed his chin. "Oh ho! A boy so young is holding a grudge against God? But why? Where does this resentment come from? You are angry with him because you believe your destiny is to be gay, that he left you no choice in the matter, and you don't think it's fair?"

I had thought along these lines many times, yet I had never actually verbalized how I felt about this—thing—I had with God. So I tried to explain it even as I tried to figure it all out myself, as I said, "Well, if it's true what most people say about God, that he rejects homosexuals, that he is angry with us, would like to see us stoned like the Bible says, and that gay folk are all destined to go to hell, then how fair is he? If he's mad at me for something I can't even help, what fairness is there in that? So if he's mad at me for what he made me to be, then how come I can't be mad back at him?"

Gandahar named my symptom: "God rage. Many of my patients infected with HIV direct their anger at their creator or a higher power. They believe if God had the power to prevent the tragedy or the power to heal such a virus, then somehow their dilemma is his fault. People afflicted with cancer, Parkinson's, and Huntington's— many people who suffer direct their anger at God who is supposed to be in charge of this universe."

"Really?" I asked, a little surprised that I wasn't the only one who really believed in God and yet was angry at him at the same time. I'd always felt really bad about these resentments. I mean, one minute I would pray and feel like God really heard me, and the next I would hold him responsible for me being gay and all the struggles that went along with this fact.

"God rage?" I tried the term out. "You must think I'm pretty bad, huh? I mean, to be gay and sometimes pissed at God."

The doctor smiled. "I think what you are is a very thoughtful young man. You have had to look honestly at yourself and have developed a belief system at a very young age. I think God is fortunate to have you for a believer in him."

I swallowed hard at that statement. "You do?"

He nodded, then got up from the couch. As he moved around to the other side of his desk, Gandahar asked, "So if you could simply accept that God accepts you for who and what you are, you would be much more confident about the future of your soul?"

Gandahar stated, "One day, you will die, Christopher. Maybe of AIDS complications. Maybe of cancer. Maybe you'll be struck by a car. All of us will die. Dying is inevitable. It's the big mystery about what's . . . beyond that troubles most of us."

Then I sorted out my real feelings on the subject of death, the after-life, and the future destination of my soul. I turned to face the doctor seated now behind his desk as I said, "I think I could be okay with all that . . . dying and facing God, if only I knew he was okay with me. If somehow I could find out that God wasn't mad at me for being gay, I could survive anything. Even the fact that I had HIV."

Gandahar looked at me. "Even stop being mad at him for who you are? Have a better relationship with him?"

"Yeah," I sighed. "Even start liking myself again, maybe. If only I knew God liked me."

He smiled that slight smile again, then nodded as if something be-tween us had been resolved. Leaning forward in his chair, the doctor pressed a button on the intercom system before him.

"Yes, Dr. Gandahar?" came the reedy sound of one of the techni-cians from the lab.

With one last smile in my direction, Gandahar spoke into the inter-com, saying, "Teresa? When will we have those test results?"

The technician's voice came through the small speaker on the doc-tor's desk: "Should be Monday, Doctor. Monday at the latest."

Doctor Gandahar offered me a pleasant smile and said, "So, we'll see you back here on Monday, Chris."

And I left his office, not knowing how I was going to survive the weekend wondering if the results were positive or negative.

Chapter Thirty-Three

Monday, November 26th

That next Monday afternoon, Jen and I sat in her room, the sounds of racing cars blaring from her TV speakers. I fiddled with the controller, watching as my Corvette crashed on Jen's television screen. GAME OVER blinked several times in bright red letters, indicating that I should press Start again, but I didn't. I couldn't. I was only two hours out of the doctor's office and still unnerved at finally receiving the results of last week's blood test.

I dropped the PlayStation controller between us. Jen sat back in her rocker situated near the bed beside me and asked, "So, you went to your doctor this morning, right? What were your test results? Can this doctor be absolutely certain of his testing?"

I asked, "Did you know that thirty-three million people are living with HIV? And did you know that based on what scientists know, that five young people are infected every minute, which results in seven thousand new cases per day, and half of those people are fifteen to twenty-four years of age?"

Jen sat forward in her rocker. "And you? Are you a carrier now like Kyle?"

I answered her question with another question. "Did you know that the human immunodeficiency virus may hide in 'several reservoirs' in the body? Did you know that there's usually a three-month window period before the antibodies appear? Did you know there are now fifteen major medications—antiretroviral drugs—used to treat HIV and AIDS? Did you also know HIV can be slowed down, but is totally incurable?"

Then I told her, "It's only been four weeks since Kyle went to Omaha. Some people test positive—develop antibodies—within a couple of weeks. But if we're trying to blame Kyle's infection on his sexual encounters up in the O, it might not be that simple. He might have contracted it months ago from Hatch."

Jen asked, "When was the last time you had sex with Kyle?"

"I thought I was safe," I blurted out. "I mean, I didn't have sex—exchange any fluids—with Kyle since he came home from the O."

Jen repeated her previous question. "Are you a carrier now like Kyle? Were your own test results positive?"

I looked Jen in the eye. "No HIV antibodies showed up in my blood. At this point, Dr. Gandahar regards my test as negative."

"Thank God!" Jen declared. Then she saw the sadness in my eyes. "But what? How come you still look like a puppy with no home?"

Blowing out a powerful breath, I explained, "But that doesn't mean I'm out of the woods with this thing yet. HIV could be hiding in my system. It might not show up right away. It all depends on two things: when Kyle became infected and whether I had unsafe sex with him after he was infected."

I added, "I remember we had a lot of fights during June, July, and August, but somewhere in there, we made up several times, and I can't quite recall the night we—"

Jen placed her two fingers beneath my chin. "You don't have to say it, Chris. But you should try to remember if you guys went all the way or not."

"We always finished what we started. But not always inside each other like you're probably thinking. Sometimes—"

Jen said, "I get the picture. What were the fights about?"

I muttered, "I suspected Kyle was seeing someone else—"

"Evidently he was!" declared Jen. "Cheating on you, maybe with Hatch! And placing you at risk, the heartless bas—"

"No." I stopped her. "Don't. Not now. Not with Kyle having it. I still care about him, even if—"

"Even if he sentenced you to death, Christopher?"

To that, I didn't know what to say. And fortunately by the look she saw on my face, Jen knew she had said too much. She whispered, "Well, where do we go from here, Chris?"

Her question was also her statement of support. *We.* She asked where we went from here. Jen meant that I was not alone in my new dilemma. I would not travel alone from this spot, fearing and dreading that I might yet have the virus. She would be with me on this step of my life's journey.

I told her, "I have to be tested again in three or four months. Dr. Gandahar tested my blood with two different types of tests: the ELISA and the Western blot. If I had the virus, very specific antibodies would have shown up in my blood."

Jen's brow furrowed. "But so far, you're clear? Tests on Kyle clearly showed these antibodies that fight HIV, right? I mean, he didn't just get sick or something and have some doctor make a guesstimated diagnosis just because he's an active gay kid?"

I shrugged. "All I know is that Kyle tested positive for HIV. Besides, Jen, it's not like you suddenly catch a cold or the flu, and then get checked because you think you might have HIV. It usually never shows symptoms that soon. There's like a ten-year incubation period between HIV infection and developing AIDS."

Jen said, "Yeah, I know. Kyle might have many years yet to live."

I grimaced at the thought of Kyle dying of this damned monster virus. My voice rose with anger as I said, "Yeah, because HIV is a smart virus but not very hardy. To any virus, we are the host. It lives off of us, like some mutant alien, feeding off of us to keep itself alive. Like for instance, Ebola, a brutally hardy virus, is so vicious it will kill off its host, eating away at all vital organs within a short amount of time. But not so with HIV, which will live off of its host, integrate itself into a person's system, and remain for maybe even ten years or longer."

Jen pointed at her computer on her desk. "When I first started reading up on HIV, I wondered if anyone had developed a patch. You know, like when my computer picks up a virus, I've got a virus detecting program or else a patch I can download to prevent that virus from wiping out my memory system. I often wondered if there weren't any antivirus treatments that might be given to clear a person's system of HIV."

"There's not, though," I told her. "A patch? I wish. But even treatments don't kill the HIV. Drugs only slow down the replication process. Somehow, the HIV always finds a way to become resistant to all treatments. And then the virus tears down the immune system's defenses and infections attack a person in full force."

Jen offered me a look of sympathy. She quickly added, "But not you, Christopher. So far, you are not infected with HIV. You are going to live long and prosper."

Maybe, I thought to myself. *Maybe just the prospect of even having HIV might have already done me some psychological damage. Maybe it woke me up, let me know how fragile the thread of life is. Maybe prepared me to approach sex with a lot more caution.*

I was close to feeling sorry for myself about all the emotions I'd experienced during my visit to the doctor, when I suddenly thought of what Kyle must be going through.

My thoughts roared, *He's been told he has the virus! He's been told there is no cure for it! He's been told that there are treatments for it and that one day his system won't be able to fight off all the infections attacking it, and then he will die!*

Poor Kyle. My poor, poor Kyle.

I let out a quiet sigh, and Jen climbed out of her rocker to hug me. And call it weird, but at that moment, I felt like God was actually using her arms to embrace and comfort me.

Friday, December 7th

I watched the sun slowly rising above the snow-covered hills to the east of town. From where I stood, at the center of Joe's Bridge, I could see miles and miles of open country. My breath trailed from my lips in gentle wisps of vapor that rose and fell, and then drifted away. It was cold, but not so cold that I couldn't enjoy the sunrise, bundled up in my parka with my ample hood drawn up. I shuffled at the snowy railroad tracks with my booted feet, and white crystals fluttered down between the ties, along with tiny bits of gravel. I watched them falling . . . falling . . . falling . . . until the shimmering crystals vanished, and the gravel plunked into the chill waters of the stream beneath the bridge.

I shuffled snow and gravel once more and heard another sound. It came from behind me. Slowly turning around, I gasped in surprise.

There stood Kyle not ten feet away.

He, too, was bundled up warmly against the winter cold, wearing coat, stocking cap, and thick wool gloves. He grinned like a mischievous elf, for he knew he had successfully sneaked up on me as I made my early morning venture. He had probably tracked me from my house and more than likely stalked me all the way down the tracks to the bridge.

"Kyle?" I whispered. "When did you get home?"

He walked up to me, wrapped his arms around me, and lightly kissed my left cheek. "Last night. Late. Or else I would have called. I got released from the Glens on account of something to do with insurance coverage. But I'll only be home for two days."

He started to step back, but I reached out and pulled him into a fierce hug. "I missed you a lot. But what do you mean two days? Where you going?"

Kyle took two steps back, and I had no choice but to release him. He looked past me to the red-orange ball of the rising sun and said, "Nice. Reminds me of all those early mornings we used to ride our bikes out here in the summer. You always did love these, didn't you?"

I turned and moved up beside him, and with our shoulders touching, we watched the red globe rise above the swells and curves of the snowy hills dotted with thick, green cedars. "Yeah. Sunsets, too. But what do you mean about leaving, Kyle?"

He glanced at me out of the corner of his eye, as he said, "God works in mysterious ways, doesn't he, Chris?"

I nodded, uncertain where this was going. During the past month, due to Kyle's behavior at the Glens, the only contact we could have were the e-mails we sent each other. He had forgiven me and basically dropped the issue about the Landan tape and, though his messages to me weren't all that warm, he had been sort of my same old Kyle.

Though he didn't seem distant now, allowing me to place my arm about his shoulders, I could sense that something between us had changed. Maybe it was on account of the virus. Maybe Kyle didn't feel it was fair to expect me to return to our normal relationship. Maybe both of us had changed. I mean, I still really loved him. But I didn't hurt for him like I used to. If that makes any sense at all.

Kyle declared, "The weirdest thing happened, Chris. You know how my parents were checking out those treatment clinics? You know, treatment places for the . . . you know . . . ?"

"The virus," I said.

Kyle nodded. It was as if he couldn't say the word. He went right on talking, not down or sad, but rather upbeat about the info he had to share. "Well, someone sent my dad registration forms for this place somewhere in Colorado. It's a real expensive treatment place, but they have a great reputation for helping people infected with it."

Not wanting to sound discouraging, I peered into Kyle's eyes and said, "Yeah, but I thought your dad's insurance didn't cover that sort of medical stuff, just like at the Glens."

"That's just it!" declared Kyle, a slight smile coming to his lips. "Someone's already paid for my stay there! These registration forms came with a signed document that claimed I could be admitted there anytime my parents wanted to check me in. Some anonymous donor took care of all the expenses! My folks don't know who, don't know why, but they're happy about it! They're taking me up there in two days."

As we turned around, walking side by side, heading back toward town, Kyle said, "God does work in mysterious ways, doesn't he, Chris?"

I nodded silently, and thought to myself, *God and Martin Ash*.

Chapter Thirty-Four

Two days later, I stood in my driveway long after Kyle and his parents drove off down the street, heading to the clinic in Colorado. I was sad to be losing Kyle for a time, but pleased to know someone would be helping him treat the virus. As good-byes go, it was not at all bitter. Just before climbing into the car, Kyle had given me a fierce hug and whispered in my ear, "Love you, Chris. Bye."

"Love you, too," I whispered back. Kyle had jumped into the car, and looked long and hard at me from the back window until his dad turned the car at the end of the block and headed out toward Interstate 80.

See two hawks along that stretch and think of us, I thought as I stuck my hands deep in the pockets of my parka.

Snow crunched under my hiking boots, and the winter wind blew bitter and cold, but I still stood there, staring down the empty street, asking God to watch over Kyle.

When I finally turned around to go in the house, I caught movement out of the corner of my eye. Looking up at the blustery skies, I saw a single hawk gliding along in swift currents. He was all alone up there, wheeling, spinning, dipping, and diving in his solitary flight. He let out a long, piercing cry and winged his way out toward the east, toward the tracks, the bridge, and the country only a mile away. He barely gave so much as a flap of his wings, for he was soaring in a current, at ease in his environment, fighting no winds of resistance nor struggling to remain aloft.

Wish I could be soaring like you, I thought. And then it hit me. *Maybe I am . . . a bit like you right now. Alone. But not lonely. In some sort of current, not fighting any winds of resistance, not struggling in my solitary flight. All alone and by myself, but okay with that fact.*

Ever since my talk with Dr. Gandahar, I had come to a conclusion about God and me. See, before when I prayed, I imagined myself walking into this courtyard filled with sparkling white mist. The moment I entered this place in my head, I was confronted by a band of tall, powerfully built, white-clad, golden-haired angels, peering at me with fiery eyes and stern gazes. As they drew their glowing swords and tightly gripped their shiny shields, looking at me, wondering what I was doing trying to talk to God, I always felt like a shabbily dressed peasant who had no right to even approach God, let alone pray and ask him for anything.

But something Gandahar said made a lot of sense to me: "If one goes through life believing in nothing or is at odds with what he believes in, that person is very alone in this world. That is a tragedy."

I could totally relate to that kind of aloneness, that sort of alienation, that kind of spiritual no-man's-land. I didn't want to travel there anymore. I wanted that part of my journey to be over with.

Gandahar also said: "Believing in God—a power beyond—a source of life—a force of love—that is a good, solid thing, a belief that builds your castle on rock."

What I had believed for so long seemed to shift every day. One moment, God hated me. The next, he was okay with me. And the same with me toward God. That had to stop.

I had told Dr. Gandahar how I felt, saying, "Well, if it's true what people say about God . . . that he rejects homosexuals . . . he is angry with us . . . would like to see us stoned . . . that gay folk are destined to go to hell . . . how fair is he? If he's mad at me for something I can't even help, what fairness is there in that?"

But who said God was cross with me? Who claimed the bridge between God and me was burned? Christian folk who quoted their Bible and claimed that I wasn't worthy to be considered by God because of who I was born to be? What gave them the right? And how foolish would I be, going through life cut off from the one thing in this world that makes a difference to me, because *they* said it was true?

The most surprising thing that Gandahar told me, and what changed my way of thinking on the entire matter, was, "I think what you are is a very thoughtful young man. You have had to look honestly at yourself and have developed a belief system at a very young age. I think God is fortunate to have you for a believer in him."

I had never had it put to me that way before. It made me feel good.

And I had responded, "I think I could be okay with all that . . . dying and facing God, if only I knew he was okay with me. If somehow I could find out that God wasn't mad at me for being gay, I could survive anything. Even the fact that I had HIV . . . even start liking myself again. If only I knew God liked me."

All of those words had passed between us, and the next night when I looked out to the starry sky and prayed, I imagined myself boldly walking into that mist-filled courtyard, actually greeted by huge angels with their glowing swords now sheathed, their shiny shields slung over their broad shoulders, and not one daring to bar my pathway to the throne beyond.

Out of the mist at the far end of that courtyard, I imagined I could see a hand actually reaching out toward me as I approached.

Now that was a good thought, a great prayer, a great way to never be alone again.

I caught one last glimpse of that lone hawk winging his way through winter winds, and then started toward the house where I hoped a bright blaze was burning in the den fireplace.

When I reached the screened-in front porch, my dad stood there waiting for me. Slowly, he swung the door open, looking down over the three steps that separated us.

He stood there silently, his eyes never leaving my face.

"Chris?" he finally said. "I just wanted to let you know . . ."

He glanced out toward the end of the driveway. "Kyle and his folks are gone?"

I nodded, knowing that's not what he had started to say. I met his gaze, and neither of us looked away.

"I wanted to let . . . to tell you . . . your mom and I talked . . . and . . ."

My dad paused, looking troubled—puzzled—like he wished someone would throw him a lifeline. He said, "Mom thinks that you think I no longer love you because of this thing . . . the thing . . . between you and Kyle."

I remained silent. A bridge was about to be built—or burned—here, and I didn't want to chance igniting a spark that would change my life forever.

Dad continued, "I don't quite understand it . . . don't really get it . . . don't know if I want to or ever really will . . . but nothing changes the way I feel about you. I don't love you any less, Chris. I just don't know about this . . . any of this."

He sighed. "Do you understand what I'm saying, Chris?"

Nodding, I responded, "Love you too, Dad."

Tears filled his eyes at that, and his hand slowly came up between us, his fingers outstretched toward me. "Come on in," he said. "Share a fire with me in the den. It's too cold to be standing out here by your-self."

I looked down at Dad's outstretched hand, thinking about when Jen hugged me and I felt like her arms represented the arms of God, and when I prayed the other night and that hand reached out to me from the misty clouds. And I couldn't help but think what that out-stretched hand might also represent: I was accepted. I was loved. I was not alone. I was okay with myself, okay with God.

Though I could no longer see clearly through the tears welling up in my own eyes, I knew Dad's hand was still there between us. Slowly, I reached out and took hold of it.

In the den, the fire glowed brightly while outside the winds of win-ter fiercely blew.

Author's Notes

I've been involved in youth care for twenty-seven years. It's never been easy. Kids can do some pretty desperate things when they're lost and struggling. I witnessed much tragedy in my first few years.

Lori, age fourteen, hung herself in her own bedroom. Daniel, age fourteen, shot himself with a .12 gauge shotgun. Robbie, age seventeen, died the same way. So too did Shawn, age eighteen.

Corey, age fifteen, died from inhaling aerosol deodorant to get high. One year from the date of Corey's death, his older brother, Todd, sat down in his bathtub, wrapped his face with a towel and goggles, and placed a lit M-80 in his mouth. One year from the date of his death, the mother of both Corey and Todd drove her car into the family garage, closed the door, and died from carbon monoxide poisoning. One year from the date of her death, three years after Corey's death, two years after Todd's death, little brother Michael, age thirteen, set his sights on following in their footsteps.

I received a phone call from a concerned friend, and I went out searching for Michael. I found him at a local park. Michael told me he didn't want to live anymore, that his family was cursed, and that he had to die on the same date as the other three members of his family. I honestly don't remember what I said to Michael in the three hours I spent talking with him. For dramatic effect, I would like to tell you that I knew just the right words, that I effectively threw Michael a lifeline. I can't recall the conversation that Michael and I had together. But Michael is still alive now, twenty years later.

My only regret is that I didn't get a chance to talk with Corey, Todd, Lori, Daniel, Shawn, and Robbie.

I was deeply moved by those tragedies. In fact, they set a course for me to follow and continually motivated me in my outreach work. In the following years, other learning experiences impacted me in profound ways, as well. One of those situations involved thirteen-year-old Billy, who placed a .22 rifle to his head and stood me off for thirty minutes. Fortunately, I was able to slowly reach out and pull the gun from his hands. Another situation was the time eleven-year-old Jessie blew out of his anger control session and led me on a five-block run through downtown city streets. Jessie ended up climbing onto the ledge at a parking garage, six stories above the streets. Scooting himself to the edge of the ledge, he clung there by his fingertips, and told me that he no longer wanted to live.

Twenty minutes of talking and one clumsy lunge by me, and I managed to prevent him from jumping. Jessie ended up being my foster son for the next three years.

During that period, I was assigned a new kid to work with in the support services I provided for Social Services. The caseworker who asked me to take the case referred to fourteen-year-old Tyler as a boy who had problems with his "sexual preferences." I was so naive then that I thought the caseworker's comment had something to do with Tyler's raging hormones, that he was simply promiscuous. Then I met Tyler, with his effeminate mannerisms, his swagger, and his sexual innuendos and come-ons that he had perfected for their shock value.

Those next few months proved to be very trying. Where for so many years I had to deal with kids who skipped school, ran away from home, stole cars, shot streetlights out with BB guns, and consumed large quantities of alcohol or smoked lots of dope, now I had to deal with a kid who went beyond delinquent acts.

Tyler sold himself to older men. He also was involved in S&M practices, which often left huge bruises on his neck and other places. Tyler also insisted on wearing a dress, complete with panty hose, bra, and dish rags stuffed into his bra cups. He was beaten up several times, and once a kid lit his spiked hair on fire. Finally, after months of working with me, Tyler was kicked out of his home, his school, and eventually the group home he was placed in.

Three years down the road, Tyler came to me on the day his doctor told him he had tested positive for HIV. Four years later, Tyler died of AIDS. And unlike Billy, who I pulled the gun away from, and Jessie, who I yanked off of that six-story ledge, I felt bad that I had not done enough to help Tyler.

On the day Tyler died of AIDS, all those old sorrows swept over me. *Another tragic story,* I thought. *Another damned tragic kid story.*

With all of this in mind, I decided to write a book about AIDS, teen suicide, and gay and lesbian youth. I discovered several sites on the Internet dealing with suicide rates among gay teenagers, sites dealing with the AIDS epidemic, and sites where many authors claimed the exact same thing I planned to explain in my new book: That the reason AIDS is so tragic, the reason that gay kids commit suicide 50 percent more often than straight kids, is that many gay kids feel totally alienated from God, from family, and from society. Many therefore commit "spiritual suicide" before they actually commit physical suicide. In essence, they have just given up and no longer care if they live or die, no longer care if they contract AIDS or not. A very sad state for any kid to be in.

I've dealt with enough tragedies in my earlier years of youth work, and with this new book, I hope to prevent more from taking place. Hopefully, if you are in a dark place at this point in your journey, this book will have allowed a little light to shine your way.

Bibliography

Bernstein, Robert A. (1995). *Straight Parents of Gay Children: Keeping Families Together*. New York: Thunder's Mouth Press.

Boswell, John (1980). *Christianity, Social Intolerance, and Homosexuality*. Chicago: University of Chicago Press.

D'Augelli, Anthony R. and Charlotte J. Patterson (2001). *Lesbian, Gay, and Bisexual Identities and Youth: Psychological Perspectives*. Oxford, UK: Oxford University Press.

Fellows, Will R. (1996). *Farm Boys: Lives of Gay Men from the Rural Midwest*. Madison: University of Wisconsin Press.

Garden, Nancy (1982). *Annie on My Mind*. New York: Farrar, Straus Giroux.

Hart, Jack (1995). *My First Time*. Boston: Alyson Publications.

Helminiak, Daniel A. (1994). *What the Bible Really Says About Homosexuality*. San Francisco: Alamo Square Press.

Heron, Ann (1995). *Two Teenagers in Twenty*. Boston: Alyson Publications.

Isaacs, Gordon and Brian McKendle (1995). *Male Homosexuality in South Africa, Identity Formation, Culture and Crisis*. Cape Town, South Africa: Oxford University Press.

Katz, Jonathan (1976). *Gay American History*. New York: Thomas Y. Crowell Company.

Leyland, Winston and Jack Fritscher (1991). *Gay Roots: Twenty Years of Gay Sunshine: An Anthology of Gay History, Sex, Politics, and Culture*. San Francisco: Gay Sunshine Press/Leyland Publications.

McNeill, Father John J. (1976). *The Church and the Homosexual*. Boston: Beacon Press.

Mondimore, Francis Mark (1996). *A Natural History of Homosexuality*. Baltimore, MD: Johns Hopkins University Press.

Owens, Robert E. Jr. (1998). *Queer Kids: The Challenges and Promises for Lesbian, Gay, and Bisexual Youth*. Binghamton, NY: The Haworth Press.

Preston, Richard (1994). *The Hot Zone*. New York: Bantam Doubleday Dell Publishing Group.

Savin-Williams, Ritch C. (1990). *Gay and Lesbian Youth: Expressions of Identity*. New York: Hemisphere Publishers.

Shilts, Randy (1987). *And the Band Played On*. New York: St. Martin's Press.

Shyer, Christopher and Marlene Fanta Shyer (1996). *Not Like Other Boys*. Boston: Houghton Mifflin Company.

Truluck, Rembert (2000). *Steps to Recovery from Bible Abuse.* Gaithersburg, MD: Chi Ro Press, Inc.

White, Mel (1995). *Stranger at the Gate.* New York: Simon and Schuster/Dutton Plume.

About the Author

Rob N. Hood has worked for the past twenty-seven years as an advocate for troubled youth. He began his career when still in high school, serving as a street contact for a runaway shelter. It was during his time as a worker at a detention facility for delinquent youth that he began writing stories for the residents. When kids began asking for sequels, Rob knew he had discovered a way to communicate and connect with troubled kids.

Rob has served as a mediator for his own truancy program and provided wake-up calls and escorts to schools for a wide mix of alternative students. In his role as a guest artist with agencies that provide care for emotionally disturbed youth, he has also developed programs that deal with conflict resolution and delinquency prevention. As an English/Drama instructor, he once produced and directed a substance abuse program which had an impact on 15,000 at-risk kids. He believes, though, that his greatest accomplishment can be summed up in the words of one troubled boy who wrote to him while confined in an institution. "Discovered your book today. It was like reading a letter you wrote directly to me. Thanks for giving me hope."

Rob currently makes his home somewhere in the Midwest, and is always busy at work on another book.